YENG PWAY NGON is a poet, novelist, playwright and critic from Singapore who has published twenty-six volumes in the Chinese language. His work is noted for its examination of the modern human condition, and has been translated into English, Italian, Malay, and Dutch. He was awarded the 2003 Cultural Medallion for his contributions to literature in Singapore, and the 2013 Southeast Asian Writers Award.

His novels published in English include *Lonely Face*, *Unrest*, *Art Studio* and *Costume*.

JEREMY TIANG has translated numerous books from Chinese, including novels by Chan Ho-Kei, Su Wei-chen, and Zhang Yueran. He has also translated Yeng Pway Ngon's novel *Unrest*. He was awarded a PEN/Heim Grant, an NEA Literary Translation Fellowship, and a People's Literature Award Mao-Tai Cup. In 2018, he won the Singapore Literature Prize for his debut novel *State of Emergency*. He currently lives in Brooklyn.

YENG PWAY NGON

COSTUME

A Novel

Translated by
Jeremy Tiang

BALESTIER PRESS
LONDON · SINGAPORE

Balestier Press
71-75 Shelton Street, London WC2H 9JQ
www.balestier.com

Costume
Original title: 戲服
Copyright © Yeng Pway Ngon, 2015
English translation copyright © Jeremy Tiang, 2019

First published by Balestier Press in 2019

Published with the support of

NATIONAL ARTS COUNCIL
SINGAPORE

A CIP catalogue record for this book
is available from the British Library.

ISBN 978 1 911221 08 1

Cover design by Sarah and Schooling

All rights reserved. No part of this publication may be
reproduced, stored in a retrieval system or transmitted in
any form or by any means, electronic, mechanical, without
the prior written permission of the publisher of this book.

This book is a work of fiction. The literary perceptions and
insights are based on experience, all names, characters, places,
and incidents either are products of the author's imagination
or are used fictitiously.

Contents

COSTUME

Part One

PART ONE

YU SAU AND GRANDPA

1. SATURDAY MORNING

THE LIFT DOORS OPEN. THE YOUNG MALAY MAN INSIDE quickly presses the door-open button and stands to one side when he sees Yu Sau with her grandfather in his wheelchair. She eases the chair in and thanks him in English. The young man smiles shyly as they swiftly descend.

Yu Sau's head is down, and her hands rest on the wheelchair handles. She looks deep in thought, or perhaps a little tired from a disturbed night. Grandpa's head sways gently, the sparse white hair barely covering the archipelago of liver spots that dot his scalp.

Three years ago, Yu Sau moved back into the five-room HDB flat (dining room, living room, three bedrooms). Her parents lived here, then her father died four years ago. Before coming here, she rented a small condo near her office with a couple of colleagues she got on well with, Geok Leng and Sandy. When her mother was diagnosed with late-stage breast cancer, Yu Sau had to take care of her, as well as her ageing grandfather. She left her friends, moved back in, and hired a Filipino helper. Her mother died last year. Now the flat contains just Yu Sau, Grandpa, and Maria.

Grandpa is eighty-eight. He was fairly healthy and chipper before Mum died. He even went for walks on his own. Not long after Mum passed away, he tripped and fell while out for a stroll, breaking a bone in his lower leg. Due to his advanced age, the doctors hesitated to put him under the knife, but after a few days in hospital, the bone miraculously knit back together, and he clamoured to come home. Surprised by this turn of events, the doctors kept him a couple more days for observation before discharging him. Grandpa's bone might have healed, but walking has become more and more taxing, and his spirits are ebbing by the day. Finding it hard to move around, he has taken to leaving the house only in a wheelchair. Even so, he insists on visiting the nearby river at least once a week. As she doesn't work weekends, Yu Sau takes him there around seven each Saturday morning.

The lift doors open, and light floods in. Yu Sau sees the stone tables and benches of their void deck, with flower beds and grass beyond. The young Malay guy presses door-open as she wheels Grandpa out, and she thanks him again.

She is a little sleepy, but the morning sun perks her up. Her steps are light as she wheels Grandpa past block after block of flats, across two roads, down to the river. They come to a halt in the shade of a tree, and she helps Grandpa up from his chair.

Leaning on his stick, Grandpa totters towards the embankment railings in the warm sunlight. Yu Sau follows slowly behind with the wheelchair. Now and then, joggers wave hello as they pass. As she strolls along with Grandpa, Yu Sau sometimes thinks of her late mother, whom she also accompanied on walks here during her illness. They went farther, all the way along the river to Bishan Park. Her mother had just been through chemotherapy, but still looked pretty good, apart from being a little paler and thinner; you wouldn't have guessed she was ill. They would stroll along in the early morning sun, small beads of sweat appearing on Mum's forehead, her pallid cheeks flushing a little from the heat, her eyes bright with life. Yu Sau often told Mum she looked healthier than Yu Sau herself.

Indeed, Mum took very good care of her body. She refused to touch meat, subsisting on vegetarian food and brown rice porridge. She ate lingzhi mushrooms every day, and drank a nourishing broth made from carrots, daikon radishes, burdock roots and Brazilian mushrooms. Her friends told her to try cancer-busting fruit and veg such as mangosteens or beetroot, and she enthusiastically took their recommendations to beat the cancerous cells attacking her body. She had a great deal of faith in all this, because she could see her body slowly recovering. Then the cancer came back, and she had to subject herself to another ordeal: chemo, electrotherapy, nausea, losing her hair. This led to despair, rage and hopelessness. She abandoned the cancer-fighting food, having concluded that the vegetarian diet, the mangosteens and beetroot, and even the lingzhi mushrooms were completely useless. She also gave up her morning walks in the park, choosing instead to hide at home, grumbling to herself. Her temper grew short, and she spent her days yelling at people.

Remembering how Mother gave up on herself, Yu Sau can't help sighing. If she'd remained as enthusiastic battling the disease after her relapse, would she have lived? She once asked the doctor what Mother ought to eat or not eat, and he replied that anything was fine within a balanced diet. Which means the cancer would have come back no matter what. She clings to this thought, because the alternative is to blame herself for not being more vigilant about Mother's diet.

After a short distance, Grandpa stops by the railings, and they stand there watching a white heron hunt its prey along the narrow, shallow river. Just as they are completely absorbed, they hear a gentle melody: someone humming Cantonese opera. She and Grandpa automatically turn to look. Not far from them is a man in a blue tracksuit, leaning against the railing and gazing at the river, singing away.

"*Let's go over to him*," says Grandpa in Cantonese, lowering himself into the wheelchair.

Yu Sau pushes him towards the young man. As they approach, his voice is like a sigh. "*Today I return to the road, breaking a willow branch in farewell. Goodbye to the beautiful maiden.*" Grandpa arrives just in time to chime in with his quavering, hoarse voice: "*Ah, how unfortunate my fate, to lose such a fine flower.*"

The man breaks off in surprise. "*Wow, Uncle, you like Cantonese opera too?*"

"*Tsuih Lau Seen's* Breaking the Long Willow Pavilion." Grandpa beams, as pleased as a little child. "*You have a good voice. My grandson had quite a hit with this song. I didn't think anyone still knew it. It's strange to hear you sing it. Tsuih Lau Seen has a few other good tunes, do you know them?*" The man shakes his head in apology, seemingly embarrassed by his ignorance.

Grandpa looks down as he rifles through the treasure chest of his memory. "*There's* Heartbreak Plaque, *and* Dreaming of Western Tower, *and* The Unforgettable Song, *and* Death at the Blue Bridge, *and, um,* The Peerless Beauty, *and, uh—* Wrong About My Beloved, *then, wait, there's more... No, I'm too old, I can't remember.*"

"*I only know* Breaking the Long Pavilion Willow," says the man, grinning sheepishly.

Suddenly full of energy, Grandpa has a good chat with him in Cantonese.

It turns out the man lives in a nearby block. He is probably in his thirties, though his thinning hair makes him look older. He used to be a Cantonese radio presenter at Rediffusion, but left before Chinese dialect programming was cancelled altogether. He jokes that it was better to resign than to get fired. "*And now, I've switched to selling insurance.*" They often played Cantonese opera recordings at Rediffusion, and he developed a taste for them. Grandpa asks if he sings, but he shakes his head: he never trained, and can only muddle his way through a line or two. He enjoys watching Cantonese opera, though he hasn't seen many.

With that, they fall into showbiz talk. Grandpa's normal muddle-headedness falls away, and his memory sharpens. He remembers every single veteran performer, and the parts they excelled in. Sit Kok Sin's *Why Won't You Return?*, Sun Ma Tze Tsang's *Lechery is the Greatest Sin*, Ho Fei Fan's *The Amorous Monk in the Boudoir*, and so on. He goes over them like family heirlooms.

"*Have you seen Lan Chi Pat 'riding the cart'?*" he asks, as smug as a boy bragging to a younger one that he saw a tiger at the zoo.

The man shakes his head. That's Grandpa's cue to go into a long account of how marvellous Lan Chi Pat's cart-riding was in *A Minister of Six Nations*. His enthusiasm makes him sway back and forth, and he even tries to lift a leg while demonstrating a move, but his joints are too stiff and his muscles too weak. Yu Sau gets flustered, afraid he'll tumble from his wheelchair. Finally giving up, Grandpa describes the gesture instead, explaining how. Lan Chi Pat rested an ankle on the opposite knee and let his leg shake casually, the picture of expansive self-possession. He lifts both hands and mimes tossing a long beard aside, gleefully adding, "*That chap could flick a beard like nobody's business.*"

The two men chat away, and somehow or other Grandpa gets onto the subject of Yu Sau's elder brother Kim Chau. It turns out the man once asked him to be on his programme. "*I think that was in '79, right after his record with* The Red Candle's Tears *came out. He sounded fantastic. I love that song.*"

"*That was originally Hung Sin Nui's song,*" Grandpa tells the man. He launches into the aria, though his voice trembles without enough breath to support it. "*My body bends like a willow branch in the wind, tossed back and forth helplessly.*" The man joins in for the next line, "*The marriage knot is easily tied, but hard to loosen. Bitter thoughts can be bought but not sold.*" And then, as if they planned it, in unison: "*Music by Wong Jyt Seng, lyrics by Tong Tik Sang!*"

The man is right: Eldest Brother was still in Singapore in

1979, though he was no longer speaking to his family by then. They heard he was singing afternoon getai at some hotel. This was Eldest Brother's darkest period, and after that he left Singapore. They didn't know where to. Some people said he went to Kuala Lumpur, others said Hong Kong. Yu Sau can't imagine her brother releasing a record. It probably didn't sell that well. Maybe that's why Grandpa never talks about it. Or did he mention it when she wasn't paying attention? Eldest Brother started studying opera when she was two or three. Grandpa doted on him. Whenever he got home from the opera troupe, Grandpa would always tell Mum to brew him some bird's nest soup. This stuck in her memory, because she got to enjoy a bowl too. He was already performing when she was in primary school. She was happiest when the whole family went to the theatre or open-air stage to watch Eldest Brother strut his stuff, not because she enjoyed traditional opera, but for the many snacks she was allowed on these outings.

Yu Sau isn't particularly fond of Cantonese opera, but doesn't hate it. Mostly she remembers the stage lights being very bright, while the drums and cymbals clashed horribly loudly. Often, she had no idea what the performers were actually singing. She adored their magnificent costumes, especially when the male and female warriors, who had pheasant feathers in their headdresses, launched into battle with their red-tasselled spears twirling like batons. She enjoyed these fights more than the actual singing. When the ingénue let rip with her screechy *eee-yah-eee-yah*, it sounded as if someone were pinching her windpipe.

In secondary school, Yu Sau stopped accompanying her family to Eldest Brother's performances. Her parents and other brother also went less frequently, leaving Grandpa faithfully attending every show alone. At home, Grandpa would praise Eldest Brother effusively, saying he was a wonderful singer. This may have been true; certainly he was quite a well-known performer of "scholar-warrior" roles. But Yu Sau was English-educated, which meant she read English books, watched Hollywood films, and listened to western music. She might occasionally give Chinese pop songs a try, but hardly ever encountered Cantonese opera.

Even now, she remembers the ingénue her brother was dating, Lily Teo. She had huge eyes, a pointy chin that tilted up a little, and spoke with exaggerated clarity, in slow, moderate tones, a little like Ng Kwan Lai, an actress she'd seen in Cantonese movies as a child. Eldest Brother also had a good friend, Lam Meng Hung, who visited often when they were secondary school classmates. Eldest Brother once told her that after he dropped out of school, everyone lost touch with him apart from Meng Hung. Grandpa and her parents were fond of Meng Hung, who joined in their mahjong games. When these went on too late, he spent the night at their home. As a little girl, Yu Sau had liked Meng Hung a lot, and would pester him to play with her. Lam Meng Hung and Lily Teo were Eldest Brother's best friends, and the three of them were always spending time together as far back as she could remember. When Eldest Brother started working in opera, Meng Hung always went to his performances. He was fairly well-off because his father ran a trading firm, so he could afford to buy entire rows of tickets and give them out to his friends. After the show, he'd take Eldest Brother and Lily for supper in his white Mercedes. Because he stayed over so often, Grandpa and her parents started treating him as one of the family, right until he abruptly got married to Lily Teo.

Like everyone else, Yu Sau had assumed Lily was Eldest Brother's girlfriend, so this was thoroughly unexpected. Eldest Brother and Meng Hung had given the impression of being as close as sworn brothers, and no one in the family, Yu Sau included, could accept the news of this marriage. They thought he was a traitor for snatching away his friend's girl, and were furious with Lily too, for being such a gold-digger.

There was one incident around the time of the wedding that Yu Sau remembers particularly clearly: Eldest Brother got into a big fight with his family over whether or not to attend. Grandpa, Mum and Dad said they weren't going, and didn't think Eldest Brother ought to go either, but he insisted on being there, and wanted to give a big red packet. They couldn't dissuade him, so the entire family went to the banquet. Naturally, they had a terrible time. Meng Hung and Lily probably sensed their disapproval, and stopped visiting after this.

A little later, Lily gave up performing, and emigrated to Canada with Meng Hung. Then the opera troupe disbanded, and without a partner, Eldest Brother was never able to get back on his feet. Shortly after that, he left home. He had a vicious argument with Grandpa just before he went, though Yu Sau can't recollect how it started or what they were fighting over. Eldest Brother never contacted them again, and they had no idea where he ended up. Yu Sau heard he'd been seen in Kuala Lumpur, but then Grandpa once said he was in Hong Kong. Second Brother lives in Hong Kong, though, and says he never saw Eldest Brother there.

Both Yu Sau's brothers left home. Second Brother, Kim Ming, went first, and then Kim Chau. (The shared first character of their names means "build," though Eldest Brother adopted "Kim" as in "sword" as his stage name.) Yu Sau is twelve and ten years younger than her brothers. She was closer to Second Brother as he played with her more often, and she went to him rather than Eldest Brother when she wanted to talk. Then the Internal Security Department came after Second Brother for his leftist beliefs. He spent quite a while on the run before finally getting caught in 1965 and deported to China the following year, aged sixteen. Yu Sau, just seven at the time, cried her eyes out because she thought she'd never see him again. Even her parents were moved to tears at the sight of her sorrow. She was twelve and just out of primary school when Eldest Brother left. Perhaps because they hadn't been as close, she wasn't as affected by his departure. Besides, she hadn't thought that she'd never see him again.

After Second Brother was sent back to the Mainland, the family heard nothing from him, though they had no idea whether he was unwilling or unable to get in touch. Around 1975, when Yu Sau was in junior college, her father mentioned he'd had a letter from Second Brother to let them know he'd moved to Hong Kong. This was their first news of him in a decade. Yu Sau wept with joy, and so did her parents and Grandpa. Right away, her father dialled the phone number in the letter, only to reach the landlord: Second Brother was at work, and wouldn't be back till seven. The family waited impatiently for evening to call him again, and this time he answered. They took turns speaking to him. When the receiver got to Yu Sau, she was so excited she could only repeat his name over and over, not knowing what else to say. After ten years without hearing his voice, he sounded odd on the phone, almost like a stranger. Two weeks later, which happened to be the June school holidays, the whole family visited him in Hong Kong.

Now that they were reunited, Yu Sau phoned Second Brother often, even after she moved to England for university. Before this, she went to Hong Kong twice more with her parents and Grandpa. On both occasions, Second Brother came to their hotel, rather than bringing them to his lodgings. Yu Sau wondered if he lived somewhere awful that he didn't want them to see. She could tell from his clothes and look of exhaustion that his life in Hong Kong wasn't easy.

And indeed, when Second Brother first got to Hong Kong, he worked at a garment factory, earning only fourteen Hong Kong dollars a day. He slept in the factory to start with, then rented a bed in a *gang fong* flophouse. That bed alone cost him dozens of dollars a month. Later, he lived in a cage home. (It was many years later before Yu Sau learnt what this actually meant: a single bed surrounded by metal wire, like a cage. If there was a fire, anyone in one of these was sure to die.) It was precisely because his life after leaving China was so difficult that he didn't want to write to his family, until he was earning a little more and could afford a proper cubicle bed.

After resuming contact, Second Brother was sure to phone his family in Singapore at Chinese New Year and other festivals. Eldest Brother, on the other hand, was never heard from again. They weren't even sure where he was, or how he was doing. When their mother was ill, Yu Sau had to take care of her while holding down a full time job, and even with Maria's help, she felt almost too busy to breathe. She resented her absent brothers, particularly the older one. Second Brother had been forced out of the country, and couldn't do anything about that. Eldest Brother was the firstborn, and therefore it was his duty to take care of his aged parents. He was shirking his responsibilities to pursue his dream. As the youngest child, she felt her big brother was being selfish, but then after her mother died, her rage washed away with the passing of time, fading away to nothing.

She misses Eldest Brother, and asks Grandpa about him from time to time. Now in his eighties, Grandpa has a touch of dementia. When they were children, he was fondest of Eldest Brother, but when she mentions his name now, Grandpa just stares blankly. Did Eldest Brother's departure hurt him so deeply? It's a shock when Grandpa mentions Eldest Brother to a man they've only just met, and talks about him without a trace of his previous indifference or confusion. When he realises this man actually knows Eldest Brother's name, when the man says the words Leong Kim Chau, she sees how excited he is. In all the years since she moved back home, she hasn't seen him like this. But then the weather suddenly turns overcast and gusty, and Grandpa reluctantly lets this man go.

*

"*How I regret acquiring this debt of sin. How could I know redemption wouldn't come easy, and time would swiftly pass? Alone with my sorrow, no longer a young girl—*" As Yu Sau pushes the wheelchair home against the wind, Grandpa continues singing *The Red Candle's Tears* animatedly. His quavery voice whips back and forth in the gale, which sweeps up the yellowing leaves from the trees and plastic bags from the pathway. The sunny sky is now inky grey, and thunder rumbles. Rain is on its way. She quickens her steps.

Grandpa finishes the aria and sighs, "*It was love that brought down your eldest brother.*" He is silent for a while, then abruptly turns to Yu Sau. "*What was that young man's name?*"

"*You didn't ask him,*" she says. Her Cantonese is a little rusty.

2. COSTUME

The rain starts as soon as they get back to the flat. Maria brought in the laundry and is folding it. When she sees Yu Sau, she hurries over to help Grandpa up from the wheelchair. Still swaying on his feet, he yells at Yu Sau to get the opera costume from the camphorwood chest. What costume? Mother chucked it out years ago, but now Grandpa insists Eldest Brother stored it there. That's his dementia talking. The moment of clarity in the park earlier wasn't typical. Yu Sau sees him getting more confused by the day. Many things and people he once talked about frequently are now completely forgotten, while he strenuously (and mistakenly) declares that certain events did take place, or claims the deceased are still living, or vice versa. Take Eldest Brother: some days Grandpa says he's still alive, others that he's been dead a long time.

Eldest Brother is twelve years older than her, which makes him forty-three. Surely he's still alive? There's been no news for more than ten years. Where could he be? His absence saddens Yu Sau. When Mum was still alive, she often complained that Eldest Brother had been such a clever child, but Grandpa kept bringing him to the opera, giving him such a taste for it he abandoned his studies to take it up professionally. Mum thought opera performers were useless, and in a fit of rage, threw away the opera costume Grandpa kept in the camphorwood chest. Yu Sau watched it go into the rubbish bin by their front door. When Grandpa found out, he dug through the bin, but it was too late, it had been emptied. He was furious, and had a big argument with Mum. They waged a cold war for quite some time after that. That's when their relationship began to chill, so Yu Sau has a very clear memory of the costume being thrown out. It's gone. To think Grandpa doesn't remember any of this!

His mentioning the costume does make Yu Sau miss Eldest Brother. On the wall of their old house, before she left for England, there were pictures of him wearing this robe: on stage during a performance, on his own, with Grandpa, with Meng Hung and Lily Teo. Grandpa had his own trove of photographs showing Eldest Brother acting or in costume, two whole albums. He showed them to Yu Sau. Since moving back into the flat, though, she hasn't found a single one of these pictures. When she asks Grandpa, he sometimes says Eldest Brother took them with him when he left (but how is that possible? This must be wishful thinking on Grandpa's part), and sometimes he sighs long and hard, lamenting that they were all in the drawer of the rosewood desk, which they sold when they moved house, and forgot to remove the albums first.

Yu Sau was five or six the first time she saw Grandpa

searching for the costume. Eldest Brother was training with the opera troupe, and she'd often watch as he pulled it from Grandpa's camphorwood chest, as if admiring some precious object, carefully spreading it open, laying it on the floor, tenderly stroking it. A long, blue robe. She vaguely recalls its design: split skirts, wide around the torso, with flowing water-sleeves, like something an ancient scholar would wear. Eldest Brother told her this was the opera costume given to Grandpa by the friend from his village who'd come to Singapore with him, the one who was now a veteran performer. It was called an "Ocean Blue", "Tilted Collar Long Jacket" or a "Taoist Robe". Eldest Brother proudly told her that Grandpa had given it to him, and he was now its owner.

THE OLD MAN

1. *CURSING, CURSING, CURSING THE EMPTY HEAVENS*

"*Helpless before the heavens we part, what sorrow, what rage; the parting heart clings to the drooping willow, goodbye tears splash the flowers.*" The old man struggles to remember the lyrics to *Breaking the Long Pavilion Willows*, humming bits and pieces. It's been too long since he's sung anything, too long since he heard this tune. When he was young, he adored Tsuih Lau Seen, particularly her rendition of this opera. Then there was Siu Meng Sing. He listened to her *Autumn Tomb* all the time, but now it completely escapes his mind. Not just the opening, every last scrap of the lyrics. Yet when Kim Chau was a kid, he taught him the whole piece! "*Half a lifetime of encounters, allowing fondness to bloom, affection thickening, dawn stained with the mist of love, adoration filling the bosom.*" He sings a few lines before realizing abruptly this isn't *Autumn Tomb*, it's *Dream of Romance*. This "horse trot" passage is also one he taught Kim Chau, but what about *Autumn Tomb*? He simply can't recall. What a shame. Kim Chau was so talented, his voice as nimble as his movements. Everything about him told you the second you laid eyes on him that he was going to be a big star: his eyes, his limbs, the way he stepped on stage. A pity he was born in the wrong place. His features were so delicate, perfect for "scholar-warrior" roles. If this had been Hong Kong, surely he'd have become a movie star! Even here in Singapore, he ought to have done well. What other performer here had his bone-deep good looks? Which "level voice" vocalist was as talented as him? The old man wishes Kim Chau could have met his childhood friend Tak Chai: Ching Siu Kai's disciple, the new Siu Kai. If that had ever happened, Tak Chai would definitely have helped him get ahead. The old man and Tak Chai went through many hardships together. Is Tak Chai still around? He's a year older. Even if he's still alive, he too would be well on his way to the grave. At the age of twenty, Tak Chai left Singapore and returned to China, where he continued performing. They haven't seen each other since.

After Tak Chai made his name as the new Siu Kai, the old man kept an eye out for news of him. He remembers the papers reporting that not long after the Japanese surrendered, the new Siu Kai moved from Hong Kong to the Mainland. Once Mainland China was liberated, the local papers rarely (in fact, almost never) reported news from there, so he had no way of knowing how the new Siu Kai was doing. There were rumours during the Cultural Revolution that the new Siu Kai had been badly tortured, that both his legs were broken. "*Tak Chai, you were an idiot,*" the old man can't help sighing. "*Things were so good in Hong Kong, why on earth return to the Mainland?*" God, if Kim Chau hadn't died young, if Tak Chai hadn't left Hong Kong, their paths would surely have crossed. Kim Chau was brought down by love. What a pity! But how did he die? The old man thinks hard, and his brain fills with memories of Kim Chau when young, striking poses as he rehearsed in their living room: pulling the mountain, retiring steps, revealing the appearance, seven star steps, waves across water, scooping step, little leap, kicking leg, striking the armour, continuous movement, washing the face, flags in the wind, circular walk. He sees every detail of each move. His ears fill with the roar of the audience as Kim Chau shakes out his flowing hair in a gesture of despair, though he can't remember which show that's from. The old man dozes. Kim Chau, then Tak Chai, flicker through his mind. He remembers, like awakening from a nightmare: someone said Kim Chau fell ill and died in a small hotel in Hong Kong. But who told him? What a shame! A wave of sadness washes over his heart. *"Not yet, not yet, not yet met my love. Cursing, cursing, cursing the empty heavens. My eyes yearn anxiously, my eyes yearn anxiously." Such emotion trembles on my lips, waiting to be told. Oh, oh, my heart is sour as the plum.* These lyrics, like uninvited guests, burst into his mind without warning, then slip from his mouth. He mumbles them raggedly, but halfway through goes blank. Shutting his eyes, he ransacks his brain, finally unearthing the rest: *"Saga seeds of longing, such jade green feelings, cruel separation, dreams follow the wild geese... shattered..."* Wild geese, shattered dreams... What comes after shattered dreams? He can't go on, partly because he's out of breath, partly because his mind is as muddled as a bowl of porridge. If Kim Chau had had someone to take care of him, he wouldn't have died. All alone in Hong Kong. Who looked after his affairs? The old man mutters tearfully to himself.

"Grandpa, lunchtime!"

His granddaughter is calling. He looks up toward the dining room, where their Filipino helper is setting food out on the table. It is already noon.

2. BUILDINGS VANISH QUIETLY BEHIND WOODEN BOARDS

AFTER LUNCH, THEIR HELPER DOES THE DISHES, AND HIS granddaughter goes out, same as every weekend. The old man sits in the living room staring into space, assailed by yawns he tries to resist. Now and then, a line of Cantonese opera wafts into his head, along with a tangle of memories. How could he have been so careless? This world is full of traps, and even before his accident on the stone steps, he'd already slipped and fallen in the bathroom, leaving his buttocks aching for two or three months, though that hardly slowed him down. Who'd have thought one tumble would land him in hospital? Though he escaped surgery, the broken leg feels devoid of energy, and he can only walk with a stick. He loathes the wheelchair, yet the stick slows him down too much, and he can't move far on it. Before turning seventy, he often bragged that he had the strapping figure of a young man, and indeed, his hair might have been a little grey, but his cheeks were ruddy and all the youngsters said he looked fifty-something at most. Once he turned seventy, though, his age revealed itself: his jowls drooped, the wrinkles in the corners of his mouth deepened, the salt-and-pepper hair at his temples rapidly whitened and thinned. His vision blurred and his ears no longer worked as well. Still, he went on getting the bus to Telok Ayer, Big Town.

There, he visited the places he'd once spent most of his time in: Chinatown and Tofu Street (that is, Chin Chew Street). Often, this would be discomfiting. His stomping ground of almost half a century now felt unfamiliar, alarmingly so. Buildings he knew well would suddenly be encircled by wooden boards, vanishing in almost no time, quickly replaced by strange new skyscrapers. The same thing kept happening, another familiar shophouse row surrounded by a wooden fence, disappearing while cut off from view, succeeded by yet more high-rise towers. They were going to surround and tear down every building he knew, one by one, like a dictator's secret police force eliminating all opposition. There'd come a day when all the places he'd lived in would be gone, the city utterly transformed, nothing familiar about it at all. Each time he saw those wooden boards rise around a shophouse or street block, the old man's thoughts turned dark. When this first started happening, he'd gather with his old friends at the coffee shop he once owned (when all his children refused to take over his business, he signed it over to a neighbour in a fit of pique, after which it became a gathering place for him and his friends). He understood that eventually this old shop would be boarded up, too, then quietly vanish while hidden from view. And indeed, that was what happened. After less than ten years, or perhaps a full decade—he can't quite remember, but what of it? It was finally unable to escape the wooden boards, the secret slaughter away from public view. The old man and his friends had to find another coffee shop. By this time, only Old Fong, Old Goh, and himself were left. The others, just like the buildings they'd once known, had departed this world.

The three men didn't particularly like the coffee shop they ended up at; the servers were rough and rude, the owner unfriendly. Unsavoury characters frequently gathered there, swigging beer, ostentatiously talking about Thai prostitutes, exchanging lewd jokes. Sometimes they'd flirt obnoxiously with female passers-by or customers. When the old men's social club disbanded after Old Goh's stroke, it felt like a relief. They'd had nothing to talk about but when their next check-ups were, or what ailments they'd acquired since last time.

Gazing at the hideous decrepitude of his two old friends, the final survivors, the old man might as well have been looking at himself. God knows they'd once been young, but those days truly felt like a dream, as if their current state had always been the reality, these heartbreaking, pathetic wrecks. Yes, better not to meet. To be honest, towards the end, the old man hadn't felt much like going anywhere. Several times, he got on the wrong bus and ended up miles from home, completely exhausted by the time he'd finally made his way back with difficulty. He can't avoid the fact that he's old. It's not just his strength, sight, and hearing that are failing, but his memory too. Things he once remembered perfectly clearly are now murky. Since his fall, he's moved around less, and he senses himself ageing even faster. Nothing is right. Every muscle and bone, every part of him, feels wrong. Sitting by himself, he hears his body gradually disintegrating, as if a termite colony is gnawing away at him from the inside. He needs assistance for so many things. He can't even make himself a cup of coffee, and needs to lean on the maid's arm to get to the bathroom. For now, he can manage a shower or shit on his own, but what about the future? Imagining how he'll become weaker and more useless, the old man grows frustrated and angry. The whole world is bullying him, setting itself against him, and now even his own body is at odds with him. He can see his future. Existence will become more painful, harder to bear. He'll put up with these torments, all so he can await the thing he dreads most of all: death.

*

THE OLD MAN WAKES FROM HIS NAP AND GLANCES AT THE dining room clock; it's almost two. He grabs the remote control from the coffee table and turns on the TV. In a kampong, a scrawny, dark-skinned, middle-aged man speaks to the camera in some sort of dialect he can't understand. What programme is this? The backdrop is a poverty-stricken village. The old man thinks about his own village, the one he left as a young man and never returned to. Since his wife Ah Yoke died— (When did Ah Yoke pass away? Too long ago, he can't remember.) It's been a long while since he thought about the village. Is it coming back now because of this TV show? Recalling the village means recalling his childhood, but he left such a long time ago, that portion of his life is blurrier than an old newspaper photo. On the screen, two boys in shorts, their torsos bare, lead an emaciated old cow by a filthy river. The sky is piercingly bright. He has a vague memory of himself and Tak Chai steering an ancient cow along a muddy bank, like they did so often. And the sky was just as dazzling then, wasn't it? He isn't sure. His memory is muddled up with what's on the screen. His head feels hot, as if the sun on the screen is the one from his childhood.

Suddenly, the TV pipes a jaunty tune. A woman dressed like a housewife is extolling some brand of washing powder. The old man nudges the button again, switching it off. Still clutching the remote, he shuts his eyes, searching for that childhood village in long-ago memories. Although he can't summon most of his experiences, certain scenes are still present: barren land, untended fields, roadside beggars starving to death. Yes, his village was extremely poor. Most people who lived there were gaunt and unhealthy-looking, their clothes tattered, no different than paupers. He was the same, patched garments and no shoes. As far as he remembers, almost everyone in the village went around barefoot. They seldom ate rice, making do with sweet potatoes and yams, often skipping meals altogether. He still remembers the rumbling agony of his famished belly, his guts trying to devour themselves. He had two sisters and a brother, all younger. He can hardly remember anything about them, only that their mother got some kind of illness that left her bedridden. Their father brewed herbal remedies, filling the house with a thick medicinal stench, as she moaned in pain on her sickbed.

YU SAU AND KAH ONN

As soon as Yu Sau walks into the coffee house, she sees Kah Onn in a corner booth. He waves, his usual smug self-confidence completely gone. His movements are slower than usual, and he looks aggrieved and a little sulky, like a schoolboy raising his hand in class to confess he's done something wrong. Yu Sau doesn't know if she ought to laugh at him or lose her temper. Of course, she's already decided to forgive him. If she were still angry, she wouldn't have come. She sits opposite him, and when the waiter comes, orders spaghetti with shiitake mushrooms. Kah Onn chooses the black pepper steak, then sits with his head down as if praying, silently staring at the beads of moisture on his water glass.

Ya Sau purses her lips, glaring wordlessly at him, like a teacher faced with a naughty student. The more she looks at Kah Onn, the more he seems like an overgrown child. Indeed, he's six years younger than her. When she decided to be with him, she said that was no problem, but in fact had to wrestle with this for quite a while. Kah Onn didn't mind her being older, of course, but what about his parents? Geok Leng also warned her: You're thirty-one and he's twenty-five. Have you thought that when you're sixty, he'll only be fifty-four? A fifty-four-year-old man is still quite young-looking, especially someone with a boyish face like Kah Onn. What happens to a woman's appearance at sixty? Just take a look at Ah Kuen and you'll know! She's not yet sixty, and even though she dyes her hair, she looks well past her prime. Good luck to you!

Geok Leng's dire prediction doesn't bother Yu Sau in the least. She has a youthful face, and thinks she looks no older than Kah Onn. Sandy says she has good skin, and she knows how to take care of herself. By the time she's sixty, she'll surely look younger than Ah Kuen now. To be honest, the age difference isn't what she's worried about. Her biggest headache is Kah Onn's insecurity. He's been unlucky in love; a year ago, his girlfriend of six years dumped him for another man. Yu Sau hasn't told Geok Leng and Sandy this detail; it might turn them off the relationship, especially Geok Leng, who'd say Kah Onn must be on the rebound, desperate to find a woman to fill the emptiness in his heart, and therefore he doesn't truly love her. When Kah Onn declared his love, she told him she didn't want to be a replacement for someone else. He insisted he was serious about loving her very much, and was afraid to lose her. He sounded so certain, he could have been in court saying this under oath.

Whether because he's afraid of losing her or because his ex-girlfriend hurt him too deeply, Kah Onn is extremely prickly about her meeting with other men, which really gets on her nerves. Yesterday, for instance, she had lunch with a former colleague, Michael. When Kah Onn found out, he spent the entire evening giving her a hard time. *So when a woman gets a boyfriend, she has to stop seeing all her male friends? I'm not even married to him yet!* The more she thought about it, the more furious she got. After going on about it forever, he finally had to admit he was uneasy because she seemed to think highly of Michael. Are all men like this, unable to accept their girlfriends might have something nice to say about other men? Or was it her fault? Has she praised Michael too freely in front of Kah Onn?

"Are you still angry?"

Kah Onn's voice drags Yu Sau back. Seeing how piteous and timid he looks, she loses her temper again. "It wasn't the first time. If you're going to be this petty, we should just break up," she snaps.

Kah Onn says nothing, just wrinkles his brow and presses his lips together, hanging his head. In the silence, she hears his deep, heavy breathing, like a sigh or low moan. He is quiet for a long time before finally saying, "Is Grandpa well?"

"Very well."

Why did he take so long to speak? Normally, he'd say something right away to smooth things over or hit back at her. What's going on in his mind? Yu Sau slightly regrets what she just said. He's already apologised, so why is she still criticising him? This is a public place. Does she really want to start another argument in front of all these people? Her temper is awful. She glances at Kah Onn, who is still frowning, staring at his interlaced hands on the table. What is he thinking? Is he seriously reflecting on what she just said? She twirls some spaghetti on her fork and brings it to her mouth. Was she too hard on him? Anyhow she'll have to remember not to threaten to break up when they fight.

"Hey," she says softly.

He looks up, awkwardly lifting the corners of his mouth into a smile.

"These mushrooms are delicious, want to try some?" she asks warmly, beaming at him.

Kah Onn has been working at their company a little over a year now. He's cheerful and always ready to help, which gave his colleagues, especially the female ones, a good impression of him. One time, when a few of them were having lunch together, Yu Sau complained to Geok Leng that it was hard to get a cab in her neighbourhood, which was troublesome when she had to bring Grandpa to the hospital. Kah Onn, sitting nearby, immediately piped up that he had a car, and as long as it was outside work hours, he'd be happy to give them a lift. Yu Sau said Grandpa made sure his follow-up appointments were on a Saturday, to suit her schedule. "That's perfect," Kah Onn exclaimed.

"Oh no, I'd feel bad troubling you at the weekend," Yu Sau protested, but Kah Onn smiled and said it was no problem at all.

That Saturday, he showed up in his car and helped her bring Grandpa to the hospital. Not only that, he started driving her, Geok Leng and Sandy home each day, claiming it was on his way, even though it wasn't really. The three of them thought he was a great guy. The only thing they didn't like was that he smoked. Finally, Yu Sau told him, and he explained that he wasn't actually hooked, it was just a habit he'd picked up after getting dumped (which is how she found out about the ex). The next day, he walked over to her desk and announced, "I've quit."

"Good for you!" she replied.

"For real!" he insisted.

"Congratulations."

He grinned at her and, coming closer, murmured, "Don't I deserve a reward? For example, you could have dinner with me." And then, with emphasis, "Just the two of us."

She agreed to the date. The following weekend, they met for afternoon tea.

The first movie he took her to was Ann Hui's *Song of the Exile*. Not long after the feature started, he reached over to her seat and took her hand. She didn't pull away. His grip was firm and warm, but she didn't really have any other feelings about it. The film was about a woman, played by Maggie Cheung, who was studying in England, which made Yu Sau nostalgic for her own time in the UK, although she was never as westernised or lively as this character. She hadn't so much as gone on a bicycle ride with any of her classmates, particularly the white ones (even the girls), nor did she drink or smoke. You could say she fit the traditional Chinese image of a good girl. But was she actually good? What about Maggie Cheung's character, Hueyin?

In fact, Yu Sau was just an inflexible, conservative woman who didn't know how to have fun or enjoy life. All that time at university, she'd gone nowhere apart from the lecture hall and library. At most, she'd stroll around the campus. When she went into London, it was just to buy groceries in Chinatown and browse bookshops, and perhaps have some mediocre Chinese food or visit a fast food joint with her classmates for burgers and coffee. She might see a musical, but only once in a while. Or she went on bike rides around the campus. The bike belonged to David, who taught her how to ride. David was a British guy she dated for a while, the only man she's ever kissed apart from Kah Onn. Her first kiss was on the university green, which is maybe why she feels so nostalgic for that lawn, sprawling on the grass and looking up at the red brick buildings and sky. She only ever kissed and hugged David. When he wanted more, she said no, and they broke up. He accused her of not being romantic. Well, maybe she wasn't. A dull, conservative Asian woman, not ready for (and also afraid of) sex before marriage.

Watching the film, she felt especially sentimental about the old tenement building that was the protagonist's childhood home, because she'd lived somewhere similar as a little girl, by a pasar (she used the Malay word; the Hong Kongers called it a street market), potted plants in the airwell and ancient furniture in the living room. "*The icy wind brings a message, the autumn night is endless.*" Grandpa's gramophone often played this old southern ballad, which shared a title with the film. It always moved her. Completely wrapped up in the movie, Yu Sau almost forgot Kah Onn was holding her hand, right until the credits rolled, and she realised he'd been clinging on all the way through.

"You looked completely absorbed," he said, smiling, as she withdrew her hand.

"The way Maggie Cheung treated her mother reminded me of mine," she said, touched. Yes, as a young woman, she hadn't got on well with her mum, and they grew further apart after she left for England. Her reasons were different from Hueyin's, though. Hueyin felt culturally separated from her Japanese mother. What was Yu Sau's reason? In the film, Hueyin accompanied her mother to visit relatives in her hometown, and finally understood why she was so isolated and lonely. Yu Sau didn't find this empathy until she had to care for her own mother when she had cancer. Yu Sau's mother had also been isolated and lonely. As they left the cinema, Kah Onn reached out and took her hand again. She let him hold it all the way to the car park.

A few days later, Kah Onn invited her to see another film. He knew she enjoyed Chinese movies and was a Leslie Cheung fan, so he suggested *A Chinese Ghost Story II*, also starring Joey Wang. The film had barely started when his hand reached out, this time for her thigh. When she didn't push it away, he began lightly caressing her. On this occasion, Yu Sau didn't pay much attention to the movie. It was just scene after scene of pursuit and killing, people and swords flying across the screen, and a chaotic series of explosions. Afterwards, Kah Onn gave her a lift home, and they hardly mentioned the film. From time to time, one of his hands would leave the steering wheel to explore her naked thigh, and when she let him, boldly crept upwards, until she squeezed her legs together and batted him away.

When they reached the car park at her place, they got out and he wrapped his arms around her, pressing her against the side of the car. He thrust against her, kissed her vigorously, ran his hands over her body, whispered in her ear how he adored her, how she enchanted him. His ardent groin rubbed hard against her. She felt scalding hot all over. Tangled together, they stumbled to the lift.

Grandpa and Maria had already gone to bed when Yu Sau brought Kah Onn into the flat. As soon as the front door closed, he began pulling off her clothes, and they stumbled into her bedroom, almost falling over the sofa in the dark. She was pretty much naked by the time they got there, and wouldn't let him turn on the light; she'd never let a man see her nude. In the gloom, she watched him take off his own clothes, and looked down at her own nakedness. They clasped their arms around each other, breathing hard, busily exploring every inch of bare skin, as if searching for something on the other person's body. And then they were in bed moaning, writhing, panting, grinding.

There was a wake downstairs in the void deck, and even with the windows shut, the mourners' conversations and Buddhist chants were audible. Yu Sau heard Grandpa cough in the next room, and wondered if he'd fallen asleep yet. And what about Maria? She tried her best to suppress her ecstatic cries, but still worried about the occasional thumping of the bed. She was a cautious person, and even in the midst of her arousal, she kept her legs shut and wouldn't let Kah Onn enter. In the end, they used their hands to extinguish each other's flames.

Remembering all this, Yu Sau reaches out and brushes the back of Kah Onn's hand with feeling. "Tasty?" she asks. Still chewing on the forkful of mushrooms she just fed him, he nods enthusiastically, looking so ridiculous she can't help giggling. He spent that night in her bed. In the morning, he was mortified to bump into Maria as he crept out, but she was completely blasé as she asked if he wanted some coffee. Yu Sau introduced Kah Onn to Grandpa. When Kah Onn said good morning, Grandpa smiled, "*Visiting Ah Lan so early?*"

"*This is my colleague. He's giving me a lift to work,*" Yu Sau explained, then turned to Kah Onn in embarrassment. "Yeuk Lan's my aunt. Grandpa often calls me by her name."

Grandpa said, "*Come visit Ah Lan whenever you're free.*" Kah Onn quickly nodded.

Yu Sau chuckled, "Grandpa's afraid no one will want to marry me." From then on, Kah Onn became a part of Yu Sau's family. He showed up at her home almost every day, hugging her in front of Grandpa or Maria, kissing her face, patting her bum.

Are things moving too fast with Kah Onn? How well does she know him? Does he understand her? Now he is gently stroking her outstretched hand.

"This morning, Grandpa met a man who likes Cantonese opera. They had a good chat," she says, sipping her coffee.

"Does Grandpa need to see the doctor this Saturday?" Kah Onn asks solicitously.

LEONG PING HUNG AND TAK CHAI

1. VILLAGE

Mr Sparrow, for 'tis he,
Flies uphill to see Auntie.
Auntie's hair is up in a bun,
Picks a red flower just for fun.
Her sash is long, her feet are small,
Such nice shoes in mud must fall.
Such good rice makes food for cats,
Such good girls will marry rats.

IN HIS OLD AGE, THIS NURSERY RHYME OFTEN POPS INTO Leong Ping Hung's mind, but no matter how he tries, he can't remember where he heard it. In the village? In Canton? On Tofu Street? Did his mother sing it to him and his siblings? He has no idea. His mother died before he was ten, and almost all his memories of her have slipped away, even what she looked like. He'll never forget he had a brother and two sisters, all younger than him. When Mother died, the sisters were eight and three, the brother seven. Their father worked hard to give them all an education, and went around looking anxious and sighing. He had an awful temper, so Ping Hung often tasted his father's fists for no reason at all, which left him seething quietly with fear and anger.

Thus Ping Hung's childhood: never enough to eat, clothes that didn't keep him warm, constant beatings. Eventually, he understood that they might eke out a living in the countryside, but would never have more than taro and sweet potatoes. In order to escape hunger and his father's fists, he decided to leave his village and find work in the city. Tak Chai, his fellow cowherd, said they ought to try Nam Yong, the south seas.

"*Lots of people from the village are there seeking gold. Nam Yong's even better than Canton,*" said Tak Chai.

"*Does Nam Yong really have gold?*" he asked excitedly.

"*The ground is covered in it!*" Tak Chai replied confidently, tilting his face up to the wide, blue sky for all the world as if he'd just returned from Nam Yong himself.

That very day, Ping Hung enthusiastically told his father over dinner that he and Tak Chai were going to look for gold in Nam Yong. To his surprise, he got a slap and lecture in response. "*Crossing the sea in a boat is dangerous. What if there's a storm? Or pirates? Forget about your gold, you'll get captured and sold off as a slave.*" Tak Chai's parents were equally opposed to the the the idea, but he refused to give up, and thought of a plan: say they were going to work in Canton, but actually get a ship from there to Nam Yong. Unfortunately, Ping Hung's dad also vetoed this plan. They were so young, he thought they were sure to get corrupted by its decadence, or kidnapped and sold off.

Life in the village got harder and harder. Ping Hung's father came home one day looking troubled, and said he was planning to sell Ping Hung's little sister to a rich family in the next village, to be their maid. Ping Hung pleaded again for him and Tak Chai to go to the city. There was simply no work in the village, and if he was gone, at least there'd be one less mouth to feed. To his surprise, his father didn't smack him this time, but was silent for quite a while before finally agreeing.

And so early one morning, before the sky was fully light, Ping Hung and Tak Chai got out of bed, ate their breakfast of roast yams, and set off on their journey. Their families followed them sorrowfully all the way to the village entrance, then watched them go with tears streaming down their faces.

Leong Ping Hung was thirteen, and Tak Chai was a year older.

2. CANTON

THE TWO BAREFOOT BOYS, WEARING BAMBOO HATS AND clutching their little bundles of possessions, finally reached the city centre.

The streets here were lined with shops and full of people, an eye-opening experience for them. They started feeling inferior, growing more uncomfortable with every step. After forcing themselves to walk around the marketplace for an entire day, they hadn't managed to find any work. Shop owners and clerks treated them with disgust, as if they were beggars. By evening, they were exhausted, but didn't dare rest in a doorway, and finally found a bridge they could spend the night under.

The light had just faded when an elderly rag-and-bone man joined them. In the pitch dark, they heard intermittent shuffling footsteps as more and more people bedded down under the bridge. The air around Ping Hung grew foul, and all night long he had to breathe the stench of rubbish mixed with piss. There were a few coughs, someone yawning, someone else snoring, farting, mumbling, but he was too tired to care. Tak Chai started snoring, and soon Ping Hung was asleep too. Some time later, the cold woke him. Tak Chai clutched his shoulders, and he pressed close to Ping Hung. "*I'm freezing*," Tak Chai stammered. "*Me too,*" Ping Hung said, teeth chattering. The opened their bundles and swaddled themselves in every item of clothing they'd brought, then hugged tightly. Even then, they couldn't get warm.

Ping Hung woke up first. It was dawn, and seven or eight other people were squeezed under the bridge with them. Two scrawny stray dogs were huddled by his and Tak Chai's legs. So that's why they'd felt some warmth against their calves. When Tak Chai woke, he kicked the dogs till they whined fretfully and scampered off with their tails between their legs. Ping Hung thought that he and Tak Chai were no better off than those dogs, which gave him a twinge of sadness. They packed up the clothes they'd used as makeshift blankets, and followed a creek upstream until the water started looking clean.

After washing their faces and rinsing their mouths, they felt much better, and returned to the bustling street to continue their mission from the day before: knocking on every door to ask for work. It was the same story: people saw their tattered clothes and grimy faces, and immediately shooed them away like beggars or stray dogs. In no time at all, the sun was setting and it was evening again. They were tired and hungry from walking all day, their stomachs growling and their lips cracked from thirst. They'd eaten the last roast yam they'd brought with them, and now had nothing apart from their tattered clothes. It finally hit them that finding a job in the city wouldn't be easy, and if nothing changed, they'd be forced to return to their village the next day on empty stomachs. Ping Hung was sure if he went back that his father would smack him, probably more than once, but that was still better than starving to death in the city.

He and Tak Chai dragged their exhausted bodies to a restaurant and loitered by the entrance. Because they were starving, it took them quite a while to gather the courage to walk in. A man in his sixties was clearing the tables. The boys walked up to him and stared timidly for quite a while before Tak Chai managed to ask if they could have any of the scraps left behind by customers. The old man crinkled his brow as he looked them up and down. They opened their eyes wide and stared at him hopefully, though deep down they didn't expect him to behave any differently to the other people they'd encountered in the last couple of days. Instead, he gave them each a bowl of leftover rice and broth. They immediately dropped to their knees to thank him, then squatted by the entrance wolfing down every last mouthful. It tasted like the best thing they'd had in years.

Afterwards, they returned their empty bowls to the man and bowed in gratitude, thanking him over and over again. The man hastily pulled them to their feet and gestured behind the counter at a middle-aged man with a goatee. *"I just work here. You ought to be thanking my boss!"* They quickly turned and kowtowed to the other man, adding that they'd be happy to help wash dishes or sweep the floor in return for the food. The boss sized them up like the first man had, and said all right, they should go to the kitchen and help wash up. When he saw they were hard-working and honest, he hired them. He was called Uncle Gat, while the assistant who'd given them food was Uncle Wah. That night, Uncle Wah said they could sleep in the kitchen.

Just as they'd been about to give up hope, they'd managed to find a job in the city that provided accommodation and two meals a day. Things were looking up for Ping Hung and Tak Chai.

3. HONG KONG

HAVING SETTLED IN THE CITY, PING HUNG AND TAK CHAI felt their eyes had been opened to the world. Clothing alone was a series of new experiences. Back in the village, everyone wore the same thing: plain blue cotton garments, patched and ragged. Here, only manual labourers and rickshaw pullers dressed like this. Almost every woman wore a cheongsam, and some even had permed hair. The men were in long-sleeved mandarin jackets. Now and then, they'd see a one in a western-style suit or a woman in a European dress holding a little parasol. The first time Tak Chai saw someone in a suit, he bragged to Ping Hung that he was going to earn some cash, and when that happened, he'd definitely have a suit made, then he'd marry a cheongsam-wearing lady. Ping Hung smiled at this fantasy. "*We're both illiterate. How would you ever earn enough money for a suit, never mind a cheongsam woman?*"

After they'd worked at the restaurant for a month, they were surprised to receive their first wages. It wasn't very much, but they were delighted. Ping Hung was so pleased that he decided the city was a pretty good place, and they should drop their Nam Yong plans. He suggested to Tak Chai that they stay. After all, it would be much easier to visit their families back in the village. But Tak Chai was still dead set on Nam Yong, and grumbled that Ping Hung was too unambitious. Their month's wages came to so little, they could work into old age and still never own a suit. Only in Nam Yong would they have the chance to strike gold, and then they'd wear suits and have beautiful brides in cheongsams. Ping Hung couldn't talk him out of it. They'd also gotten to know some fellow villagers, Ah Chiu, Ah Chuen and Ah Hoi, who worked in the nearby bakery and medicine shop and likewise hoped to get rich in Nam Yong. This strengthened Tak Chai's resolve.

After two months at the restaurant, Ping Hung said they should ask Uncle Gat if they could visit home. Tak Chai said, "*The village is so poor. In the time we've been here, we've already seen quite a few people from home come here for work. Anyone could do our jobs. If we go back home so soon, what if Uncle Gat hires someone else to replace us?*" They decided to wait a little longer before asking for time off. But as time went on, more and more people arrived from the village. Ah Chiu, Ah Chuen and Ah Hoi didn't dare step away from their jobs, so of course neither did Ping Hung and Tak Chai.

The two boys stayed in Canton for a year. By living frugally, they managed to save up enough to pay for the passage to Nam Yong, and got ready to say goodbye to Uncle Gat and Uncle Wah before catching the train to Hong Kong with Ah Chiu and the others. Once again, Ping Hung suggested to Tak Chai that they should go back home for a visit. He reckoned they were leaving the restaurant anyway, so why not see their parents before departing? Tak Chai was still against the idea. What if something or other came up while they were home, and they ended up stuck in the village? They could forget about Nam Yong then.

This made sense, but after so long in town without a single trip back home, Ping Hung was troubled. And Tak Chai? He must have felt the same, but his determination to reach Nam Yong was even stronger, and you'd never have guessed from his appearance that he was feeling the slightest bit uneasy. *"We'll make some money in Nam Yong, then go back home in our fancy clothes. Just think how grand we'll look!"*

And so Ping Hung and Tak Chai made up their minds to set off for Hong Kong; Uncle Gat and Uncle Wah couldn't persuade them to stay. Before they left, Uncle Gat gave them each a red packet, and Uncle Wah came to see them off. He gave them flatbreads to eat along the way, and warned them to be careful not to get swindled or kidnapped. Ping Hung found himself a little reluctant to say goodbye to Uncle Wah (and of course, to the city), but luckily Ah Chiu and the others were on the train, so he had a few more companions his own age, and wasn't as sad and lonely as when they left the village.

The train pulled into Tsim Sha Tsui. They stepped out of the main train station, into Hong Kong.

Hong Kong's streets were much livelier and busier than Canton's. People carried baskets on their shoulders, hawking their wares by the side of the road, while rickshaw boys dashed along with their passengers. Now and then, there'd even be a private motorcar rumbling by, horn honking loudly. It took them a while to find an inn, where they crammed into a small room with bunk beds. They stayed there for two nights, till they could get boat tickets to Singapore.

4. SINGAPORE

Ping Hung and Tak Chai squashed into steerage with all the other passengers who looked just as poor as them. The air in this part of the boat was foul with the sour stench of sweat and vomit. They endured the awful rocking for about four days, before finally arriving in Singapore.

Singapore was a British colonial possession, and foreign labourers first had to pass through the quarantine centre at Pulau Sakijang Bendera, where they were disinfected with sulphur. And so, before actually alighting on Singapore proper, the steerage passengers first had to take a little boat to Saint John's Island, as it was also known.

Quite a few people had vomited prodigiously during those several days in the hold. Ping Hung and Tak Chai didn't get seasick, but the reek of sulphur at the quarantine centre made them heave. Even before reaching the promised land, Ping Hung was already feeling mistreated. With a twinge in his heart, he worried that Nam Yong might not be such a paradise after all, and regretted coming here. He grumbled to Tak Chai that they should never have left Canton, a place for Cantonese people where everyone spoke their language and shared their way of life. If you were willing to work hard, you'd definitely be able to feed yourself. Uncle Gat and Uncle Wah had treated them so well, why had they ever quit the restaurant? Singapore was far from home, and they knew no one here. The language was unfamiliar too. What if they ended up begging, or worse, starving to death in the street?

Tak Chai didn't seem anxious at all. He believed it would be easy to make a living here. They'd found jobs within two days of arriving in Canton, so surely they'd have no problem in Singapore. Ah Chiu and the rest agreed that they were young and strong, and weren't afraid of hard work, so they definitely wouldn't starve to death. Ping Hung was less optimistic. He reckoned they'd been very lucky to meet their benefactors so quickly in the last place, and might not be so fortunate in Singapore. Starvation seemed distinctly possible. Tak Chai was the sort of chap who didn't worry about anything; if the sky fell on him, he'd use it as a blanket. He was constantly having to comfort Ping Hung, telling him not to worry, the boat straightens as it approaches the dock. Where did he learn that proverb? Even if it were true, Ping Hung's concern was that their metaphorical boat would sink long before it got near a harbour, and then what would they do? He went around frowning, sunk in worry. After a week of anxiety, they were finally allowed to leave Saint John's Island.

As they approached the mainland, Ping Hung noticed some tall, skinny trees on the shore with leaves like giant combs sprouting from their tops. They looked bizarre. A man standing next to them said these were coconut trees, and they could be found in China too, on Hainan Island. A short while later, the boat docked.

The sun-drenched shore was full of porters, dock workers, and people waiting to meet the ship; a noisy tide of humanity that heaved and surged. Ah Chiu, Ah Chuen and Ah Hoi were immediately surrounded by relatives and family friends, chattering rapidly about this or that. Ping Hung stood next to Tak Chai, stunned to be in the midst of so many strangers. He felt the loneliness and fear of arriving in a strange place. When Ah Chiu and the other two had departed, he remained sunk in gloom, feeling as if he'd somehow been cheated. Whom by? Those three boys? They hadn't claimed not to know anyone here, but also hadn't mentioned that they did! He and Tak Chai had blundered here without knowing a single soul. If they starved to death, who'd be to blame?

Yet Tak Chai was chatting away cheerfully, insistent that their boat would straighten itself out any minute now. Ping Hung watched people passing by and decided he couldn't trust a single one of them. They'd have to rely on themselves. That's fine, that's what they'd planned to do anyway. No point feeling defeated just because the other guys were lucky enough to know people here. Unfortunately, almost everyone they met spoke Hokkien, which they didn't understand, so it was extremely difficult to talk to the locals. Even so, they managed to find a hostel near the quay that had a couple of beds available.

As Ping Hung and Tak Chai put their luggage on their bunks, the middle-aged man in the next bed came over to say hello. He was tall and sturdily-built, and seemed the bluff, hearty sort. He said in Cantonese, *"My name's Ah Keung, just call me Brother Keung!"* He was older, so they called him Uncle Keung instead, which he seemed equally happy with. He told them he was also a bachelor from Canton, and had been here more than four months. He worked as a labourer at the docks, carrying sacks of rice. He warned them that Nam Yong was very hot, and it was best to bathe three times a day. If they ever started feeling unwell, throwing water on themselves would help.

Uncle Keung asked if they had family in Singapore, and they shook their heads. What about jobs? They shook their heads again. *"All right!"* he said, the two befuddled young men a thumbs-up. *"No one's taking care of you, yet you made it all the way to Singapore without getting kidnapped and sold as slaves! Lucky chaps. Well done! Well done!"* He nodded and smiled so much it looked like he was making fun of them, but when he was finished saying well done, he smacked them on the shoulder and added, *"Come with me to Boat Quay tomorrow morning, they're hiring coolies."*

Having just arrived, Ping Hung and Tak Chai didn't dare go wandering too far. After washing up, they went for a quick look around the neighbourhood, watching passers-by from a nearby verandah. They were curious about one man's appearance: he was in a white shirt, with a white cloth wrapped around his waist, and had very curly hair. His skin was the colour of charcoal. Back at the hostel, they described him to Uncle Keung, who said, "*That was an Indian. Didn't you see any of them on Pulau Sakijang Bendera?*" They shook their heads. Ping Hung had been so dizzy from the sulphur fumes at the quarantine centre, and so distracted by his anxiety, he wasn't sure if he had or not, and it was only in talking to Tak Chai later that he remembered some men with darker skin, but their clothes had been different. When they came ashore and the other boys' families descended like a swarm of bees, he'd been so uncomfortable surrounded by these strangers that he hadn't taken in who else was on the quay. Seeing how solicitously the other three were being cooed over, he'd felt awful, confused and lonely, his future uncertain. How could he have paid any attention to his surroundings?

Uncle Keung explained that apart from the Chinese, Singapore also had other kinds of people, namely the Indians, the Malays, and the Ang Moh devils. This land belonged to the Ang Moh, so their status was the highest. Tak Chai suddenly remembered the dark-skinned Molocha people he'd seen in Canton with their hair bound up in cloth, though their clothes were different from the Indian just now. Did the Molocha count as Indian?

"*If their heads were wrapped up, they were Bengalis,*" said Uncle Keung.

Ping Hung and Tak Chai hadn't had a decent night's sleep in a while, neither in steerage nor on Pulau Sakijang Bendera. After dinner, they chatted a little more with Uncle Keung, bathed, then climbed into their bunks. In the middle of the night, Ping Hung's neck, back and shoulders started itching. He called out to Tak Chai on the upper bunk, who he was feeling it too. They got up and started scratching, only to find they were covered in little bugs that gave off a terrible stink when squashed. Sleep was now impossible. They sat on their bunks catching insects, cursing and grumbling so loudly they eventually woke Uncle Keung. He yelled through the darkness, sounding annoyed, *"Those are just bedbugs. Just grit your teeth and put up with it, you'll get used to this."*

The two boys stayed up all night getting bitten by bedbugs. They didn't dare lie down again, so just sat on the edge of their beds, yawning. Ping Hung shut his eyes and dozed off a little, blearily hearing the rumble of an electric tram outside the window. It was daybreak. Tak Chai crawled out of his bunk and, in the daylight spilling into the dorm, they looked at each other's necks and faces, which were covered in little bumps. There were more bite marks on their arms and legs, and their forefingers and thumbs were stained with bedbug blood. The filthy bedspread was bloody too, some fresh from the night before, some so old it had turned black. *"We've been attacked by vampires!"* Tak Chai grumbled. They went to the shared bathroom to wash up. As Ping Hung poured water over his body, he discovered two more bedbugs on his chest and belly. Tak Chai probably had some too! Afterwards, they washed their dirty clothes, ate a bowl of congee with a few bits of salted vegetable and tofu, then followed Uncle Keung to Boat Quay.

5. CARRYING RICE SACKS

EVEN THOUGH IT WAS ONLY APRIL, THE TEMPERATURES quickly started rising after nine in the morning. Ping Hung spent all morning hauling rice sacks, and by the afternoon break, his clothes were so sweaty he looked like he'd been dunked in water. Following some colleagues, he and Tak Chai went to the public baths on South Canal Road to wash up, yet when they stepped outside, the scorching sun left them perspiring again before taking a few steps. This felt like a pot of boiling water, like their brains were being roasted. Everyone said it was summer year round in Nam Yong, and every day would be this hot. Would they get heatstroke? Uncle Keung smiled and reassured him, "*It may be summer all year round in Nam Yong, but one rainstorm will turn it into autumn.*" He was right—it started raining after dinner, and the falling water washed away all the heat of the day.

When Ping Hung and Tak Chai returned to the hostel each evening after a long day of hauling rice sacks, they were both exhausted and aching all over. Ping Hung felt as if his bones were ready to fall apart. While everyone else in their dorm bathed and got ready to go out on the town, these two only wanted to stay in and rest. Their only entertainment was sitting by their beds with a half-full basin of water, catching bedbugs. One by one, they'd pick the insects out of their blankets, their pillows and the wooden slats of their bed frame, then fling them into the water. They did this till seven, lights out, after which only the lamps in the dining hall remained on. They were at work all day, so could only kill bedbugs for a couple of hours after dinner. It took a week before they saw a difference. The first day or two, their basins were full of floating bedbug corpses. The numbers decreased over the week, and the boys slept more comfortably at night, no longer itching all over. By the end of their first week, they no longer had to spend their evenings hunched over a basin of water.

6. KOPITIAM

PING HUNG AND TAK CHAI WERE THE YOUNGEST OF ALL the coolies. It was hardest on Ping Hung, the scrawniest person there, who found the work most arduous. With the sacks pressing heavily down on him, his legs trembled when he walked, and soon he couldn't even stand upright. After a couple of weeks, Uncle Keung saw how much he was suffering, and told him he'd heard a coffee shop in Big Town was looking for assistants. He gave them the address and sketched out a simple map on the back of a calendar page. They skipped the quay the next day and went there instead.

Following Uncle Keung's map, they found themselves in Kreta Ayer. It turned out this neighbourhood was full of Cantonese people, which immediately made it feel familiar, as if they were back in Canton. If only they could find work here. They asked directions, and soon arrived at the kopitiam. Inside, they met a tall, skinny, middle-aged man who spoke perfect Cantonese. Tak Chai respectfully called him Uncle, told him their names, and asked if the shop was hiring. The man studied them both for a while, and asked how long they'd been in Singapore. Less than a month, Tak Chai answered glibly. They were hefting sacks of rice at the docks, but they'd worked at a restaurant in Canton before, and would do well at the kopitiam. The man asked how much they earned at the moment, and Tak Chai answered honestly.

This tall, thin man was the coffee shop owner. He told the boys that his assistants got paid less than dock workers, and he was only looking to take on one person at the moment. Ping Hung hastily assured him they didn't mind about the wages, as long as they got something to eat and a place to sleep, but could he please take them both? The boss folded his arms and looked them up and down. Ping Hung thought back to Canton, where Uncle Gat and Uncle Wah had scrutinised them the same way. They'd had nowhere to go at the time. Hunger and desperation had taken away their confidence, filling them with fear. Now, perhaps because they were older, perhaps because they had their jobs at the docks to fall back on, they were able to face the kopitiam owner's gaze impassively, even though they wanted very much to work here. When he finally said, *All right!*" they were as overjoyed as they'd been when Uncle Gat took them on, and bowed in thanks again and again. The boss was called Ong Kwok Kin, but told them to call him Uncle Kin. They'd start work the next day. "*Thank you, Uncle Kin!*" they chorused.

Although they'd be earning less for longer hours, life still felt a lot better, mainly because room and board was included. They rushed back to the hostel, hoping to say goodbye to Uncle Keung, but he was still at the docks, so they just settled their bill and took their meagre possessions to the kopitiam, stopping on the way to have their hair cut at a roadside barber stall. They started work that very day, and that night slept on canvas camp beds in the shop, along with the manager and his assistant.

At five the next morning, Ping Hung and Tak Chai were kicked awake by the manager. Literally kicked awake: rather than calling them, he booted their beds. Ping Hung was so startled he almost fell to the ground. Naturally, he was furious, but by the time he got up the manager had made coffee, and was setting mugs on the table next to them, telling them to drink up and put away their beds. This was Ping Hung and Tak Chai's first ever taste of coffee. They immediately loved this piping hot, aromatic brown fluid, with its hint of bitterness through the sweet condensed milk. Coffee was delicious.

While Ping Hung and Tak Chai climbed out of bed and drank their coffee, the manager sat nearby, smoking glumly. The overhead lights were still off, so the only illumination came from a small lamp in the kitchen and the tip of his cigarette flickering in the dark. The man's bony face came in and out of view through the puffs of smoke. When they said good morning and thanked him for the coffee, he just nodded silently. After he was done smoking, he went into the kitchen and started work. They didn't know his name; everyone just called him Number One. Later on, they heard some customers refer to him as Pretty Boy, a nickname that could only be a cruel joke: he was in his sixties, short and scrawny, and couldn't be described as "pretty" by any stretch of the imagination. They finished their coffee and brought the cups into the kitchen, where Number One's assistant was brushing his teeth in the attached bathroom. They didn't know his name either, and said, "*Good morning, Number Two,*" when he emerged. Number Two was about twenty years old. He had a head of thick, curly hair, and narrow eyes that made him look perpetually drowsy. He'd come back very late the night before, so their first night of sleep in this shop was interrupted by his knocking. (Later, they would learn that this was a regular occurrence.)

That day, Ping Hung and Tak Chai heard Uncle Kin and the other two speaking a language they didn't understand. Afterwards, Number Two informed them this was Hainanese. Uncle Kin was from Hainan, as were his manager and assistant. On their second day, Ping Hung and Tak Chai met the boss's wife. Numbers One and Two called her Big Sister Kam, so the boys followed suit. She'd brought four pairs of striped blue trousers and four white T-shirts for Ping Hung and Tak Chai, two sets each. These were their uniforms that they would change into each morning before the shop opened. The boys had never had new clothes before, only hand-me-downs. Thrilled, they thanked her, and Ping Hung asked if they could wear them outside of work. Big Sister Kam giggled and replied, "*It's up to you, but everyone will know you work at Wing Fong Kopitiam!*" She was Cantonese, which explained why Uncle Kin was so fluent at the dialect.

Big Sister Kam was a cheerful, witty woman, and capable too. She started gabbing away the minute she arrived, and though she had a loud voice, she was never fierce. Still, the staff were more afraid of her than of Uncle Kin, who was placid and had a slow manner of speaking. Ping Hung watched him discussing things with Kam, and noticed that he usually gave way to her.

After a couple of days at Wing Fong, Ping Hung and Tak Chai realised that everyone in this neighbourhood was Cantonese. No wonder everyone they'd asked directions from whilst trying to find their way here had spoken their language!

7. TOFU STREET

Ping Hung and Tak Chai worked six days a week, but had to alternate their days off. There weren't many places to go, so mostly they just wandered round the neighbourhood in their clogs.

Ping Hung's favourite pastime was to watch the dough figurine maker on Tofu Street. Each morning around ten, he appeared at the street corner wheeling an old bicycle with a wooden box strapped to its rack, a sharp-chinned middle-aged man with a little goatee and a cigarette drooping from a corner of his mouth. He'd stop by the drain, and slowly open up the box, which folded over the bicycle to make a little table. Then he'd sit on a folding chair, still smoking, narrow his eyes, and spread out his colourful array of doughs. Then he'd get to work.

In the man's hands, these clumps of colour became, like magic, tiny figurines. As each one came into shape, he'd stick it onto a wooden skewer, holding that in his left hand while his right brought the cigarette to his lips between two fingers. He'd take a deep breath, then let out a stream of white smoke that blew over the figure. As it dispersed, he'd study it a bit longer, tap the ash off his cigarette, return it to his mouth, prod the figurine here and there, give it a final look, then wedge the skewer into a crack in the box so it stood upright.

He went through the exact same motions to make each figurine, almost like a ritual, which made the puff of smoke that enveloped it take on a magical aura, as if he was breathing mystical life into each one. Ping Hung would stand next to the bicycle, watching all sorts of dough figures come vividly into being: generals with war banners waving behind them, the Monkey King with his gold-banded staff, pretty maidens with elaborate hairstyles, young gentlemen fanning themselves. It was like a play, watching these characters appear on the wooden box as if it were a stage. Ping Hung could sit there for an hour or two without getting tired of this, so enchanted that the bustle of the crowds and the hawkers calling out their wares seemed to disappear, and he didn't feel people jostling him. When they yelled at him for getting in their way, he just smiled foolishly. When he animatedly described all this to Tak Chai back at the kopitiam, Tak Chai said he'd seen the dough figurine man too, and was just as fascinated.

"*Did you notice how, when he's at work, his jaw goes up and down like a mouse?*" Tak Chai imitated the movement.

"*That's right!*" Ping Hung burst into laughter.

Uncle Kin's kopitiam didn't sell liquor, so it closed in the evening. After work, Ping Hung and Tak Chai liked to walk around Tofu Street, where the hawkers would be selling the last of the day's bedraggled fruit and vegetables at a discount, and second-hand clothes (this is where they got their shirts and trousers). At this time of day, the last of the setting sun spilled lazily over the road like fortified wine, elongating everyone's shadows. People started coming outdoors, setting their stools up by their doorways so they could cool off and trade gossip. The men smoked hookahs and played Chinese chess, while the women held babies to their chests and waved palm leaf fans, or sat with their sewing. Children squealed as they chased each other through the streets, while hawkers' voices wove through the clatter of wooden clogs. When the kids got too rambunctious, one of the adults would yell at them to behave, and they'd quiet down for a while before starting again.

"*Fatty fatty fat old thing, buy some pork as offering, shit*

yourself just halfway there, go home change your underwear."
The children's song drifted through the intoxicating twilight,
and a little yellow dog ran excitedly amongst them in a frenzy
of barking.

One time, they saw a woman in her thirties let down her
bun and start combing it, thick black hair cascading down to
her chest, covering her pale face, like a veil over her delicate
beauty. Ping Hung and Tak Chai were mesmerised, their hearts
suddenly thumping. Every evening after that, whenever they
saw a woman on Tofu Street brushing her hair, they hoped it
was her, but most of the time it was someone else. There were
women who looked like ghosts with their hair down.

As the sky darkened, if the boys didn't feel like an early
night, they went to listen to the storyteller on Banda Hill.
They'd drop two cents into his tin, grab stools from the pile,
and find a space for themselves in the crowd. The storyteller
was in his forties, a scrawny, craggy man with a big nose and
high cheekbones. His eyes blazed expressively as he regaled
them with countryside legends, tales of strange happenings,
and excerpts from Qing dynasty novels. By the faint light of
his table lamp, his facial expressions shifted along with the
story, becoming the upright Qing official, the impetuous
ruffian, the sly villain, the mild-mannered scholar, the gravel-
voiced old man, the coquettish woman, and many more. The
boys particularly remembered one rendition of a Justice Bao
story, during which he turned his paper fan into a gavel and
thumped it hard on the table, eyes wide and voice raised in a
thunderous roar, stunning the audience into complete silence.
When he made his voice high-pitched to play a woman, no
matter whether it was a gossipy old grandma or a pretty young
miss, he'd have the audience rolling about with laughter. His
gift for mimicry ensured his stall was always packed. He'd
light an incense stick and tell stories until it burnt out. If they
wanted to stay for more, they had to put another two cents

in the tin. Everyone was constantly tossing money in there, unwilling to leave. Even the frugal Ping Hung and Tak Chai found themselves unable to stop at just one instalment.

Before he started his main programme, the storyteller gave them a digest of recent news and current events, and this was captivating too. Although Ping Hung and Tak Chai heard some of this when customers chatted with Uncle Kin, it was only fragmentary, not clear and digestible like when the storyteller laid it out. After a few sessions, the boys learnt the storyteller was named Ah Boon, and had quite a large following, but unfortunately his opium habit consumed most of his earnings.

After a month at the kopitiam, they were settled in, and Ping Hung began to grow homesick. Whenever they walked past the arcade with the herbal tea stall on Tofu Street, and saw the man who read and wrote letters home, he and Tak Chai would linger there, wishing they could send word back to their families, but neither knew their home addresses. Besides, their parents were illiterate, like most people in their village, so how would they decipher a letter? Their families believed they were still in Canton, and were probably worried after so much time without any contact. Would they search for them in the city? The boys regretted not going home for a visit, but it was too late now. No matter what, they had to write home soon to let their families know they were in Singapore and doing well. Yet they never got round to visiting the letter-writer.

8. IF YOU HAD A GRAMOPHONE, YOU COULD DEFINITELY AFFORD A SUIT

PERHAPS BECAUSE THEIR FATES WERE ALIGNED, OR PERHAPS because Ping Hung and Tak Chai were clever, hard-working and obedient, Uncle Kin and Big Sister Kam grew very fond of the boys. The couple had no children of their own, and in less than six months, Kam was treating them as if they were her own kids, affectionately calling them "Hung" and "Tak" like a mother calling to her brood.

The couple lived in a flat above the kopitiam, and whenever Kam brought down some broth or cooling tea for her husband, she almost always had a portion for the boys too. "*Tak, Hung, here's some watercress soup for you, come get it while it's hot.*" Their hearts felt toasty warm when she spoke to them like that. Ping Hung, particularly, wished he could just call her Mum.

Big Sister Kam liked watching Cantonese opera, and though Uncle Kin was Hainanese, she'd managed to get him interested too. Now and then, they'd bring Ping Hung and Tak Chai to a show. The boys lost count of how many times they'd seen *Blue Sky Birthday Wishes, A Minister of Six Nations, The Minister Leaps Into Promotion* and *Heaven's Concubine Bids Her Son Farewell.* They learnt that a veteran performer in *Heaven's Concubine* was singing with a Central Plains accent; of course, it was Kam who told them that. She always got Tak and Hung to sit next to her, and would explain the ins and outs of the show to them. Sometimes, she sang along with the female lead's falsetto. Apart from these outdoor shows, Uncle Kin also brought them to the fifth floor of the Great Southern Hotel for the performances there. (He also took them up to the sixth floor, where Peking Opera was performed. After seeing the martial artists there turning somersaults, Tak Chai exuberantly announced to Ping Hung that one day he'd learn this style of movement too.)

A few times, Uncle Kin and Big Sister Kam took them out to supper after the show. They went to a market near the hotel, where even at this late hour, the streets blazed with light and seemed perpetually crowded. Big cars were parked by the roadside. Kam told them many rich men came here for supper, accompanied by rouged women with permed hair and alluring cheongsams: dance hall girls.

Before the new year, the boys went upstairs to help Uncle Kin with the spring cleaning. That's where they saw a gramophone for the first time.

This was a little box with a trumpet-shaped speaker fixed to it; on the box was a turntable with a stylus. Big Sister Kam put a vinyl record on, cranked the handle, and the turntable started to revolve. She gently dropped the needle onto the edge of the black disc, and music came through the speaker, as if a soprano and her entire orchestra were hidden in the box. A startling invention. Kam left the music playing so the boys could listen as they worked. Seeing how distracted they were, she didn't put on any more records after the second one finished playing. *"Pay attention to your work, you can listen to music when you're done,"* she said. With the trumpet falling silent, they obediently turned their minds back to spring cleaning.

When they were done, Tak Chai whispered to Ping Hung, *"As soon as I've earned enough, I'm going to buy one of those."*

Ping Hung replied, *"Me too."*

"Great, we'll have one each."

"What about suits? Are we still buying suits?"

"If you had a gramophone, you could definitely afford a suit!" said Tak Chai, raising an eyebrow.

They galloped cheerfully down the stairs, certain they would soon have a gramophone and a suit apiece.

9. TAK CHAI JOINS THE OPERA TROUPE

UNCLE KIN WAS GOOD FRIENDS WITH THE VETERAN performers and musicians of the local opera troupe, and would often meet them at a teahouse or for a mahjong session. Many of them also frequented Wing Fong Kopitiam, where they'd gossip with Uncle Kin about the troupe and popular singers such as Lan Wah Hang, Chan Fei Nung, or Ma Si Tsang.

Uncle Kun, a musician from Hong Kong, loved coming to Wing Fong and describing the teahouses of Central in Hong Kong, where the customers sipped their tea and listened to music. *"We charged fifteen cents a person, and there was never an empty seat in the house,"* he said. *"Then there's Shek Tong Tsui, where all the famous whorehouses are. That's where rich Hong Kongers spend their cash!"* Ping Hung was surprised to hear this, because they'd experienced a very different Hong Kong from the one Uncle Kun was describing. Then again, they'd only spent two days there. Even so, they'd seen a couple of men in suits and women in dresses out in the streets, but most people had been wearing faded cloth outfits like Ping Hung and Tak Chai, and looked like regular workers. When they'd gone to eat near the guesthouse, they'd overheard complaints that Hong Kong had more people than jobs, and it was hard to earn a living here, unlike in Canton. They also heard about the soaring cost of rice that July, leading to hoarding, so people had to eat yams or sweet potatoes instead. That's why he and Tak Chai were so eager to follow Ah Chiu and the rest out of there. He quietly wondered what Uncle Kun was doing in Nam Yong, if there was so much money in Hong Kong? Of course, he never dared to ask.

One of the actors, a "warrior performer" called Law Siu Kai, was very fond of Tak Chai. One time, Tak Chai was standing nearby after serving coffee, when Master Law abruptly turned around and asked if he liked Cantonese opera. Tak Chai not only replied that he loved it, he even sang a "long phrases, flowing water" passage. Law Siu Kai said that was wonderful. He felt Tak Chai's temples and the back of his head, then asked him to swing his arms around, so Tak Chai did a "pulling the mountain" move. Master Law nodded and smiled, and asked if Tak Chai wanted to come study opera with him. Thrilled,

Tak Chai answered at once that he'd love to, but he had to ask Uncle Kin first. Master Law turned to Uncle Kin and said he'd like to take Tak Chai as his disciple, if Uncle Kin would release him? Uncle Kin was delighted, and Big Sister Kam even more so. They agreed right away.

Just like that, Tak Chai joined the opera troupe, leaving Ping Hung behind to continue working at Wing Fong.

Whenever Tak Chai had some free time, he came back to visit Uncle Kin, Big Sister Kam and Ping Hung. He told them about his life at the troupe: rehearsals, vocal training, pressing a wooden stick to his belly to strengthen his diaphragm, lying on the ground to practice "the bowing fish", headstands, somersaults, the splits. The training left him exhausted, but he still had to wait on his mentor afterwards, lighting his pipe, giving him backrubs, making him tea.

"*Is that how they treat young people?*" Ping Hung was shocked, and thought Master Law was being cruel.

"*That's how things are in the troupe,*" said Tak Chai. One of the older performers had told him he actually had it pretty good. When Law Siu Kai was an apprentice himself on a red boat, he was everyone's skivvy. He had no position or wages, and the rest of the troupe were free to give him orders, so he fetched water, did laundry, and picked up groceries for the seniors, all of whom could discipline or scold him. At night, he wasn't allowed a bunk, but had to sleep in the "sand street", that is the boat's passageway. Law Siu Kai's mentor had to perform and attend events, and didn't actually have time to give him lessons. Master Law learnt his skills by asking the older performers for tips as he lit their opium pipes, or by observation as he worked backstage. He also had to wake up at dawn to study martial arts with a fight director. Tak Chai was better off as his mentor personally taught him singing and stage combat.

Tak Chai was also full of anecdotes about the troupe. For

instance, how they would pray to the White Tiger before performing for the gods, or how they had to "seal the stage" after a show. One time, Tak Chai brought Ping Hung backstage during a show, and even many years later, long after Tak Chai had become the famous singer known as "the new Siu Kai", Ping Hung could still remember every moment of the experience, watching the old hands performing from the wings as Ping Hung murmured an explanation of everything around them. *"That's the seat we leave vacant for the deity Master Wah Gong, that's the trunk for our stage weapons, that's the running order prompt."* He pointed at a slip of paper clipped to a rope with a wooden peg. *"The stage manager writes out the story, the scene order, the music, the entrances, and who's playing what roles."*

Ping Hung leaned closer and saw dense rows of characters. *"You can't even read that!"* Tak Chai exclaimed, dragging him to the other side of the passageway, which was full of trunks. *"That side was for props,"* he said. *"This is the wardrobe side, where we keep our costumes."* In the cramped space, the performers were standing by their individual boxes, busily getting changed and adjusting their make-up, ready for their next entrances. Ping Hung and Tak Chai darted amongst them like minnows swimming through river grass; the old hands cursed at them whenever they got in the way. Ping Hung worried that Tak Chai would get into trouble with his mentor, so although he'd had a lot of fun on that visit backstage, he never went again. It all seemed like a magical dreamland to him: the clashing of gongs and cymbals, the old hands taking their first steps onto the red carpet, the dazzling opera costumes, the rouged performers waiting in the wings to make their entrances.

He longed to follow Tak Chai into the opera troupe. Big Sister Kam kept praising Tak Chai's talent. Every time he visited, she'd tell him that as long as he worked hard, he'd surely become as famous as Law Siu Kai himself. Ping Hung

was filled with envy, especially as he'd been a Cantonese opera
fan long before Tak Chai. He remembered one year, on the
twenty-eighth day of the ninth month, Master Wah Gong's
birthday, Uncle Kin and Big Sister Kam had taken them to
see *Happy Returns on Fragrant Flower Hill*. Tak Chai hadn't
known the story, so Ping Hung had happily explained the
eighteen transformations of Kwan Yin and so on. That was the
beginning of Tak Chai's fascination with opera. Ping Hung
had confided then that he wanted to train to be a performer. It
was all because of Ping Hung that Tak Chai was in the troupe
now. Ping Hung was certain he was the more talented of the
two, and he was much better at "long phrases, flowing water".
If only Master Law had asked him to demonstrate, rather than
Tak Chai.

Ping Hung was jealous of Tak Chai's luck, and wished he
could find an opportunity to ask Law Siu Kai if he, Ping Hung,
could be his disciple too. But he didn't dare. He was afraid
Uncle Kin would be angry. Not long after Tak Chai left Wing
Fong, the assistant manager quit too, and Uncle Kin promoted
Ping Hung to assistant manager. He learnt to roast coffee
beans, and when the manager was on a break, he was in charge
of making the coffee. Uncle Kin clearly thought he deserved
this responsibility. If Ping Hung announced he wanted to
leave and train as an opera performer instead, Uncle Kin
would be furious, and Ping Hung didn't want to think what
the consequences of this fury would be. On one of Tak Chai's
visits, Ping Hung confided in him about his aspirations, first
swearing him to secrecy. Tak Chai said it would be better if he
stayed at Wing Fong and learnt to run the business, because
Uncle Kin and Big Sister Kam were very fond of him, and
needed him. Life in the troupe was very difficult. In the six
months Tak Chai had been there, between practising and
serving his mentor, he was barely getting three hours sleep a
night. If he performed badly, his mentor would slap him. He'd

had to learn all the moves: the soldier jump, opening the alley, the flower door, the bridge of hands. It would be a long time till he'd be allowed to do pushing or pulling, and who knew when he'd ever get to play a second or third warrior role.

If Master Wah Gong didn't deign to let you earn a crust, you'd spend your life in poverty, without so much as a bowl of congee. It was an unstable life. Even if you were talented, if the timing wasn't right, you'd still end up starving. Even someone as famous as Ma Si Tsang had spent a long time unemployed after offending some older performers, and ended up selling herbal medicine in the street, being a miner, and working behind a shop counter. Tak Chai said he actually slightly regretted joining the troupe, though he didn't dare tell Uncle Kin and Big Sister Kam.

After Tak Chai turned nineteen, Law Siu Kai decided to return to Canton, so of course Tak Chai had to go with him. Before going, he presented Ping Hung with a blue robe as a memento: the costume his mentor had given him the first time he went on stage to perform for the gods. Tak Chai was planning to visit their hometown before starting his new life on a red boat. Ping Hung took him to a photo studio and got pictures taken of the two of them as well as his own portrait, and asked Tak Chai to give his father these photos along with some money for his family.

Two months after his departure, a letter arrived for Ping Hung. The writing was so regular and neat, it was obvious Tak Chai hadn't written it himself. Ping Hung asked Uncle Kin to help read it: Tak Chai had gone back to their hometown, and done everything Ping Hung asked him to. The village was still as poor as ever, but Ping Hung's father and siblings were well; Tak Chai's own father had passed away. After this, two or three letters came with sketchy details of Tak Chai's life in the troupe. He had to travel often with performances, and was still leading quite a rough existence. Then nothing further.

Ping Hung continued watching Cantonese operas with Uncle Kin, which made him miss Tak Chai, and he still longed to be a performer himself. Sometimes he daydreamed about becoming a famous singer, or even a movie star. Although Ping Hung wasn't as tall or well-built as Tak Chai, he thought he was more handsome. Tak Chai played young warrior roles, but Ping Hung was better suited to being a young gentleman or even a scholar-warrior. He'd surely make it big if he went into the profession. But after spending a long time weighing up his options, he couldn't bring himself to abandon his current life to join a troupe and start all over again. He had to admit he was comfortable where he was, and accepted that he wasn't the sort of person who took risks. He came up with several excuses for this, most prominently that he was already in his twenties, which was too old to start training. The real reason, though, was what Tak Chai said about how hard a life it was, and how you might end up starving if you didn't become famous. He was still enamoured of this world, but didn't want to give up his stable existence.

And so he continued helping Uncle Kin in his work. When the manager retired and went back to Hainan Island, Ping Hung was promoted to be the manager of Wing Fong Kopitiam.

LEONG PING HUNG AND AH YOKE

1. AH YOKE

Three years after Tak Chai's return to Canton, when Leong Ping Hung was twenty-one, he told Uncle Kin he was very fond of Ah Yoke, the daughter of Chan Kwok Tai who owned Kwong Heng Loong Provision Shop. He hoped Uncle Kin would arrange the match for him.

Her full name was Chan Peck Yoke, meaning "jade", but everyone called her Ah Yoke, and that's what Ping Hung knew her as. She had pale skin and an oval goose-egg face, with large eyes, a slender nose and thin lips. She was often to be found behind that counter, helping her dad mind the shop. She didn't speak much, and even when she did, her voice was wispy, as you'd expect from a rather sheltered girl. Ping Hung wasn't the only one who liked her, Tak Chai did too. Before he joined the opera troupe, the two boys would jostle to be the one to go when Uncle Kin needed something from Kwong Heng Loong (mostly spirits). Their objective, of course, was to see Ah Yoke, and they felt let down if she wasn't at her usual spot.

Whether it was Ping Hung or Tak Chai, when one got back to Wing Fong after such an errand, the other would only need to look at his expression to see if he'd gotten what he was after: a glimpse of Ah Yoke. If the kopitiam wasn't too busy when Uncle Kin needed something, he'd let them both go to Kwong Heng Loong, and if they encountered Ah Yoke there, the two of them would animatedly dissect the encounter just before bedtime: her every peal of laughter, every slight movement, every utterance.

Ah Yoke was the woman of Leong Ping Hung's dreams, and Tak Chai's too. Being more glib, Tak Chai was better at bantering with her, and he'd frequently leave her laughing quietly through closed lips, which made him very full of himself. Ping Hung didn't like this. Could Ah Yoke be taking more of a shine to Tak Chai?

Both boys called Ah Yoke's dad Uncle Chan. He was strict with his daughter, and whenever he heard a male customer attempting to chat her up when he was in the next room, he'd step back in and fix his eyes on her. Uncle Chan had thick brows and bulging eyes, and his high cheekbones made his long face look even gaunter. Even when he wasn't in the shop, Ping Hung and Tak Chai could feel him glaring whenever they spoke to Ah Yoke, and so neither of them dared to ask her out. They only managed to see her outside the shop after Tak Chai got into the opera troupe.

One evening, the boys made a detour to pass by Kwong Heng Loong after work, hoping for nothing more than a sight of Ah Yoke's face. If they had a chance to speak to her, they'd be more than satisfied. They were very lucky: Uncle Chan wasn't on the premises at all, Ah Yoke said he'd taken her little brother Tat Yan to see some friends in Small Town, and wouldn't be back till eight.

Tak Chai boldly asked if she'd like to come out with him. *"Ask Ah Chuan to keep an eye on things. We'll just go for a stroll around Tofu Street for a couple of hours. You'll be home before your dad gets back. That's all right, isn't it?"* said Tak Chai. *"I'm leaving Wing Fong soon to join the opera troupe. I won't have many chances to come back here after that. Call it a farewell dinner for me, how about that? I'll treat you to ding ding tong and malt candy."* Ah Yoke declined at first, but Tak Chai kept pleading and pestering. Eventually, she gathered the courage to come with them, though she only agreed to one hour.

At Tofu Street, Tak Chai bought them each some candy. Ah Yoke licked at it, not saying much. Tak Chai was the opposite: he wouldn't stop talking, trying to cheer her up, pulling all kinds of faces. He even sang silly tunes like, *"Chilli sauce the king won't eat, bean sprouts fried with piggy feet."* He coaxed a giggle out of Ah Yoke from time to time. In the golden twilight, her smile was like a delicate flower being shaken by the breeze. Her bright eyes and smile, her pale skin and flushed cheeks, were intoxicating to Ping Hung and Tak Chai, teenagers still in the process of becoming men.

Unfortunately, she was so worried about her dad getting home early that she started to look anxious after just thirty minutes, and wanted to hurry back. In order to calm her down, Ping Hung and Tak Chai did as she asked. In the end, they'd only spent about forty minutes on Tofu Street, but that stretch of time strolling along, eating candy, would be the sweetest shared memory the two boys had.

From then on, they never saw Ah Yoke when they walked past Kwong Heng Loong. Once, they saw Tat Yan, but when they asked where his sister was, he just shook his head and refused to open his mouth. They knew she must have hidden as soon as she saw them approaching, and though they had no idea why, they guessed that Ah Chuan must have told his boss about their little excursion, for which Ah Yoke would have received a scolding, or worse, a beating.

Those forty minutes on Tofu Street were the first and last time this trio went out together. Not long after that, Tak Chai entered the opera troupe. Whenever he came back to see Ping Hung, whether or not they went to Tofu Street, they'd end up talking about their outing with Ah Yoke.

Tak Chai seemed to grow up very quickly once he entered the opera troupe. There was something more mature and grounded about him, and he was no longer as mischievous or playful as before. After three years, he was a fairly accomplished "little warrior" performer. When his mentor decided to return to Canton, he naturally had to go along too. His mood was dark when he went to Wing Fong one last time to see Ping

Hung, who understood how he felt, and in fact was sad himself. They were like brothers, and had been together since they were children, from the village to the city to Singapore, living through so much sadness and joy together. Now they would be torn apart, with no idea when they'd see each other again. Tak Chai said he wanted to see Ah Yoke before he left, and asked Ping Hung to bring her along when he came to say goodbye. Ping Hung wanted this too, but despite several trips to Kwong Heng Loong, he didn't manage to see her. Even if he had, she might still not have been allowed to come. In fact, her father would definitely have refused. And so, the day Tak Chai left Singapore, Ah Yoke wasn't there to see him off. He was filled with sadness and disappointment as he boarded. At the last moment, he suddenly grabbed hold of Ping Hung's arm and frowned as if in great pain. It took him a few moments of struggle before he was able to say, "*Tell her to wait for me. She has to wait. I'll work hard to earn money in Canton, then I'll come back south and marry her in no time at all.*"

These words shocked Ping Hung. What right did Tak Chai have to speak like this? Was he engaged to Ah Yoke? He, Ping Hung, liked her too! This was a bitter pill to swallow. So Tak Chai had been lying to him: after entering the opera troupe, he hadn't just been coming back to visit his old friend and Uncle Kin, he'd been seeing Ah Yoke too. They must have become intimate, and he'd been in the dark the whole time. He felt deceived, and even some time after Tak Chai's departure, he still couldn't let go of his agitation. He no longer felt like visiting Kwong Heng Loong, and even when he had to, he'd just scurry in and out, dreading running into Ah Yoke.

After a couple of months of this, he could no longer keep a lid on his thoughts of Ah Yoke, and went back to Kwong Heng Loong. Yet when he saw Ah Yoke, all he said was hello, lacking the courage to actually speak to her, let alone pass on Tak Chai's message. He noticed Ah Yoke seemed a little grumpy and taciturn. Why was this? Had she really pledged herself to Tak Chai? When had they done that? How had Ping Hung not known? He felt sad and heartbroken. Should he go on liking Ah Yoke? Even in his despair, because he wanted to see her, he continued visiting Kwong Heng Loong. Ah Yoke was now more attractive to him than ever before. He cherished her. Finally, he gathered his courage and spoke to her. Of course, Uncle Chan was in the back room as they chatted, and would glower at them from the doorway every now and then.

They had to be careful with their words, particularly at the beginning. Ping Hung didn't dare say too much. Without Tak Chai by his side, he was much less bold. That was part of the reason, but more importantly, Tak Chai's parting words remained like a thorn in his heart. They amounted to a warning: Ah Yoke is mine, and if you regard me as your brother, stay off my turf and don't even think of having designs on her. These thoughts assailed Ping Hung constantly, so even though he liked Ah Yoke a lot, more so than when Tak Chai was here, he couldn't summon the will to ask her out, not even after Tak Chai had been gone a long time. Kwong Heng Loong and Wing Fong were on the same street, separated only by a dozen or so shopfronts. Whenever he had a spare moment, he'd itch to walk over and see her, but he never said more than a few words before leaving again. He couldn't make himself ask her out (how easy Tak Chai made it look, that time they all went for a stroll down Tofu Street!). He thought of asking Uncle Chan for permission, but that would require even more courage. And so the only words he spoke to Uncle Chan were polite greetings.

Ping Hung began showing up at Kwong Heng Loong more often, and gradually realised Uncle Chan didn't actually hate him, and might even be a little fond of him. This may have been because he often took it upon himself to help out around the shop, climbing or stooping to rearrange the tins on the shelves, lugging heavy sacks of rice or sugar out from the back room. Uncle Chan's long face was no longer as fierce as before; in fact, he was always smiling. Now Ping Hung boldly laughed and chatted with Ah Yoke, though of course he never told her Tak Chai's parting words. The effect of those words on him wore down over time, fading away to nothing. Ah Yoke wasn't Tak Chai's fiancée, which meant Ping Hung had the right to pursue her. It was now clear to Ping Hung that he wasn't doing anything wrong, and this had nothing to do with Tak Chai or loyalty. Having resolved this ethical dilemma, Ping Hung was able to go after Ah Yoke with a clear conscience, determined to win her heart.

Sometimes, Ah Yoke would ask about Tak Chai, and Ping Hung would burn with jealousy at this sign she still cared for him, though he never showed this. Tak Chai hardly ever wrote, but that didn't stop Ping Hung making up stories about him to tell Ah Yoke: he was doing well and earning some money; he was seeing a rich girl and would marry her soon. He spoke repeatedly of Tak Chai's impending nuptials without even a glimmer of guilt, as if he believed they actually existed. He wanted Ah Yoke to think Tak Chai had forgotten her and was leading a very happy life with another woman. Was Ah Yoke disappointed? Ping Hung studied her reaction closely, but couldn't see any strong emotions in her placid eyes. She just stared at him in silence, expressing no thoughts of her own. He worried that she could see through his lies, but reassured himself that he sounded so natural there was no way she could tell. Besides, these might not even be lies. Tak Chai was a good-looking chap, and surely had women after him. Ping Hung was sure Ah Yoke must feel let down. At least, he hoped she did.

At long last, Ping Hung plucked up the nerve to ask Uncle Chan's permission to take Ah Yoke out, and he actually said yes. Even though Uncle Chan's attitude had softened, this still came as a surprise. He privately surmised Uncle Chan might have watched him long enough to have judged him hard-working and honest, and so was allowing him to be with his daughter.

Ping Hung and Ah Yoke's outings were mostly to movies, opera performances, Great World Amusement Park and, most often, New World on Jalan Besar.

The main reason they went to New World was to ride the ghost train. For ten cents each, they sat in a two-person carriage that hurtled into the darkness of the wooden structure, where they'd hear ghostly cries as well as the screams of the other passengers when female ghosts with long, straggly hair, grisly skeletons, and hanged men with protruding tongues abruptly appeared before them. Sometimes these spectres would grab their heads (actually it was ropes or willow branches dangling from the ceiling brushing against them). Each apparition made Ah Yoke screech and clutch Ping Hung's hand tightly, at which point he'd take advantage of the moment to pull her into his embrace, wrapping his arms firmly around her. Several rides on the ghost train later, she no longer objected to holding his hand in public. He asked Uncle Kin to broker the marriage, and Uncle Chan agreed right away.

2. MARRIAGE

It was only when Ping Hung married Ah Yoke that he learnt her full name, Chan Peck Yoke. He sent Tak Chai a copy of their wedding photo: him in a suit, her in a cheongsam. He waited a long time, but there was no reply. Perhaps Tak Chai was leading a peripatetic life, following his mentor on tour? His next few letters also got no response. Was that because he'd married Ah Yoke? True, Tak Chai had liked Ah Yoke a lot, but he'd been away from Singapore for so long, how was Ah Yoke supposed to know when he'd be back? Was she supposed to just sit at home and wait for him? Tak Chai was an opera artiste, and surely had other women after him. Maybe he'd married one, like in the story Ping Hung made up for Ah Yoke. If Tak Chai wanted to sulk, there was nothing Ping Hung could do. He loved Ah Yoke too, after all! And Tak Chai surely knew that. They'd once been close as brothers, and survived all kinds of hardships together, only to fall out over a woman. Then he'd comfort himself by remembering this was just a guess; the truth might be different. What was it, then? His letters were vanishing into the void, and he hadn't received a single word back from Tak Chai, so he stopped writing. Worried that Ah Yoke might still prefer Tak Chai, he even started hoping to never hear from him again.

After the wedding, Ping Hung and Ah Yoke moved into the third floor flat, while Uncle Kin and Big Sister Kam had the second floor, just above the kopitiam. There were five rooms on the third floor. Three of them were rented out to families, while the other two had been used for storage. Uncle Kin got Ping Hung to clear one of them out, moving everything into a single store room, and bought a new bed, wardrobe, table and chairs: everything necessary to give the newlyweds a beautiful home. This was his wedding present to the couple. For as long as Ping Hung kept working at the kopitiam, he could live there rent-free. Ping Hung was extremely grateful for this.

3. ACCEPTING A HEAVY BURDEN

WHEN PING HUNG AND AH YOKE HAD BEEN MARRIED THREE years, their son Kung Man was born. One evening, after adding up the accounts, Uncle Kin asked Ping Hung to help him carry the day's takings up to the second floor. Big Sister Kam was up there, sitting at the dining table and smiling warmly. When Uncle Kin had finished locking the money away in the safe, she poured out three cups of tea and said in her motherly voice, "*Goji berry and longan tea. Drink up, it's nourishing for your blood and skin.*" Ping Hung and Uncle Kin sat down and sipped their tea.

Uncle Kin paused to gather his thoughts, then told Ping Hung his news: a close friend was opening a restaurant in San Francisco, and he and Big Sister Kam were going over there for a while. They wanted Ping Hung to take over the kopitiam while they were away, maybe for a year or two, until the restaurant was up and running. Ping Hung's eyes opened wide with shock and uncertainty, then he grimaced. Not long after Tak Chai's return to China, Uncle Kin had gotten Ping Hung to handle the accounts, and he'd recently been more or less responsible for running Wing Fong. Still, he'd never thought of actually being in charge, and Uncle Kin's words made his heart thump with anxiety. What if he wasn't up to the challenge?

Uncle Kin saw his hesitation, and lightly touched the back of Ping Hung's hand. He and Big Sister Kam had no children of their own, he explained, so they'd always treated Ping Hung like their own son. They knew him well, and felt safe leaving him to run Wing Fong. Moved, Ping Hung put his other hand on top of Uncle Kin's, not knowing what to say. Big Sister Kam chimed in, "*We believe in you, Hung. You can do this.*" Uncle Kin explained more: from the following month, Ping Hung would receive a one-fifth raise in his salary. He'd pay regular expenses such as rent and wages out of the month's takings, and stow the rest in the safe. Ping Hung protested that he'd just had a raise after the child was born, how could he accept another one so soon? Besides, a fifth was too much. Uncle Kin said he'd been planning to do this anyway, because Ping Hung would soon find he needed more money, with a wife and kid to support. Ping Hung thanked him repeatedly, adding, "*If business isn't good, I'll take less."*

Uncle Kin smiled. *"That's up to you. You'll be the boss, and whatever you say goes."*

To set his mind at ease, Uncle Kin told Ping Hung that if the kopitiam started losing too much money, they wouldn't blame him if he dismissed the servers and terminated the lease. That was the worst case scenario, though, and Uncle Kin didn't believe it would actually happen. Ping Hung nodded. *"I'm going to work hard. Don't worry, I won't let you two down."* There was no reason to say no, so he accepted.

The three of them talked a while longer. Uncle Kin said he and Big Sister Kam had no heirs, so the business would be Ping Hung's after they died, as long as he was willing to look after it in the meantime. Ping Hung felt a wave of gratitude at such affection and trust, and promised over and over that he'd do a good job. When the clock struck ten, Big Sister said she was going to bed, and Ping Hung returned to the third floor.

Uncle Kin walked him to the landing, and patted him on the shoulder, repeating his encouragement: running a small business like the kopitiam wouldn't be difficult, as long as he was diligent and smart. It was easy to earn money in Nam Yong. Hard work wouldn't necessarily make you rich, but it would definitely keep you out of poverty. The main thing was not to pick up bad habits: drinking, smoking, gambling or whoring. There was no harm indulging in a drink or two when you were flush, or maybe the occasional prostitute, as long as you didn't make a habit of it and it didn't affect your family. No gambling or opium, though. Many people worked hard all their lives, only to end up dying in the street because they couldn't resist the opium pipe or card tables.

For the next month, Ping Hung was busy helping Uncle Kin and Big Sister Kam buy the clothes and other items they'd need for their trip. Then the moment came to see them off at the dock, and Ping Hung didn't know what to say. They'd treated him like their own child, and although they said they'd be back in a year or two, he was reluctant to let them go. When Big Sister Kam told him to take good care of Ah Yoke and their son, his eyes reddened. She touched his face. *"Silly boy, what's the point of crying? It's not like we won't be back!"*

Her fingertips on his cheek were all it took to set him sobbing.

4. DOWNTURN

Before setting off, Uncle Kin had warned Ping Hung not to offend anyone from the Hong Gate Secret Society. Ping Hung already knew this, having seen what happened to people who got on the wrong side of the clan. Uncle Kin had always kept up a good relationship with them, and Ping Hung did the same, dispensing gifts and red packets at the appropriate moments. And so, even after Uncle Kin left, no one came to cause trouble at Wing Fong.

The kopitiam had its regulars, and there was no change in the business immediately after Uncle Kin left. Unfortunately, Singapore was going through a downturn. That July, the price of rubber dropped to just over 14 cents; in August, more than two thousand navy dockworkers went on strike to protest falling wages; in September, the owner of a small rubber plantation on Upper Serangoon Road hacked his family of nine to death, then set himself on fire; in October, two well-known rubber traders went bankrupt, one after the other. By the end of the year, rubber had fallen to 13.5 cents. The following year, 1931, Ping Hung's second son Kung Woo was born, and rubber fell to four Straits dollars a picul. Around this time, his younger brother Kit wrote to say their father had passed away, and also that their sister was married and had a five-year-old. Life was hard in the village, and Kit hoped Ping

Hung would find a way to bring him and their other sister to Singapore.

Kit's letter left Ping Hung shocked and guilty. In the blink of an eye, more than ten years had passed since his coming to Nam Yong. He'd asked Tak Chai to bring some money to his family, but after that, his comfortable life here had led him to forget all about them and his village. Tak Chai hadn't mentioned the Leongs' current address. They'd exchanged a handful of letters, but Ping Hung had never asked. Now he rebuked himself for being so thoughtless. The letters from Tak Chai had stopped coming, so he hadn't even been able to tell them when he got married. Had he been away so long that he'd grown cold towards them? Even hearing that his father was dead, he felt only a little sadness, not real grief. After so much time here, his hometown felt far away and unfamiliar. His siblings had all been little when he left. Kit was the youngest, and Ping Hung had to struggle to summon even a vague outline of his face. Of course, he'd only been a child ten years ago. What did he look like now? And his two little sisters? Kit must have got his Singapore address from Tak Chai. Yet why was he only writing now, so many years after Tak Chai's return to Canton? Had Tak Chai only now revealed his address? Or had it taken this long for Kit to find someone to write a letter on his behalf? And why hadn't Tak Chai written himself?

Ping Hung held his brother's letter, his heart full. Although he couldn't grieve his father's passing, he was still gripped by regret. Naturally, he knew how hard life in the village was. His siblings probably thought he was leading a cushy life in Nam Yong, and it was true. He was much more comfortable than them. He wanted to help them—indeed, he had to—but didn't know how. What could he do? Because of the downturn, business was getting worse by the day, and he didn't know how he would keep the place going. He could barely feed his wife and two children. If only Uncle Kin and Big Sister Kam would come back soon, so he could hand the kopitiam back to them and focus his energies on helping his siblings.

Uncle Kin's letters were invariably short. It was to discern from those few lines how things were going in San Francisco, though Ping Hung had a vague sense that it was choppy. Sure enough, the most recent letter said the restaurant was in a bit of a complicated situation, and they might not be able to return within two years as planned. Complicated how? He never said, though he did suggest that Ping Hung and his family move down to the second floor, rather than leave it unoccupied. Ping Hung did as he said, though he also kept the third floor room vacant rather than renting it out, so they could move back up at short notice if Uncle Kin returned. To reassure him, Ping Hung wrote that despite the downturn, business at Wing Fong was all right.

In fact, it was becoming more of a struggle, but Ping Hung gritted his teeth and clung on. He was determined to keep his promise to Uncle Kin. The problem was, keeping hold of Wing Fong made it difficult to take care of his siblings back home. The Singapore government had recently started restricting immigration from China, and he used this as an excuse not to bring them over, sending scraps of money instead. He felt awful about doing so little.

Kit continued to write from time to time. About a year later, he told Ping Hung that their nephew had died of malnourishment, and their grieving sister had killed herself. Kit begged to come to Singapore with their remaining sister, no matter what it took. Life in the village was unbearable, and they'd surely starve if they stayed. This was in 1933.

On April 1st, the government had put in a new restriction: each ship could only bring in 25 immigrants per country each month, making it more difficult to bring over Kit and their sister than before. He wrote back to tell Kit about the new law, and said he would think of something, but actually there was nothing he could do. Kit's letters all said the same thing: Ping Hung needed to find a way to bring them to Singapore. He didn't know what to say, and finally he hardened his heart and stopped replying altogether, not even to send money. The fact was, he was overstretched himself. Between running the kopitiam and caring for his wife and kids, he had no energy left for his siblings.

Now he had constant qualms and suffered from nightmares, which made him short-tempered. Naturally, the brunt of his anger fell on Ah Yoke and the kids, as well as the servers. Sometimes he even blew up at the customers, and lost quite a few regulars that way.

The letters from Kit stopped coming, which only increased his guilt. What happened to his brother and sister? Had they starved to death? For a long time after this, he was tormented by his conscience.

YU SAU

1. YU SAU'S DREAM

EVER SINCE GRANDPA'S ENCOUNTER WITH THE MAN WHO sang Cantonese opera by the river, he's been calling for Yu Sau to fetch the costume from the trunk. Each time, she drags the camphorwood chest from the cramped storeroom and opens it to show him it contains only an old suit, and no costume. Then Grandpa insists it's in Eldest Brother's schoolbag, even though Eldest Brother left school after Secondary Two to join the opera troupe, and as far as Yu Sau remembers, he stopped carrying his satchel even before that. Anyway, he moved out when they were still at their old place, so how could his bag possibly be anywhere in this flat? Yet Grandpa keeps saying it's in the storeroom, sounding so certain you'd have thought he put it there himself. Frustratingly, he makes Yu Sau search for it again and again.

Perhaps because of his non-stop pestering, Yu Sau dreams of performing on stage in the costume. She's never sung opera, but is perfectly in tune and rhythm, striking all the right poses. Grandpa is in the audience with her parents, clapping loudly. Someone nearby says, "*What a voice Kim Chau has.*" Kim Chau? Have they mistaken her for Eldest Brother? She feels muddled when she wakes up, but there wasn't any confusion in the dream: she *was* Kim Chau, Eldest Brother. For a long time after that vivid dream, she remembers the sensations of that performance. From then on, whenever Grandpa asks about the costume, she wishes it were still here. She wants to put it on, to see what she looks like. Perhaps she'd look like Eldest Brother.

Yu Sau makes a more thorough search of the storeroom.

She wants Grandpa to be right: that Eldest Brother's satchel is somewhere in here, and the costume in it. But the bag never shows up, so of course nor does the costume.

The dream also makes her miss Eldest Brother. Where is he? And how is he? Surely he didn't die young, as Grandpa said? She feels uncertain and a little sad. She calls Second Brother in Hong Kong to ask if their brother could have passed, but he says he hasn't heard anything, and doesn't know where he is either. "If he died, Mum and Dad would have said something," she says, trying to reassure herself. "But they never mentioned it."

"*Grandpa spoiled your big brother, and so did Grandma. They were the same, they doted on him,*" her mother said, a few months before her death. "*He was so clever back then!*" Before he even started primary school, she taught him to recite the *Three Character Classic* and *Book of Ancient Aphorisms*, which he did perfectly. It was only because he got hooked on Cantonese opera that his schoolwork suffered. "*What kind of future can you have, singing opera in Singapore?*" she frequently complained. "*By the time he joined the troupe, no one was watching those shows! Or even if they did, they'd want stars from Hong Kong. Back then, Sun Ma Sze Tsang, Ng Kwun Lai, Mak Bing Wing, Law Yim Hing, Lan Chi Pak and other big names would tour to Singapore. Who on earth would still watch our local performers?*" And indeed, by the sixties, television had come to Singapore, and there were quite a few cinemas. With so many entertainment options, and a faster pace of life, not many people had the patience for the slower rhythms of Cantonese opera. It was different with the Hong Kong stars, they were celebrities who also appeared on TV and in films, so naturally their fans showed up. Mum was actually far more rational than Grandpa, and correct to oppose Eldest Brother's decision. When Grandpa told her that Eldest Brother was a well-known performer in '67 or '68, that was probably his own delusion. Mum added that it wasn't easy for an opera troupe to survive in Singapore, and the only ones who did it were the amateur ones attached to clan associations. All the others had disbanded.

2. I WANT TO DRINK KOPI-O

"*WHERE ARE CHAU AND MING? WHEN ARE THEY COMING back?*" Yu Sau remembers how Mum looked the day she died, the sadness and confusion with which she suddenly asked about her two sons. The day before, she'd been in so much pain the doctor gave her morphine, which knocked her out till Yu Sau came to visit the next morning. She said she wanted to brush her teeth, so Yu Sau handed her a glass of water and her toothbrush. After a couple of swipes, she asked for toothpaste, and Yu Sau squeezed some onto the brush. Her mother stared blankly at the window, her shrivelled chicken-foot hand moving slowly up and down. Then she stopped abruptly and turned to Yu Sau. "*Where are Chau and Ming? When are they coming back?*"

Yu Sau was surprised to hear her mention Eldest Brother. They hardly ever said his name these days, even when they phoned Second Brother in Hong Kong, as if he really were no longer in the world, or at least no longer a part of this family. How did Yu Sau answer? As far as she remembers, she didn't say anything. Just stared at her mother's foaming mouth, the white froth trickling down onto her chin. The image burned into her mind; for several days after her mother's death, she couldn't stop thinking about her dribbling toothpaste. She held out an empty cup for her mum to rinse, and dabbed her mouth dry with a face towel.

Staring at her like a little girl, her mother said, "*I want to drink kopi-O.*" Her voice was wispy, like a violin bow brushing lightly over the strings, but Yu Sau heard these words clearly. She can still hear them now. She left the ward and hurried down to the hospital canteen. When she returned with the coffee, the doctor said her mother had lost consciousness.

Yu Sau put the styrofoam cup on the bedside table and took Mum's hand, whispering in her unwieldy Cantonese, "*I'm back, Mum. I have your kopi-O.*" She stood there a long time, gazing silently at her mother, listening to her rattling breaths. She still remembers every moment. What was she thinking? Of her mother slowly cleaning her teeth? Her eyes fixed on the window? (And again, Yu Sau recalls the sadness and confusion with which she asked about Eldest Brother.) She knew her mother would never wake up again. Her last words were, "*I want to drink kopi-O.*" And now Yu Sau remembers replying, "*All right, I'll go get you some kopi-O.*" Her mother nodded enthusiastically, like a little child. Did she already know she was about to die? Couldn't she have said something more important? Whenever Yu Sau thinks of this, she feels a moment of heartbreak.

She had an old classmate, Hui Yee, who died of cancer. Just before she passed, she told Yu Sau how sad she was to leave her and their other good friends behind. Yu Sau hadn't seen Hui Yee very often, but they'd always been there for each other at times of need. When Yu Sau needed someone to talk to, she never thought of her mum, who was just the person who'd given birth to her, never her friend.

Even after she left her rented flat and moved back home, she barely saw her mother. She felt separate from her family, particularly her parents. She did her duty as a daughter, giving them money for the household expenses (a little reluctantly at first), but never took them or Grandpa out for a meal. The kopi-O was the first and only drink she ever bought her mother, but she never even got to take a sip. Yu Sau had never bought her mum so much as a cup of coffee. When her mum sent her away, she must have known she was dying. What was she thinking? Who was on her mind? Was there someone she couldn't let go of? Eldest Brother, perhaps. She'd been furious when he abandoned his studies to go sing opera, but actually she was very fond of him, and must have missed him as she slipped away. *"I'll bring him back for you, Mum,"* she vowed, looking at her unconscious mother.

Did she really say that to Mum? Yes, Yu Sau is certain that's what she said, *"I'll bring him back for you, Mum."*

3. WHY HAVEN'T WE SEEN THE MAN WHO SANG *BREAKING THE LONG WILLOW PAVILION*?

YU SAU SEES THE OPERA-SINGING MAN QUITE A FEW TIMES after that, on her regular Saturday morning strolls by the river with Grandpa. Sometimes he's stretching on the grass, other times he's jogging along the pavement. Once or twice, he runs right by them. She never sees him leaning against the railing and singing opera again, though.

Although Grandpa demands the costume in the chest from time to time, when the man who triggered these memories passes by and says hello, Grandpa just stares blankly, not recognising him at all. And yet, he occasionally asks Yu Sau, *"Why haven't we seen the man who sang* Breaking the Long Willow Pavilion? *Has he moved away?"* She tells Grandpa that the man's still around, but Grandpa insists he was never here. He says with great certainty, *"If I set eyes on him again, I'd definitely know who he was."* What can Yu Sau say to that? From then on, whenever Grandpa asks, she just says the man must be busy. Grandpa's memory is worsening, and Yu Sau worries that eventually, he won't even know who she is. Already, he often calls her Ah Lan, mistaking her for her aunt Yeuk Lan.

4. THE JAPANESE PLANES ARE ATTACKING! THE JAPANESE PLANES ARE ATTACKING!

ABOUT A MONTH BEFORE NATIONAL DAY, FIGHTER PLANES roar through the sky during rehearsals for the parade. Grandpa is napping the living room when one of them startles him awake. He points to the sound and screams, "*The Japanese planes are attacking! The Japanese planes are attacking!*" Yu Sau scrambles to shut the windows as he shouts that the Japanese devils will send bullets flying in. With the jets rumbling by so often, Grandpa no longer dares go down to the river. He refuses to leave the flat, and won't let Yu Sau go out either. The Japanese planes are attacking, and bandits are taking advantage of the chaos to rob people.

Even after National Day, when there are no longer any fighter jets, Yu Sau still has to spend quite a while each morning explaining to Grandpa that it's 1990, and the Japanese surrendered four decades ago. Only then will he let her go. "*Surrendered! The Japanese devils surrendered! At last, thank god,*" he mutters to himself.

"*What year is it?*" he often asks. "*How old are you now, Ah Lan? You're not young any more, you should find someone to marry. Don't get left on the shelf.*"

And Yu Sau will explain once again that she's his granddaughter, not Aunt Yeuk Lan.

"*Auntie got married long ago. She's in China now,*" Yu Sau says.

5. AUNT YEUK LAN

AUNT YEUK LAN ACTUALLY LIVED IN HONG KONG, AND DIED almost twenty years ago. It was her second brother Kim Ming who told Yu Sau she killed herself. When Yu Sau first got back from England, although she didn't see or speak to the rest of her family much, she often called Second Brother. During one of their conversations, she asked about their aunt. Second Brother had mumbled something indistinct at first, but finally came out and told her about the suicide, though he said she shouldn't tell their parents or Grandpa as this would sadden them. Yu Sau kept it to herself, and didn't even mention it to Geok Leng or Sandy, nor her ailing mother and grandfather when she moved back in with them.

Second Brother gradually gave her more information. In 1955, when Yeuk Lan was twenty-two, she and their uncle took part in the Hock Lee Bus Company workers' strike. The police attacked some stewards, which led to violence breaking out. The colonial government was arresting leftists who'd taken part in the protests, but Yeuk Lan managed to hide from them, only to get detained in February 1963 by the Internal Security Department, who were arresting leftists opposed to the formation of Malaysia. Uncle was captured too, but escaped into the jungles of Malaya. Second Brother said, "Eldest Brother was fifteen, I was thirteen, and you were just three. You might not remember this. Some time after she was detained, they deported her to China."

Yu Sau found the whole thing ridiculous. Her aunt had been a socialist, but managed to escape the colonial-era detentions, only to get deported by the Singapore government for being against Malaysia. Second Brother said this government had been brought to power in the first place by the support of leftist students and workers, and the leaders had even taken part in the anti-colonial struggle! Yet the same people turned on Yeuk Lan and her husband. What happened to Yeuk Lan after being sent back to China? She'd been fine, hadn't she? How had she ended up committing suicide in Hong Kong?

Second Brother said that starting in '66, the overseas Chinese in Guangzhou were allowed to emigrate to Hong

Kong, so their aunt moved there and started working at a print shop. Second Brother met her a few times after coming to Hong Kong himself, in '73. She seemed a little dazed and was clearly in despair. "One day, she finally told me that a fellow protestor from Singapore had given her the news: her husband had been shot dead in the jungle by his own comrades, in a counter-revolutionary purge. They called him a traitor, but Aunt didn't believe that could be true. She kept blaming herself, saying she was responsible for his death." How was she responsible? Second Brother didn't explain. "Uncle's death hit her really hard." Second Brother sighed. "Now I wish I'd spent more time with her when I realised what a bad state she was in. A few months before she did it, we were talking about souls, and she insisted that our spirits linger after we die. How could a socialist believe in the existence of souls? I should have understood this was a warning that she might kill herself. I'd just come over from China then, and my mind was full of my own problems. I didn't have time to worry about anyone else. She told me she couldn't sleep, because she kept hearing voices. I advised her to see a doctor. She did, and stored up the sleeping pills she was prescribed, then took them all at once."

"*Your second brother was influenced by your aunt,*" said her mother, thinking Yeuk Lan was still in China. "*I don't know how your grandfather could have had a daughter like that. Your dad always said his dad was strict, and Yeuk Lan used to be an obedient girl. Her mum didn't give her much leeway either. But in secondary school, she fell in with some leftist classmates, and stopped listening to them.*"

Grandpa's version of events was different: after the Japanese surrendered, he let her go to Peace School ("*Just next to Great World,*" Grandpa said) and she was influenced by the leftist teachers there.

Her mother said Yeuk Lan had wanted very much to go to Pre-U after secondary school, but girls are just going to get married and have kids, so what's the point of studying so much? That's why Grandpa hadn't let her continue her education, but made her work at the kopitiam instead. Yeuk Lan refused, and ran away from home. *"If your grandpa had let her keep studying, she wouldn't have ended up like that. Maybe with more qualifications, she'd have found a better job, and met a better man to marry than that Communist coolie."*

Yu Sau couldn't understand why Grandpa and her parents hated and feared the Communists so much, while Second Brother and her aunt and uncle loved Communism. She didn't understand politics, and wasn't interested anyway. The whole thing seemed like a ruse to her. When Second Brother and her aunt were deported to China, when her uncle fled to the jungles of Malaya, they would have felt sad to leave their home, but surely also a sort of excitement: they were finally realising their dreams of revolution, though they couldn't have imagined the abyss that their passion and idealism would push them into.

Not long after their mother died, Yu Sau went to visit Second Brother in Hong Kong. He was upset that he hadn't been able to come back to Singapore to see their parents one last time, so she brought him everything their mum had saved for him: old photos, his report cards, the essay he'd published in the newspaper. His eyes moistened and he said, "I always thought Mum and Dad didn't love me and never thought about me. But they did, after all." Yu Sau understood how he felt, because she'd thought the same thing: that their parents had been so busy quarrelling, they had no energy left for their children, especially Second Brother, who was always running off and staying with his classmates. What made him angry was that they didn't even notice he was gone. Yu Sau envied him for his lawlessness. She'd once tried copying him and spending the night at a friend's place, but her parents gave her a beating. "Maybe I did as a kid and forgot, but I can't remember ever touching our parents. I wish I could hold Mum's hand, or hug her," said Second Brother, running his fingers over the newspaper clipping. Yu Sau started weeping. She'd never hugged their mother either, and she'd had plenty of opportunities, but even as she'd stood by her deathbed, it never occurred to her to reach out.

On that trip, Yu Sau stayed at a hotel in Tsim Sha Tsui. She met Second Brother for dinner at a nearby restaurant, and then they went for a walk along the waterfront to the east. It was almost Christmas, and the skyscrapers were decked out in colourful lights. They wore jackets against the cold winds. Their conversation turned to everyone in their family, and eventually they got to their aunt. Yu Sau asked why she'd wanted to work elsewhere, rather than helping at the kopitiam, and Second Brother explained that Yeuk Lan had loved her freedom. She hated people telling her what to do, and most of all, she didn't get on with Grandpa. Did you know she worked in a glass factory for a while, and got a scar on her arm? (Second Brother absently rubbed his own arm, as if he'd been scalded by molten glass too.) Her wages always were low, less than two dollars a day, and the hours long, so she ended up changing jobs often, wandering all over Malaya: from Singapore to Johor Bahru, Kuala Lumpur and Ipoh. Apart from glass, she also made shoes, clothes and biscuits. "Her life was pretty hard, but she could take it. I have a lot of respect for her." Second Brother's voice was solemn, and Yu Sau could tell how much he admired their aunt, but she was still puzzled. Wouldn't she have been better off working at Grandpa's kopitiam? It would have been a much easier life. Did she really have more freedom running around looking for work? Why was freedom so important, anyway? Yu Sau asked Second Brother this string of questions, because she found it incomprehensible that their aunt had really preferred being exploited and bullied by her bosses rather than working in the family business. Second Brother just repeated, "She didn't get on with Grandpa." Yu Sau wasn't satisfied with this answer, but didn't ask any more.

Second Brother hadn't got on with Grandpa either. Like Yu Sau, he hadn't been able to stand their parents. He stayed away from home all the time, and naturally would never have served drinks at the kopitiam.

After secondary school, Second Brother worked at a construction site. "Mum said Aunt Yeuk Lan made you into a leftist. Is that true?" Yu Sau asked, wide-eyed and earnest. He laughed, "She left home when she was fourteen or fifteen, just after I was born. I was still a child when she got thrown out of Singapore, and I barely saw her even before that. But do you remember? Dad talked about her all the time when we were kids. She became a sort of legend to me."

Had Dad talked about his sister? Yu Sau couldn't remember, but then in her memory, her father hadn't spoken much to her at all. "She was my heroine," said Second Brother, looking at the glittering lights of Hong Kong Island across the water. "Or you could say she was my spiritual inspiration. I idolised her. All the time I was studying in secondary school, I wanted to be like her. By the time I tracked her down in Hong Kong, she was middle-aged, and I think she hadn't yet heard about Uncle's death when we first met. She looked desolate, but still very beautiful, as strong as noble as Wang Xiaoyan in those movies I used to watch. I felt so emotional seeing her, finally meeting my childhood idol. Maybe Mum was right and I was influenced by her. The sad thing was, her personality was so stubborn and unyielding, she suffered unnecessarily, but that's exactly why I was so mesmerised by her." Second Brother paused, still staring at the jewelled city across from them. He sighed, thoughtfully. "Why did they have to tell her about Old Liu? Did they see him get shot with their own eyes? If it was just a rumour, did they have to pass it on? That makes them responsible for her death."

Second Brother fell silent. Yu Sau sensed that he wanted to say more, but he just gazed into the distance. The waves dashed themselves against the breakwater with a susurrus like a sigh.

Second Brother always referred to Yeuk Lan's husband as Old Liu. (What was his full name? Yu Sau never asked.) The first time Old Liu asked Yeuk Lan out, she declined. She found him coarse, lazy and unprogressive. But after getting to know him better, she realised he was kind and caring, and was always helping his friends out. He was concerned for her too, of course, and during her wilderness years, he was always on the lookout to help her find work. One day, he told her he liked her a lot, and wanted to marry her. He'd joined the Party, and hoped she would too. She was full of passion and righteousness, and having spent so much time with Old Liu and his friends, had started thinking like them. She'd formed a much better opinion of trustworthy Old Liu, and agreed to marry him and join the Party. Their colleagues threw a simple ceremony for them (basically, just dinner at their place), and then they were a couple. Grandpa and Grandma didn't even know she was married, and nor did anyone else in the family. They'd had no news of her once she left home. It's the same with Eldest Brother now. Nobody has any idea where he is.

"Aunt and Eldest Brother are tragic figures," Yu Sau muttered.

"Not just them, Second Uncle too," said Second Brother. "He's in China now, but no one knows where."

LEONG PING HUNG

1. IF I'D HAD THE CHANCE, I'D BE FAMOUS NOW!

In July 1937, the Marco Polo Bridge incident began Japan's invasion of China, and overseas Chinese rushed to donate money to the war effort, to help injured soldiers and refugees in the fatherland. With the encouragement of the China Relief Fund, the Singaporean Chinese organised many fundraising events, selling flowers and so forth. Not only did every organisation and school take part, so did regular folk, even the working girls on Keong Saik Road.

Leong Ping Hung had three children now. Kung Man was ten, and Kung Woo seven. They were only in primary school, and already doing their bit. Their little sister Yeuk Lan was only five, and even she helped her big brothers to sell flowers around Wing Fong. Business had declined badly, but everyone had to do their wartime duty. Whenever there was a fundraising event, Ping Hung gave as much as he could spare. He was very concerned about the situation in the fatherland, and read the papers every day, having taught himself to read. When Uncle Kin put him in charge of the kopitiam, he kept up the practice of subscribing to a paper, partly for his customers' reading pleasure, partly for his own. After so many years, he'd learnt quite a few words, and would sometimes glean enough information that he could discuss affairs of state with his customers. He read that some famous Chinese opera performers had raised money in the States for the anti-Japanese war effort, and was excited that one of them was the new Siu Kai, Tak Chai's stage name. He looked at the photo below the article, and sure enough, there was Tak Chai in a suit. He was much more handsome and imposing than before, and his face shone with spirit. The picture was small and not particularly clear, but Ping Hung picked him out at once from his stance and determined chin. Tak Chai was famous now, wearing a suit and performing in America, and still a patriot too.

Along with his exhilaration, Ping Hung felt anger that Tak Chai hadn't written for so many years. He was still living above Wing Fong, so his address hadn't changed, but ever since he'd written to say he was getting married to Ah Yoke, Tak Chai had fallen silent. Ping Hung's subsequent letters might as well have dropped into the ocean. It seemed petty of Tak Chai to forget an old buddy now that he was famous. Ah Yoke tried to defend him: Tak Chai, like Ping Hung, had never learnt to read. Maybe he could decipher an opera score, but not a letter, and a celebrity like him could hardly go to a street scribe. *"You like Cantonese opera yourself,"* she said. *"Big Sister Kam encouraged you to look at the newspaper every day, and taught you. After all these years, you've learnt so many words, but still can't write a letter!"*

Ah Yoke's words only made him even angrier. She was a quiet person and hardly ever argued with him, but whenever he complained about Tak Chai, she'd intervene. Ping Hung met her at the same time as Tak Chai, and it had always bothered him to think she might have preferred Tak Chai. She was his wife now, why was she standing up for another man? Why couldn't a celebrity go to a street letter-writer? Her argument didn't even make sense. Ping Hung sneered, *"Rubbish. So what if he's famous? I can sing opera too. Before Tak Chai joined the troupe, I was better than him. I just didn't get my break. Law Siu Kai never asked me to sing for him. If I'd had the chance, I'd be famous now! Do you know, the first time Tak Chai went on stage, he was so nervous he forgot all his lyrics. He actually didn't have that much talent, he was just lucky. Fuck him!"* Ah Yoke didn't try to argue with him, just walked away to wash some cups in the back room. She found it frustrating that every mention of Tak Chai had to end in a quarrel.

Tak Chai was like a sharp knife between Ping Hung and Ah Yoke. If they weren't careful, one or both of them ended up getting hurt. This left Ping Hung angry and suspicious. How far had Tak Chai actually gotten with Ah Yoke? The question drove Ping Hung mad. He once dreamt that Tak Chai told him he'd asked Ah Yoke out, and he'd screamed, *"Ah Yoke's my wife, how dare you date her!"* He was still full of rage when he woke up and saw Ah Yoke sound asleep next to him. He rolled over on top of her, angrily ripped her clothes off, and rode her all night long.

Ping Hung's envy made him put down Tak Chai in front of Ah Yoke, but when talking to other people, he praised Tak Chai to the skies, especially if he ran into an old performer he knew. For them, he had nothing but good words for the new Siu Kai. Of course, he never neglected to mention he'd been childhood friends with the new Siu Kai, recounting how they'd herded cows together in the village, then come to Canton looking for jobs and virtually ended up begging, until they were lucky enough to find salvation working in a restaurant, then how they'd carried sacks of rice in Singapore before ending up at the kopitiam. After going through his entire history with the new Siu Kai, he'd move on to bragging that his mentor Law Siu Kai had been old friends with Uncle Kin, the proprietor of Wing Fong. He, Ping Hung, had known Master Law too, it was only that Tak Chai had had better luck, and been called on to sing "long phrases, flowing water" in front of him, and become his disciple that way.

There were times when Ping Hung would lament to the old performers he knew that he'd wanted very much to sing Cantonese opera too, and hint at how talented he'd been in his younger days. If only he'd had an opportunity. None of them showed any sympathy. They told him their lives seemed glamorous, but were actually filled with suffering and uncertainty. If Uncle Kin was giving him so much more responsibility, that meant he would leave the kopitiam to him sooner or later, which would be a much better future than going into opera.

Ping Hung disagreed. He knew life in the troupe was difficult to start with, but only till you'd established your reputation. As it was, the very best he could hope for was to be the boss of a little coffee shop. How could that compare with being a famous performer?

Perhaps because Tak Chai had been away for too long, the torments of his training seemed to slip Ping Hung's mind. He forgot the bruises and scars Tak Chai showed him, the agonies of doing the splits, the whisper that Tak Chai's voice became after he'd exhausted it practising. Most of all, he forgot the panic and fear these induced in him, so now he was able to tell his friends how much he regretted being so afraid of hardship and reluctant to leave his stable life that he'd missed his chance to train as an opera singer.

Ping Hung also had a strange idea: he'd missed his chance to be a performer, but why not train his own children instead? Wing Fong wasn't doing very well, but he still found the money to bring the boys to performances frequently. They weren't bad-looking, and every bit as intelligent as Tak Chai. If Tak Chai could be an opera singer, so could they. Besides, they'd both had a good education, and were more cultured than Tak Chai. This meant they'd surely be better at opera than him. Yet this was never more than an idea. When the older boy Kung Man turned ten, the ideal age to start training, Ping Hung tried to teach him a few lines, but he was never interested. Kung Woo was only seven, too young still. Then there was his little daughter Yeuk Lan, just five years old. Maybe in a few years? For all he knew, she might end up as a famous performer of "flower roles" someday.

2. GREATER TENSIONS IN THE FAR EAST

AT THE START OF SEPTEMBER 1941, THE JAPANESE INVADED
Vietnam, leading to greater tensions in the Far East. Singapore
began preparing for the worst. The colonial government
began carrying out evacuation and air raid drills, and put in
place blackout measures; cars and trains had to hood their
headlights so nothing could be seen over the horizon. People
had been talking about the anti-Japanese war in the fatherland
ever since the Marco Polo Bridge incident, but although the
discussion now turned more to Singapore and Malaya, none
of the kopitiam customers seriously believed Japanese forces
would actually come this far south. Besides, a couple of weeks
later, the Sin Chew Jit Poh published a quote from British Far
East Command that the Dutch East Indies had strong enough
defences to keep Malaya as secure as a boulder.

In the middle of November, the customers described vividly
how they often looked out of their windows to see British
naval ships firing anti-aircraft guns, and people were starting
to get more concerned about the situation in Singapore.
Some thought the Japanese might show up to bomb them
any day now, while others said it wouldn't happen so soon.
Most believed the British defences were strong, and even if
the Japanese did show up, there wasn't too much to worry
about. All they could do was go on living their lives. By the
start of December, though, one item after another appeared
in the newspapers to make it clear the war they feared was no
longer a faraway occurrence, but coming closer and closer. The
colonial government declared a state of emergency in Malaya,
and Britain's largest battleship, the Prince of Wales, was sent
to Singapore. Meanwhile, the Japanese-language newspaper
closed down, and the Japanese in Singapore were rapidly
decamping. Shenton Thomas, the Governor of the Straits

Settlements, announced a mobilisation of volunteer troops due to the rising tensions worldwide.

3. THE JAPANESE PLANES ARRIVE

ON THE EVENING OF 7TH DECEMBER, PING HUNG WAS playing mahjong with the third floor tenants, Third Auntie, Ah Hoi and Uncle Ho. They went back upstairs after the game finished around ten. Ah Yoke heated up the watercress soup left over from dinner, and the couple sat chatting in the living room as they drank it. The kids were all asleep by then. Ah Yoke went to bed first, while Ping Hung had a shower and a nightcap of ginseng brew. Then he turned in too, and all was quiet. This lasted till a little after four in the morning. The streetlamps still shone on the silent roads, and most of the island's inhabitants were, like Ping Hung, lost in their dreams.

Then the war they'd discussed so eagerly during their waking hours burst upon their sleep.

Ping Hung was startled awake by planes roaring overhead and explosions like thunderclaps. He scrambled out of bed. Outside the window were thick smoke and flames, and the air smelt of gunpowder. He stared at the collapsed buildings and fire, unable to work out what was going on. There were more blasts and gunshots. Only now did he hear the screams and sobs of people outside. The houses across the street had been hit. Something flew in the window, perhaps debris or a bullet, and shattered the dressing table mirror, flinging shards of glass across the floor. As if waking from a dream, Ping Hung realised he was in danger.

The children ran into the bedroom, Kung Man and Kung Woo frantic, Yeuk Lan weeping. Ah Yoke jumped out of bed and rushed to them, a mother hen protecting her chicks. She picked Yeuk Lan up and clutched her tight to her bosom.

"*Get down! Get down!*" Ping Hung shouted at the children. Kung Man and Kung Woo seemed mesmerised by the sight, mumbling, "*The Japanese planes are attacking! The Japanese planes are attacking!*"

"*Get down!*" Ping Hung called again.

They crouched behind the bed. The walls and floor shook with each explosion, as if they might collapse at any moment. Terrified past endurance, Ah Yoke and their daughter began howling. A moment later, Yeuk Lan managed to stop, and began comforting her mother. More airplanes rumbled overhead, and there was an enormous crash close by. Ah Yoke and the children screamed, and Ping Hung thought his heart would leap from his throat. Through the clouds of smoke, he saw their wall clock lying on the floor. "*It's Uncle Kin's clock,*" he said shakily, looking helplessly at his trembling wife. The explosions continued sounding outside, accompanied by chilling cries. Didn't the British have good defences at sea? Where were their anti-aircraft guns? How could the Japanese planes have arrived so quietly, without anyone noticing?

Later, Ping Hung discovered it wasn't just their neighbourhood of Big Town that had been affected, but many areas around the city too. Raffles Place, Clifford Pier, Clarke Quay and Fort Canning Hill had also been hit, and several of the boats in harbour had been sunk. Worst of all, the air bases at Seletar and Tengah had come under fire, destroying the planes and airstrips. In other words, they'd lost control of the airspace over Singapore and the peninsula. The Japanese would be able to carpet bomb to their hearts' content, and life was about to get much more difficult. Would Singapore fall to the Japanese devils? Ping Hung was filled with anxiety. What would happen if they conquered Singapore? His wife and kids might be the first victims. What would he do?

The days after that were dreadful. From that first bombing on the 8th, the air raid sirens sounded frequently, and everyone felt they were living in a nightmare. Many didn't dare go out, while others spent like crazy, afraid the currency would plummet. People often got together to talk about what was happening, so business at Wing Fong was fairly good. The cinemas were booming. Everyone wanted to watch movies, never mind what about, though they often had to evacuate halfway through a screening when the sirens went off, to run to the nearest shelter. One evening around eight, the sirens sounded, more Japanese planes soared overhead, and quite a few buildings in Big Town were bombed, amongst them the New Star Theatre on Smith Street.

New Star used to be known as Lai Chun Yuen; Ping Hung and Ah Yoke had watched many Cantonese operas there. When it became New Star, it started screening movies too. Just that September, they'd watched *The White Whirlwind* starring Cheung Wood Yau and Lam Mui Mui. New Star also staged plays, which Ah Yoke's brother Tat Yan enjoyed watching. Not long ago, he and Ping Hung had seen a few anti-Japanese dramas there. The day of the bombing, there'd been eight or nine air raid warnings. Everyone was jittery, so the theatre closed early, as did Wing Fong. Tat Yan and Ping Hung often caught a show after work, when they weren't staying in for mahjong. If the theatre had stayed open, the two of them might well have been killed in the explosion.

4. ESCAPE

WITH THE JAPANESE DEVILS BOMBING THE CITY, MANY people worried their homes would be hit next, or that they'd be injured by flying debris, like the proprietress of the medicine shop catty-corner to Wing Fong. She was in her kitchen cooking when a bomb struck a fabric shop a short distance away, sending a piece of shrapnel through the window and into her forehead. More and more shopkeepers in their neighbourhood abandoned their businesses to hide in the countryside. Ping Hung and Ah Yoke contemplated doing the same, but that would mean leaving their home to the looters. They mulled it over for a few days: Ping Hung thought the city was no longer safe, while Ah Yoke didn't want to give up all their possessions. Ping Hung said those were just things, and their lives were more important. In the end, he got his way.

Where would they go? Their closest neighbours had decamped to Bukit Timah, but Fatty Wing from the pork shop said he'd heard there was no more accommodation available there, and Hougang might be a better bet. They packed up their savings, jewellery, rice and other provisions, and followed Fatty Wing and few others to Hougang. Ping Hung asked his father-in-law to join them, but Chan Kwok Tai's shop was full of tinned food, alcohol, cigarettes, and rice, not to mention premium goods like abalone and shark fin, so he decided to stay and guard them. Without anyone there, mice would eat all the food. Besides, Singapore was so small, if war started in earnest, everywhere would be equally dangerous. When the bombing started, he started sleeping in the shop, reasoning that with two storeys between him and the roof, he was less likely to be killed in a direct hit. Tat Yan decided to stay with his father, and wouldn't come with them either.

Public transport was no longer running, so after breakfast that day, Ping Hung and his family gathered their belongings and joined the stream of people walking out of the city. Every step of the way, they were terrified the planes would return with more bombs. Yeuk Lan grew too tired to walk, and Ping Hung had to carry her on his back. Kung Man and Kung Woo were also exhausted, but managed to help carry some of the lighter bundles. Fortunately, the air raid sirens remained silent. Instead, the sky darkened, and it began to rain. Even though it wasn't heavy, everyone felt thoroughly miserable huddled beneath their umbrellas, listening to the spattering and dragging their sodden shoes through the mud.

Jeeps full of British soldiers occasionally sped past, splashing them. Soon, Ping Hung's clothes were soaked. He stared after the offending vehicles, but felt no anger at all. He'd heard the men singing a rousing tune, and although he couldn't understand the lyrics, the music made him feel a bit less anxious, even hopeful. Surely these vigorous troops would be able to hold this small island, and keep their home secure.

Ping Hung had rented an attap hut before they'd set out. It was of course much less comfortable here, with the five of them squashed into a rather dilapidated room. There was no running water, just a well, and kerosene lamps instead of electricity. At night, mosquitoes buzzed around their ears and attacked them like miniature fighter jets. They lit mosquito coils, but even then, it was hard to get to sleep. There were only public outdoor bathrooms, which made going to the toilet at night inconvenient. No one cleaned out the shit pits, which began to stink after a while, and most people chose to relieve themselves in the nearby undergrowth instead.

Just as Ping Hung's father-in-law had predicted, the countryside wasn't entirely safe either. They still saw Japanese planes flying overhead, making their zinc roof rattle. There was an air raid shelter here too, a trench about human height covered with wooden boards weighed down with sandbags. Everyone dived in when the sirens went off. It was pitch dark in there. Ping Hung and Ah Yoke groped their way, following the crowds, comforting their sobbing daughter. When the bombs went off, dirt and pebbles were dislodged and landed on their heads. They squatted in silence, waiting for the all clear. Sometimes, they'd get back to the hut only to hear the sirens again, and they'd have to rush to the shelter once more.

Late one night, yanked out of sleep by yet another air raid, Ping Hung grabbed his daughter while Ah Yoke got the boys, and they stumbled blearily along the dirt road to the shelter. He hugged his wife and children as they huddled in the suffocating darkness with the other refugees. He couldn't see the people around him, only feel their warmth, their breath, their smell. The roaring planes and explosions mingled with coughs and murmurs, and the weeping of small children. The reek reminded Ping Hung of the night, many years ago, when he and Tak Chai couldn't find a place to stay in Canton and slept under a bridge. It was just as dark then. The space wasn't as cramped, and there were no ear-splitting explosions, but the blackness before his eyes was the same. Only now, the person pressing against him wasn't Tak Chai, but Ah Yoke. How cold it was, that night in Canton! Ping Hung sighed. *"Are you cold?"* he asked tenderly, moving his hand from Ah Yoke's shoulder to her chilly face. *"No,"* Ah Yoke and the children answered at the same time. Ping Hung reached out to hug his children, glad they'd been dressed warmly enough when they'd run outside.

"I wonder how Daddy and Tat Yan are doing," Ah Yoke murmured, her voice trembling with uncertainty and sorrow.

5. IT WAS OVER, THERE WAS NO HOPE

PING HUNG HEARD THAT BY THE MORNING OF 8TH DECEMBER, when the Japanese planes attacked Singapore, their troops had already reached Kota Bahru. On the 10th, the battleships Prince of Wales and Repulse, which had been defending the peninsula's coastal waters, were sunk by Japanese aircraft. In quick succession, Alor Setar, Trengganu and Penang were also taken.

The more bad news he heard, the more he fell into panic and despair.

On the 20th, the Japanese claimed Kelantan, followed by

Taiping and Ipoh. It got worse in the new year. Between the 3rd and 15th of January, Kuantan, Kuala Lumpur, Klang, Seremban, Tampin, Gemas, and Malacca fell one after another. By the end of January, the retreating British troops had pulled back all the way from Johor to Singapore. It was over, there was no hope. British Far East Command's pronouncement that Malaya was "as secure as a boulder" now felt like a cruel joke. He and Ah Yoke blazed with anxiety, while the children didn't quite seem to understand what was going on. They kept asking when they could go home, because life in the countryside was so awful.

6. A HELL-LIKE INFERNO

AS THE BRITISH FORCES RETREATED TO SINGAPORE, not only did they blow up all the buildings along the Johor Bahru shoreline, they destroyed the causeway too. This meant cutting off the pipes that delivered drinking water, leaving Singaporeans reliant on the island's reservoirs. The water shortage left hygiene facilities in a parlous state, particularly the toilets, which were overflowing. At least the countryside didn't have flush toilets, so Ping Hung and his family were spared this. As long as they were careful, rainwater and well-water supplied all their needs.

The Japanese now occupied the entire peninsula, and at the start of February, they began firing on the northeast of Singapore from Johor Bahru, while the air raids continued. In Hougang, Ping Hung heard the thunder-like roar of gunfire and felt the ground tremble. Singapore would soon be in the hands of the Japanese devils. Ah Yoke was constantly worried about her father and little brother in the city, while Ping Hung felt confusion, anxiety and fear, as well as anger. How could this have happened? He felt as if he'd been lied to and abandoned.

Yes, Singapore's fall was imminent. On 7th February, the Japanese occupied Pulau Ubin, and the next day began heavily bombing and firing on the mainland. They destroyed more than three hundred fuel depots, turning the island into a hellscape of flames and thick smoke. That night, Japanese troops landed on the west coast and overwhelmed the defences there, and on the morning of the 10th, they marched on Seletar Air Base, joined by reinforcements who swarmed across Kranji River and the Straits. On the 11th, Kallang Airport was devastated by bombing, and Japanese soldiers marched down Thomson Road to seize the reservoir. They now controlled Singapore's only water source. Like the rest of Singapore, Ping Hung and the other refugees in Hougang were being showered in pamphlets urging them to surrender, dropped from Japanese planes.

Like a hot knife through butter, the Japanese cut off Bukit Panjang and Bukit Timah, and by the 12th, they were encroaching on the city. It was said they'd unleashed more than four thousand fighter jets, dropping over seven hundred tonnes of explosives. Several days of this, and the sky was blocked out by a thick layer of smog. Even in the afternoon, the streets were dark as night.

TAT YAN

FINALLY, THEY WERE HERE

FROM THE CLAN ASSOCIATION, TAT YAN FRANTICALLY pedalled his bicycle through the explosions and flames, hurtling through debris and smoke. He saw the crumbling remnants of buildings, orphans weeping by their dead parents' bodies, cars abandoned in the street, some with corpses still in the driver's seats. Other vehicles sped recklessly along, engines screaming. Uniformed British soldiers crouched by the buildings, bleeding and moaning, wandered the streets in a daze, or roared as they fired their guns fruitlessly into the sky. Nasty-looking thugs broke down shop doors and grabbed furniture, bedding, clothes, sacks of rice, crates of tinned food, cigarettes and alcohol. Tat Yan sped up, worried that the provision shop had been targeted too, anxious for his father's safety. Finally, he got to their street. Turning swiftly down the back alley, he jumped off, tossed the bicycle to one side, got out his keys, and unlocked the back door.

Pushing the door open, he heard a commotion from the front: voices, and objects being moved. His father was lying in the airwell, mouth open and eyes wide with fear, fresh blood soaking his head and clothes. Tat Yan almost cried out, *Dad!* but clapped his hand over his mouth and swallowed the word. He bumped into the wooden door.

"Someone's coming!" called a voice.

He quickly stepped back outside, closed and locked the door, got back on his bike, and headed to Wing Fong.

Using the spare key Ah Yoke gave him, he went in through the back door, and dragged the rice and biscuits they'd left behind up to the third floor. He carried his bicycle up there too. The looters would show up sooner or later. Next, he got a cleaver from the kitchen and kept it by his side as he sat on the stairs. Fear, sorrow and guilt were welling up inside him. He buried his face in his hands and burst into tears, cursing himself for being a coward. He'd fled for his life, leaving his father in a puddle of blood. Eventually, he calmed down and comforted himself. His father was already dead, and getting into a fight with his killers wouldn't have changed that. He'd have accomplished nothing but cutting short another life: his own. More explosions rumbled outside. He didn't know how long he'd been sitting there when, amidst the intermittent bombing, he heard something bang against the front door. Finally, they were here.

He jumped to his feet, shut the wooden door to seal off the third floor, and pushed two heavy tables against it. Soon after that, he heard a loud crash: the front door had been rammed in. Then he heard voices and more noise: people had entered and were helping themselves to everything that wasn't nailed down. He held his breath, shaking hard, and stared at the barricaded door, the cleaver clasped firmly in his sweaty hands.

THE FALL OF SINGAPORE

WING FONG KOPITIAM HAD
MIRACULOUSLY SURVIVED

ON 14TH FEBRUARY, THE EVE OF CHINESE NEW YEAR, THE customary racket of firecrackers was replaced by shelling, bombing and gunfire. Ships all down the coast were engulfed in a sea of flames, and deafening explosions took over the city centre.

On the 15th, Chinese New Year, the exhausted British troops were still valiantly fighting on in the early morning, but the ammo dump on Alexandra Hill had been bombed into non-existence, leaving them short of ammunition and fuel. They only had enough food left for three days, and almost no bullets. So many pipes had been destroyed that there was now no water in the hospital, and the streets were full of injured soldiers with no one to tend them. In fact, the whole island had almost run dry, and clinging on could only lead to more casualties.

At 9.30am, the British commander Lieutenant-General Percival called an emergency meeting at Fort Canning Hill. At 7.15 that evening, Percival surrendered to the Japanese. That night, the Japanese flag hung like a medicinal plaster from the tallest building in Singapore, the Cathay.

The next morning, Singaporeans witnessed the Japanese rolling onto their island in tanks, singing victory songs.

Thus began the Japanese Occupation of Singapore. On 18th February, they proclaimed that the island would be renamed Syonan-to. After the ceasefire, Ping Hung and his family dragged their weary bodies and despairing hearts from Hougang back to their street. Along the way, they caught their first sight of Japanese soldiers and army vehicles, bombed-out buildings, and streets full of debris. Some of the walls were still smeared with blood and brain matter. The ruined roads were littered with corpses. Ah Yoke kept stopping to vomit. Ping Hung covered his daughter's eyes so she wouldn't see, but she caught glimpses of the carnage, as did her brothers. Ping Hung didn't know what effect so much death would have on his children's minds. For the next few days, they couldn't force down any food, and their sleep was plagued with nightmares.

Many of their friends and neighbours were dead, but Wing Fong Kopitiam had miraculously survived. Of course, the door had been smashed open and the shop stood empty. Not even the furniture was left. When they fled, Ping Hung had only managed to bring a sack of rice, some biscuits, tinned food, coffee and sugar. Everything else was gone now, even the canvas folding beds. It was like the shop had been stripped bare by locusts. But perhaps they'd forgotten the upper floors? They went up to the second floor, where the heavy items like beds and wardrobes still remained, but everything movable, including clothes, chairs and even the crockery, was gone. The third floor looked untouched. Best of all, Ah Yoke's brother Tat Yan was there.

Scrawny and filthy, Tat Yan looked as startled as a feral cat leaping out of a rubbish bin. He embraced Ah Yoke and sobbed, "*I thought I'd never see you again.*" He told them about Chan Kwok Tai's death, and that he'd heard the Japanese had shot quite a few resistance fighters in Bukit Timah, including old people, women and children. Tat Yan hadn't been sure if Ah Yoke and her family had fled to Hougang or Bukit Timah, and had been filled with anxiety.

"*Hougang, we went to Hougang,*" Ah Yoke managed to say, weeping as she held her brother's hand.

THE OLD MAN

1. GUNFIRE BEHIND THEM

THE JAPANESE TIE HIS HANDS BEHIND HIS BACK WITH WIRE, along with several other men, and lead them in a line onto an army truck. Everyone's head is down. In the gloom, he can't make out their faces. Their keening sobs are like an erhu's plaintive notes. Like a premonition, he feels he can't breathe. He is icy cold, teeth chattering. The truck rattles along for a while before stopping. He looks out but can't tell where they are, there's nothing in sight but the oppressive sky and sea. The Japanese soldiers shout at them to get down. His mind is murky, his heart full of panic, and his legs wobbly. He tumbles to the ground, more a roll than a jump. The row of people, tied together, can only move in unison like a skewer of meat.

He feels no pain even as he hits the dirt. They struggle to their feet as the Japanese, wielding guns, hustle them to the shore and make them run into the waves. As the captives stumble into the ocean, there's a spate of gunfire behind them. They scuttle like cockroaches being sprayed with insecticide, colliding and getting entangled in each other's limbs. He feels a sharp pain in his back, and knows he's been hit. His legs go limp, and he falls into the water. He struggles, but his arms and legs won't do as they're told. Salt water enters his lungs, choking him. He is sinking, sinking into the cold and dark, to the bottom of the sea—

Abruptly, a piercing beam of light cuts through the black waters.

"*Grandpa, Grandpa!*"

Someone is calling him from within the light, and shaking his shoulder.

He opens his eyes.

This isn't the bottom of the sea; he's in his bedroom, and the lights are on. No wonder he felt cold, the blanket is by his side.

A woman stands next to him. The light is disorienting, and he's feels as if he's still underwater. Her figure wavers. He can't make out her face. She says something and pulls the blanket over him. After a while, his eyes adjust to the light, but he is still half in his dream, and can faintly hear the rat-tat-tat of gunshots and terrifying cries.

"*Are you okay, Grandpa? You were screaming really loudly.*" Another woman has come into the room, and is speaking gently to him.

"*What time is it?*" he asks blearily.

"*Four o'clock,*" one of the women answers.

The dream is still clear in his mind. It's a familiar one. He must have had the same dream years ago, more than once. It feels like an old movie that comes back for a repeat screening when he isn't sleeping well. Each time, he feels the same when he wakes up: alone, sad, regretful. As if the Japanese actually had shot him in the back.

"*Why didn't I die?*" He's confused. The room looks alien in this yellow light. "*Turn the lamp off,*" he mutters, then shuts his eyes. Even so, he can still see the Japanese soldiers glaring at him.

Didn't someone say the Japanese surrendered? Have the devils given up or not? His heart is a terrified muddle, and his head is jumbled too. It takes him a long time to quieten down. When he opens his eyes again, the lamp is off, and the two women are moving around the room. In the dark, he can make out a glass of water and small jar of Tiger Balm on the bedside table. One of his shirts hangs over the back of the chair. This is the bedroom he knows. He lives in an HDB flat in Bishan now, not the old place in Big Town.

He misses the flat above Wing Fong Kopitiam. Though the

family fled to Hougang during the bombing, they returned when the Occupation started. Uncle Kin and Big Sister Kam passed away one after the other in San Francisco, soon after the war ended. Wing Fong was now his. At the start of the '50s, business took a turn for the better. He saved up some money and renovated the second storey a couple of times, turning it into a four-room flat with a large kitchen and a long living room, in which he placed rosewood furniture and calligraphy scrolls. (Later, these would be joined by photographs of his grandson Kim Chau in costume.) A gramophone and some records stood on a little shelf in the living room. He owned quite a few Cantonese opera recordings (where are they now?) that he would often regale visitors with as they drank and played mahjong. Sometimes, he felt guilty: he wouldn't have any of these things if not for the kopitiam, but Wing Fong was Uncle Kin and Big Sister Kam's. All his possessions were actually theirs; he was a cuckoo in their nest.

He thinks of the rosewood dressing table he bought Ah Yoke, the bed he slept in with Ah Yoke by his side. Yes, Ah Yoke should have been Tak Chai's wife, but Ping Hung loved her so very much, especially after she died and he truly felt the pain of losing her. He didn't cherish her enough when she was in the world, but gave her a hard time out of jealousy that her heart belonged to Tak Chai. She didn't welcome him on their wedding night. At first he thought she was shy, but then realised she was pushing him away. She spent the whole of their first time silently weeping, which made him feel vexed, embarrassed, humiliated, as if he were forcing himself on her. He asked if it hurt, but she shook her head. She must have been thinking of Tak Chai, which meant she must have been intimate with him. The thought drove him near insane, and he grew frantic with jealousy, trying to guess what happened.

He and Ah Yoke were terrible together in bed. She went through the motions as if it were just a bureaucratic hassle, more mechanically than the prostitutes on Keong Saik Road. At least the whores knew how to fake passion. Ah Yoke just lay there, cold as a slab of ice, mortifying him. But he loved her. No matter how angry and hurt he was, the most he ever did was sulk or grumble. He never once hit her. In order to satisfy his urges, he made several trips to Keong Saik Road, but that felt dirty. Over time, Ah Yoke quietly learnt how to please him. Had she acquiesced to her fate? He didn't know, but tried his best to be good to her too, more caring. Yet whenever he remembered it was Tak Chai she loved, not himself, he'd get angry, and take it out on her. Without mentioning any names, he'd lash out at her with sharp words. He called her a loose woman who didn't know the meaning of chastity, then regretted it afterwards. That's how he tortured her: tenderness when he liked her, harsh words when he didn't.

When she got gravely ill, he felt remorse for everything he'd done. After her death, his guilt and self-recrimination deepened. Had his ill-treatment weakened her body? What a good wife Ah Yoke was, he sighed. She'd quietly suffered through the Japanese Occupation with him. Although the saying goes that a poor couple have a hundred sorrows, they were actually happiest together when they had the least. When they lived in constant fear of the Japanese, trying desperately to survive, he didn't have energy left over for jealousy, and they managed to be loving amidst this deprivation. Ah Yoke must have been happiest in Syonan-to. In peacetime, their material life got better, and he began picking on her again. Ah Yoke really was a good wife. She hadn't uttered a word of complaint during the hard times, and painstakingly raised their children whilst helping him to run Wing Fong. Whenever he misses Ah Yoke, he berates himself for being so heartless, treating fine timber as kindling.

He once dreamt that Tak Chai wrote to him after his marriage, with a thick stack of banknotes as a wedding gift. He never told Ah Yoke about this, because he suspected it wasn't a dream, but something that actually happened. Maybe Ah Yoke knew, but kept it to herself. The dream made him uneasy. He felt like a criminal or a cheat who hadn't been found out yet. Sooner or later, someone would uncover his guilt. For some years now, he's been uncertain which of his memories are dreams, and which actually happened. For instance, he's recently started dreaming that Ah Yoke and the children are still upstairs at Wing Fong, but he hasn't been back to see them for a long time. This makes him anxious. How are they doing? Who's taking care of them? It feels so real, not at all like a dream.

The two women stay in the room a little longer, say something to him, and leave.

Who are they? Not Ah Yoke and Ah Lan, surely.

Ah Yoke has been dead a long time. And his children? Kung Man is dead too, he thinks. And there's Kim Chau, Kim Chau's dead too. What about Kung Woo? And Kim Ming? And Ah Lan? Is Ah Lan still alive? He thinks hard, growing lost in fragments of time and shards of memory. After a long while, he remembers that he saw Kim Ming in Hong Kong many times. So he's probably still there. Kung Woo said he was going to China after leaving Singapore. He remembers giving Kung Woo the location of his village, and telling him to visit his uncles and aunts. The bastard left Singapore so many years ago, and there hasn't been any news from him. Where is he now? Did he ever go to the village? What about Ah Lan? Where is Ah Lan now?

Deep in the maze of memory, he finally dredges up the names of the two women who were in the room earlier: his granddaughter Yu Sau and their helper Maria.

A whole family, dead or dispersed. Maybe he brought the curse on them. Is heaven punishing him? Is this retribution? A tide of desolation sweeps over him.

2. INSPECTION

"*I HAVE TO QUEUE UP FIRST THING IN THE MORNING FOR THE inspection. Tat Yan died during his.*" The old man turns over, as if Ah Yoke is beside him in bed. "*I'm sure his death has something to do with those people, the Nightblooming Drama Society. He spent so much time with them, and they staged anti-Japanese performances. The chap who ran the society and some of the others went for the inspection and never came back.*" He sighs long and hard, then rolls onto his back and stares at the ceiling, only it's no longer the ceiling, but a screen unfurling in his mind. The scrambled memories are sharpening. Something from decades ago, crystal clear before his eyes:

He had a large bag of biscuits and a bottle of water as he made his way at dawn to Upper Cross Street, the gathering point for the inspection. Early as it was, there were already quite a few people there. The road was surrounded by a metal fence and piled with sandbags, on which machine guns rested. In the field where the inspection would be carried out were armed Japanese soldiers, and a tank was parked nearby. He found a patch of grass to squat on. At least he'd gotten there early enough. Soon, there'd only be room on the road, which would grow hot from the sun by afternoon.

He hadn't considered that as the queue moved, he'd end up on the scalding hot road. They inched along, and were only allowed to squat, not stand. No one was allowed to leave once they were here, not even if they needed the toilet. He was usually a very clean person, but when his bladder couldn't hold out, he had to do the same as everyone else and pee where he was. After some time, his legs grew too tired to keep squatting, and he had no choice but to sit in his own piss. They were like animals in a cage, their bums smeared with shit and urine. The Japanese yelled orders and whacked them with their rifles to make them move forward. The only thing distinguishing them from beasts was that each held a form containing their personal details.

Terrified, he stood before the Japanese soldiers carrying out the inspection. He stank of piss, which made him ashamed. He stammered out a greeting in Japanese. The soldiers glared nastily at him for quite a while, then barked out questions. "Name? Occupation?" They made him hold out his palms to be inspected, then marked his body with a stamp, and shoved him to one side.

"*They put a mark on my shirt. I wore that marked shirt from then on,*" says the old man to the empty pillow next to him. "*I didn't dare to take it off or wash it.*" He stares at the space beside him for a long time, then rolls back and shuts his eyes.

Many people never returned from their inspection. They were pumped full of water and tortured to death. That's probably what happened to the drama society members. Anyone who didn't get a mark on their clothing was dragged into the sea and shot dead. Tat Yan was summoned the same morning as him. When he got home that evening, there was no sign of Tat Yan, not even at dinner time. This wasn't good. He'd been worried during his own inspection that the Japanese would ask about Tat Yan, but they hadn't. Still, he remained anxious they'd give him trouble in the future. He never told Ah Yoke about these fears.

Exhausted, he went to bed immediately after dinner, but was too scared and uneasy to sleep. The next morning, Tat Yan wasn't there, but Ah Yoke insisted he'd been back in the night. After Ping Hung went to bed, she did the washing up, and when she came back out, there was Tat Yan in the living room, staring at her without a word. She said, "*What are you doing there? You gave me a fright.*" His face was stark white. He looked fear-stricken, and very tired.

"*I told him to sit down, and turned back to get him a bowl of soup from the kitchen. Before I got there, I heard him say*

behind me, 'I'm leaving, Sis.' I said, 'Leaving? Where to? Why
are you rushing off like a scalded cat?' He said something about
the drama society people waiting for him, they had something
urgent to do. I said he should eat first, but he was in a hurry.
And just like that, he rushed out the front door."

The old man can see Ah Yoke saying this, as if it happened
yesterday. She went to the door and called after Tat Yan, but
he'd already disappeared down the stairs. She ran after him, but
found the street silent. No sign of Tat Yan, just the concertina
wire blocking the road and the two Japanese sentries. "He'd
vanished like a ghost," she said.

They never saw Tat Yan again. Oh yes, the old man
remembers now: the night after the inspection, he had a bad
dream. He was tied to some other people, forced into a truck,
and driven to the sea, where Japanese soldiers fired at them
from behind. But the "him" in the dream was actually Tat Yan.
Later, he told Ah Yoke what he believed: that Tat Yan had been
killed during the inspection, and was already dead when she
saw him that night. Ah Yoke burst into tears. For many years
after that, whenever she remembered that night, she'd say, "He
came back just to give me a fright," and start crying again.

"You can't bring the dead back to life, no point howling about
it." The old man's dried-out eyes stare into the darkness of the
room as he mutters, "I told him not to spend so much time with
those theatre people, didn't I?"

3. SO FEW CHANCES TO BE DRUNK,
WHY MISS THIS ONE?

"AH SAU!" DURING LUNCH, THE OLD MAN WANTS TO TALK TO
Maria about Syonan-to again. He often calls her Ah Sau. "Back
when this was Syonan-to, every front door had a Japanese
sticker. If not, you were in trouble. The Japanese would come

and hassle you, and if they suspected you were in the resistance, that would be the end of your life."

Ever since National Day, the old man has been babbling about Syonan-to, mostly to himself, sometimes to Yu Sau and Maria. He often calls Yu Sau by her Aunt's name, Ah Lan, and at some point he started calling Maria by Yu Sau's nickname. Yu Sau corrects the old man each time, reminding him that she's his granddaughter, not Aunt Yeuk Lan. Maria doesn't mind what he calls her, she can't understand a word. Now he's done it again, and Maria stares dubiously at him, saying in her rudimentary Cantonese, *"Eat! Eat!"* The old man ignores her. His hands are shaking so much that the bowl of rice in his left hand is a little boat in choppy waters, while the chopsticks in his right hand are like the elongated beak of a bird, pecking at something in mid-air. *"You think we had such good rice to eat back then? I ate broken rice, adulterated rice, rice with sand in it. Even then, we had to queue up with our ration cards."*

The old man scoops up some rice and stuffs his mouth. As he slowly chews, his muddy, dried-out eyes are fixed on the stir-fried pea shoots on the plate. He slips back into his shattered memories. Just before the Japanese surrendered, prices had soared to unbelievable heights, while the value of banana currency fell, sometimes several times a day. You had to bring a sack of banknotes to go shopping. Even though life was extremely hard on Syonan-to, Great World and Happy World amusement parks stayed open, and were filled with gambling stalls: chap ji kee, word flowers, dominoes. Early in the Occupation, there was no way to open the kopitiam right after the looters had taken everything, so he worked as a guard at a gambling den for a couple of months. The old man chews vigorously, and finally manages to force down the mouthful of rice. His eyes are wide open, and he says to Maria as if in a dream, *"Luckily Uncle Kin warned me not to gamble or go near opium. I saw it happen with my own eyes, so many people ended up in the street.*"

He thinks of Wing Fong after the looting, of his father-in-law's provision shop picked bare, the stalls that sold old clothes and other goods on Market Street. Someone told him their stolen possessions ended up at one of these stalls. The old man blurts out in rage, "*Damn them, everything they sell is stolen, we should steal it back!*"

Maria smiles uncomprehendingly. "*Grandpa, eat!*" she says. That's about the extent of her Cantonese. The old man looks at her, confused. He gets angrier the more he thinks about this. Most people were very poor back then, yet there were those who caroused every night: gouging merchants, or straight-up traitors. How else could they have made their money? He shakes his head and sighs at the injustice of it. His existence in Syonan-to actually wasn't too bad. The money and jewellery he and his wife brought when they fled were enough to restore Wing Fong, and he was able to re-open before too long. After a while, they could even afford to watch Cantonese operas at New World and Great World. He heard performances by the likes of the scholar-warrior Chan Yin Tong, the ingénue Lau Lai Ho, the female impersonator Lee Tsui Fong. Of course, they're all forgotten now. Swirling through his mind is Yoshiko Yamaguchi singing, "*So few chances to be drunk, why miss this one? After we say goodbye tonight, when will the gentleman come again?*" Yes, she was often on the radio, that's probably why he can still remember her songs. He hums to Maria, "*Beautiful flowers seldom bloom, beautiful times quickly pass.*" Then he mutters, "*I used to hear this every day. The singer was famous, but I can't think of her name. That's what happens when you're old!*"

4. DO WE HAVE ANY MORE JAPANESE MONEY?
BURN IT ALL!

THE HUNGRY GHOST FESTIVAL COMES SOON AFTER NATIONAL
Day. During Ghost Month, the old man and his daughter-in-
law used to burn offerings on the pavement outside Wing
Fong Kopitiam. They did the same even after moving into the
flat. After his son died, his granddaughter came back to live
with them, but she never took part, probably thinking it was
just superstition. Then his daughter-in-law took a turn for the
worse and couldn't get around easily, so when the old man
made his offerings that year, the granddaughter had no choice
but to help him. He told her to bring everything down to the
side of the road: cooked food, fruits, joss paper, hell money.
She resisted at first, maybe because she'd studied overseas. This
probably seemed ridiculous, or even embarrassing, to her. She
initially agreed only to help him bring the things downstairs,
but when she saw what a hard time he was having, she helped
him lay them out too, then set the joss paper alight. Out of
reluctance, she was moving as fast as she could, as if she was
doing something shameful.

When his daughter-in-law died, that seemed to change the
girl's mind. She even said to him that Ghost Month was like
the Grave Sweeping Day, an occasion to remember the dead,
nothing superstitious about it. And sure enough, at Ching
Ming, she went with the old man to pray at her parents' and
grandmother's grave. Like her mother used to, she now talked
to the dead, begging her father's forgiveness for not taking
better care of him, asking her parents and grandma to protect
her and Grandpa, and give them good health. Now the old
man sits in his wheelchair, watching his granddaughter kneel
by the side of the road, chanting as she burns joss paper. Ash
dances through the smoke like a flock of black butterflies.

He says to her, pausing between sentences, "*When the*

Japanese devils were here, so many people were killed. They all became restless spirits, and to this day I'm still praying for them. Did you know? The day they surrendered was the Hungry Ghost Festival. We all burnt Japanese money for the dead, like it was hell money. Japanese currency had become worthless, you see."

His granddaughter listens quietly. This is all very strange. Ever since National Day, when the fighter jets roared past outside, her grandpa returned to the Japanese Occupation. Although he's confused, he remembers the period with perfect clarity. Of course, she has no way of knowing if his memories are accurate. All this happened before she was born. Still, she believes everything he's saying about the Occupation. Just as she's wondering why his mind is sometimes so sharp, he shouts at her, *"Ah Lan! Do we have any more Japanese money? Burn it all!"*

LEONG PING HUNG

THE JAPANESE SURRENDERED

On 18th August 1945, the Japanese surrendered.

Before this happened, Leong Ping Hung had spent most of his banana notes on groceries and other essentials, so when the Japanese currency became scrap paper, he didn't lose too much. He'd squirrelled away enough Straits dollars that when Singapore was restored, they still had enough to live on.

The Japanese had governed Singapore very strictly, and any infraction of their laws could lead to the death penalty. Even burglars were executed. Once, Ping Hung was walking across Coleman Bridge when he saw decapitated heads hanging from the railings, with placards stating what crimes they'd been killed for. He was nauseated and terrified, and it was a long time before he dared walk that way again. Everyone behaved with extreme caution. Never mind overthrowing the Japanese, they didn't even dare misbehave. You didn't even have to break the law to get into trouble. If you were walking down the street and forgot to bow to a Japanese soldier, he'd slap you across the face, or worse. Ping Hung saw a man who must have offended the occupiers in some way, being forced to strip naked and hug an oil drum by the side of the road. Under the sun, the scorching metal soon left him covered in sweat. His face was contorted, and Ping Hung could imagine what torment he was in.

After American atom bombs fell on Hiroshima and Nagasaki on 6th and 9th August 1945, even though the Japanese hadn't officially surrendered yet, the fight went out of them, and there were barely any soldiers to be seen in the street after that. Anarchy descended once more, just as it had before the British surrender. Shops were looted and there were gunshots everywhere. Even the Japanese encampment was set on fire. Ping Hung kept the gates of Wing Fong firmly locked, and only went outside to buy food. Order returned with the British, and the kopitiam could open its doors once more. That's when he got a letter from Big Sister Kam in San Francisco, telling him Uncle Kin had passed away and she was too ill to travel, so she wouldn't be returning. The kopitiam was now his. He asked his son Kung Man to write back with his condolences, and to tell Big Sister Kam all the terrible events she'd missed by leaving Singapore. Wing Fong was still standing, even after being cleaned out by the looters, and he would work hard to restore the business. He hoped Big Sister Kam would recover and return, so he could hand it over and go back to working for her. He was sad he had to stay and run the shop, rather than going to San Francisco to care for her. He sent some money and told her to buy nourishing foods. He also said the kopitiam belonged to both her and Uncle Kin, and any profits he made were hers.

He never knew if Big Sister Kam received the letter, and the money he tried to remit was returned. He never heard from her again, nor was there any news from Uncle Kin's brother in San Francisco. He thought Big Sister Kam might have died too, and felt a pang of grief. She'd been very fond of both him and Tak Chai, but Ping Hung had always got on better with them than Tak Chai, and in fact thought of them as his adoptive parents.

There were no more letters from Tak Chai either, but he'd long given up hope of that. Occasionally, he read something in the papers about the new Siu Kai, who had apparently taken refuge in the French concession of Kouang-Tchéou-Wan during the war, then moved to Hong Kong when peace resumed. As a "young warrior" performer, he'd made quite a few martial arts movies, and now had a bit of a reputation in the film world, whilst still singing opera. Ping Hung admired but also envied him. Tak Chai had entered the profession at the age of sixteen and returned to Canton at twenty. In the blink of an eye, two decades had passed and they were now middle-aged men of forty. His old acquaintance was the new Siu Kai, star of stage and screen, while he was still an ordinary kopitiam uncle leading a mundane life. Yet when he thought about it, he'd been much luckier than many others. And really, he ought to be grateful to Tak Chai: he'd just been an illiterate country boy, and would never have had the courage to leave for Nam Yong if he hadn't been following his fearless friend. He was an ordinary person destined to lead an ordinary life. Seen in that light, owning a kopitiam was a pretty good fate. That's not what he thought most of the time, though. Instead, he resented Tak Chai's success when he, Ping Hung, was the more talented one. When he saved up enough to buy a gramophone, this didn't just seem like the fulfilment of the wish they'd made twenty years ago, it also shored up his belief in his own singing abilities.

The gramophone was for his eldest son's wedding, a newer model than Big Sister Kam's, with much crisper sound. As the mellifluous voices rose from the records, he would sometimes stand before the mirror and sing along, studying his face and figure with satisfaction. He was really not bad-looking, and would have made a good young male lead. Why hadn't he thought of this at the time? Once again, his jealousy of Tak Chai flared up.

When Kung Man and Kung Woo were little, never mind that there was a war going on and money was tight, Ping Hung would bring them to see Cantonese opera. Maybe they didn't go often enough, because the kids never seemed as enraptured as he was. It was Kung Man's son Kim Chau who, many years later, would fall in love with the art form. Kim Chau started accompanying him from around the age of four. This was in

1951, the year Kung Woo got married. Bak Yuk Tong came to Singapore and performed his famous role in *Wong Fei-Fu's Rebellion*. That was Kim Chau's first trip to the opera, and from then on, whenever Ping Hung said he was going to a show, the boy would clamour to come along. He was completely enchanted. It wasn't just the performers in their magnificent costumes, their voices, their gestures, their expressions, even the music with its drums and cymbals had him spellbound. At home, he would walk around the living room with a towel round his shoulders, copying the performers striding around the stage, singing passages with utmost earnestness. His childish voice full of determination, he told his grandpa Ping Hung that he would be like them one day, performing on stage in a beautiful costume.

Ping Hung was delighted, of course. At long last, he could open the wooden trunk and get out the robe Tak Chai had given him. He told Kim Chau, "*This was given to Grandpa by a good friend, the new Siu Kai, who sings opera. He's also a famous film star.*" Kim Chau stared at him, eyes wide. He had no idea who the new Siu Kai was. Ping Hung was surprised by his puzzlement, but then realised he hadn't seen any news of Tak Chai in the newspapers for quite some time now. The rumour was that he'd gone back to China, and word from there had been hard to come by since the Communists took over. How was he doing now? Looking at the costume, Ping Hung couldn't help sinking into melancholy. His feelings for Tak Chai were complicated: envy at his accomplishments, rage that Ah Yoke loved him and not her own husband, but also affection for the time they'd spent together in their youth, the hardships they'd survived. He gently stroked the robe where it lay on the ground, and his voice filled with emotion as he said to Kim Chau, "*This is yours. Grandpa will keep it safe for you, and when you're grown up, you can wear it on stage.*"

Tak Chai had once taught Ping Hung how to perform

water sleeves, and now Ping Hung passed the lesson on to his grandson. Kim Chau learnt quickly. Whenever he took the opera costume out of the camphorwood chest to look at it, he'd always fold it carefully afterwards, and put it back neatly where it belonged.

YU SAU AND GRANDPA

1. GRANDPA TALKING LOUDLY AT NIGHT

MARIA TELLS YU SAU THAT SHE ISN'T SURE WHY, BUT Grandpa seldom speaks during the day. Yu Sau has noticed this too. When she gets back from work, he's always sitting blank-faced in the living room. He doesn't seem to be napping; his eyes are wide open. It's more like he's sunk in thought. Now and then, he'll sigh deeply. If she calls out to him, he might turn to look expressionlessly at her, but never says anything. Sometimes Kah Onn comes home with her, but when he calls out a friendly greeting, Grandpa just ignores him, as if he's angry with Kah Onn for some reason.

Grandpa didn't use to be like this; he always liked Kah Onn. When Kah Onn called him "Grandpa", he seemed to mistake him for her second brother Kim Ming, and asked him all sorts of questions: was he married yet? Was he moving back home to live? Yu Sau explained again and again that Kah Onn was her boyfriend, not her brother. He nodded each time, seeming to understand, but a short while later he'd ask Kah Onn, "*Is your big brother in Hong Kong or not? When did he go there? Why didn't you tell me?*"

Maria says he used to be talkative at mealtimes, but now he doesn't say a word, just silently shovels rice into his mouth. Or else he stares at the food, as if he sees something moving in it. He doesn't eat very much, just a few mouthfuls, then he'll put down his chopsticks. Maria grumbles that she doesn't know what to cook for him any more. He won't eat, though he does drink water. Whenever Maria brings him a glass, he gulps it down right away, then just sits there, like a philosopher lost in thought.

The trouble is, though he's quiet in the day, he becomes very active at night. Around ten o'clock, he'll start swaggering around the living room with his walking stick, talking loudly to himself, like a sea captain shouting orders to his crew over a raging storm. This goes on till midnight, and really does sound like he has a whole gang of people following his instructions. Sometimes Yu Sau gets home at eleven, and he'll still be shouting away in the living room. He seems to be calling out names, mostly of people she doesn't know, though she's certain most of them are dead. Perhaps they're former employees at the kopitiam, or people he used to know. She recognises the name Ah Yoke, her grandma, and also his old friend Tak Chai and her brother Kim Chau. Sometimes, she hears him talking to "Sai" and "Kit", which agitates him to the point of tears. Yu Sau doesn't know who they are, but he mentions "their" dad. Could these be his siblings? They seem very important to him, just like Grandma, Eldest Brother and Tak Chai.

He makes this racket every night, before finally going to bed after twelve. Maria is terrified, convinced he's communing with the spirits. She complains to Yu Sau that it's not just Grandpa's voice she hears, there are also other people speaking too. There's nothing Yu Sau can do, even though Grandpa keeps her awake too, stomping round the living room shouting. Even worse, Maria tells Yu Sau one morning that the flat is haunted. She woke up the night before to see an old man standing at the foot of her bed. Not Grandpa, another old man. He was staring ferociously at her, screaming in a language she couldn't understand. She was scared out of her wits, but couldn't move. It felt as if something heavy was pressing down on her. Yu Sau says this was a nightmare, the sort of bad dream you have when you're not well, nothing to do with ghosts. Then a few days later, Maria reports that Grandpa was sitting on the sofa when he crinkled his nose, opened his mouth, and let out a roar like a wild animal, then blurted out a long speech in a language she was sure wasn't Cantonese. He sounded the same as that other old man. Yu Sau tries to reassure her. Grandpa's old, and he can't help talking to himself when he gets lonely. His brain is stuffed full of memories. Perhaps this is the dialect of the village he grew up in? If he's caught up in remembering something unhappy, of course he might sound upset. Maria doesn't buy this explanation. She insists that the flat is haunted, and she's petrified.

Two weeks later, Yu Sau gets home from work, and Maria lunges at her as soon as she opens the door. At lunchtime, Grandpa grabbed her hand, and started wheezing alarmingly. It took her a lot of effort to break free. Maria is still agitated, and a little incoherent, as if she can't control her voice. She's clearly been through a great shock. After some time, she calms down enough to explain to Yu Sau that she asked a Filipino friend, who told her a man in his eighties couldn't possibly have so much strength. Grandpa is obviously possessed. She once saw someone get possessed in her hometown, and he behaved exactly the same as Grandpa now. Maria's friend knows an exorcist, and she urges Yu Sau to give this person a call. Maria's words make Yu Sau's hair stand on end, but she fobs her off with a vague assurance that they'll wait and see. Maria seems disappointed that Yu Sau clearly doesn't believe her. Indeed, Yu Sau isn't superstitious, and the only strange behaviour she's witnessed is the loud late-night talking. She's never heard these bestial cries and unfamiliar languages, nor has Grandpa ever grabbed her hand. Why would he do that to Maria? It makes no sense. Maria has no reason to lie, but at the same time, it's very hard to believe her stories.

One morning, Maria finally hands in her notice. She tells Yu Sau she woke up on the floor. If she'd fallen out of bed, she'd surely have startled herself awake, but no, she was just on the floor this morning, as if she'd gone to sleep there. She rarely stirs in her sleep, she says, and this has never happened.

A demon must be playing pranks, and she's terrified at the thought of what it will do next. At this point, even Yu Sau's scepticism begins to sway. She hasn't experienced any of the things Maria is describing, but that doesn't mean the flat isn't haunted. Perhaps Maria is one of those people her mother called "badly fated". Yu Sau does her best to assure Maria that she believes her, and offers to give the exorcist a call, but Maria is determined to leave at the end of the month.

Once Maria leaves, who's going to take care of Grandpa while Yu Sau's at work? She's reluctant to put him in a home. When she was studying in England, her father had a stroke, and her mum took care of him all by herself. Whenever she phoned, her mum would grumble that she wasn't well herself, and this was taking such a toll on her, she might even die before him. Yu Sau got fed up listening to these complaints and suggested that she put him in a home. Her mother did as she said, and he died there. Yu Sau didn't even get to see him one last time. Her parents' marriage had always been fraught, so when her mum said she was ill, Yu Sau assumed that was just an excuse, and the truth was that she didn't want to take care of her dad. It was only when it came her turn to take care of Grandpa that she realised what a demanding task this was. And at least she had Maria's help, whereas her mum had done it all by herself. Her dad had still been relatively young, but it might actually be easier to take care of an old person than a younger one who'd had a stroke. When she'd told her mum to put her dad in a home, were those just angry words, or what she actually thought? She'd grown up watching her parents quarrel. They were both bad-tempered, and most of their arguments were over money, often tiny sums. Her dad was unemployed for a long time, and her mum would make cutting remarks about that. Neither of them would take a step back, which ended up with them banging the table and throwing crockery. Once, her mother pulled a pair of scissors from the drawer and waved it in his direction. Yu Sau can't remember now what provoked her to such an extent. She'd rushed over, grabbed her mum's hand, and carefully pried the scissors from her fingers. She was just seventeen then, still in JC. Yu Sau hated her family, and going to study in England was a form of escape. It was frustrating that her mum kept calling her to complain about having to care for her dad. Yu Sau felt angry with her brothers: as men, they ought to be responsible for their parents, but instead, they'd both selfishly left home.

2. GRANDPA SPOILT ALL THE MEN IN THIS FAMILY

AFTER HER FATHER'S DEATH, YU SAU WAS FORCED TO RETURN home to care for her mother, who had breast cancer, and her elderly grandfather. She was unwilling at first, but after spending more time with her mother, began to understand her better, which made her more sympathetic. She now knew her mum had developed her bad temper because of this family, particularly Dad, and to a lesser extent, Grandpa too. Mum was always grumbling that Grandpa had spoilt all the men in this family. This was a reasonable complaint. Mum and Grandma had mostly been in charge of helping out with the kopitiam, essentially as cheap labour. After Grandma died, Mum was left with almost all the work. Not only did she have to wipe the tables, wash the dishes and sweep the floor like a skivvy, she also did the accounts each night, handed the daily takings to Grandpa, and sometimes even had to go to the market with their cook, Sister Ngan. Grandpa did next to nothing; his only responsibility seemed to be sitting with his friends as they aired their opinions. Dad and Second Uncle were busy with something or other elsewhere, and in fact, Yu Sau hardly ever saw them in the kopitiam from when she was in primary school onwards. Dad only showed up at mealtimes, while Second Uncle's rare visits came when he wanted to borrow money from Grandpa. If Second Aunt came with him in all her finery, they'd leave after fifteen minutes at most. (He's been married twice, but Yu Sau has only ever met the first Second Aunt. The second marriage took place in England, and Yu Sau doesn't even know what this wife looked like, they separated before they'd been married two years, and got divorced soon after.)

It wasn't so bad that Dad never helped out. What really annoyed Mum was when his own business failed the year he turned forty, and he turned into a complete wastrel after that, always bloviating about this or that rather than going out and finding a real job. He'd started out in her other Grandpa's export business, but was too ambitious to work for someone else, especially not his father-in-law (whose company he thought was too small, and had no future). He resigned after two years, borrowed money from Grandpa, and set up his own firm. Later, he had an affair with a female employee. That's around the time Mum's temper started worsening, and her frequent arguments with Dad turned a little hysterical.

With Dad long-term unemployed, the low wages Mum brought home from Grandpa's kopitiam weren't enough to keep the household running. As for Eldest Brother, even though Grandpa claimed he was a star performer of the opera troupe, he wasn't contributing much either. The family was perpetually broke. Because Dad had already burnt through a pile of Grandpa's cash with his failed business, Mum's sense of pride made her refuse to ask Grandpa for more. Her father realised what was happening, and because he was very fond of his daughter, started helping the family out financially. Once Eldest Brother left home, it was Yu Sau's other grandpa who more or less supported them. That's how Yu Sau was able to finish secondary school. She promised herself that she'd be financially independent after that, and find a way to escape this embarrassing family. Soon after graduating, she found a job as a secretary at a trading firm. She got a bursary to attend university in England, but paid the bulk of her fees out of her savings. While studying, she also worked as a part-time sales assistant and a nanny. That's why her mum always said Yu Sau was the most capable person in their family, unlike all these useless men who'd been cosseted by Grandpa and ended up frittering away his money.

Second Uncle was the worst offender. According to Mum, he'd been very clever when he was young, and did well at school, so Grandpa was most fond of him and happy to spend a large sum of money to send him to an American college, where he studied Business Management. He had more than ten jobs after returning to Singapore, but didn't last more than two years in any of them. Quite a few ended within three or four months. He asked Grandpa for money to open a business, but spent all his time carousing. He'd visit dance halls every night, and hang out in the barber shop by day, leaving less than two hours to actually put in an appearance at the office. Some days he didn't even show up for work at all. Soon, all the money Grandpa had given him was gone, and he owed lots of money besides. Grandpa had to rent out both the kopitiam and the flats above it to clear these debts. Luckily, Dad had previously applied for a government flat, so the family had somewhere to stay. Mum would talk emotionally about how Grandpa had to wind up his kopitiam after so many decades there, which left his old employees in a bad situation. Sister Ngan, who had no family, ended up moving into a nunnery, and dying soon after. Uncle Kam got diabetes and died in a home. Second Uncle subsequently got into more debt after losing money on the stock market, but this time Grandpa refused to help him, no matter how much he pleaded. Grandpa didn't have much money left, in any case. In the end, Second Uncle fled Singapore to escape his debts. According to Mum, soft-hearted Grandpa slipped him more money before he went. They didn't hear from him for a long time, then two years ago he contacted Second Brother. He said he was in Shanghai now, and had tried to look up Second Brother on previous trips to Hong Kong. Later, he moved to Guangzhou, and phoned again to say his life was going well. It should have been easier for Second Brother to see him now, but they never actually managed to meet.

When Yu Sau was last in Hong Kong, she asked Second Brother about this, and he said, "Second Uncle's a strange guy. At the start of the year, he phoned and said he wanted to meet me in Guangzhou, but wouldn't tell me his address. He said to call him when I got there. So I went to Guangzhou and phoned him, but he said he was in Shenzhen, so I said, okay I'll come find you in Shenzhen. He said okay, but when I called him from Shenzhen the next day, he said he was already back in Guangzhou. I don't know what's going on with him." When Yu Sau phoned Second Brother a while ago, he said he'd gotten a call from Second Uncle recently to say he was handling a sale that could net him a million yuan. Second Brother asked where he was now, but he refused to give his address, with the excuse that he was never at home because he often had to travel to Beijing and Shanghai. Yu Sau asked what kind of business he was running, and Second Brother said he wasn't sure, only that it was something to do with property management. He thought Second Uncle wasn't very pragmatic. He wasn't young any more, but it wasn't clear if he had a partner, or if he'd married again after his two divorces.

Yu Sau doesn't know why Second Uncle is always avoiding Second Brother. She asked Second Brother if he'd lent their uncle money, and he admitted that yes, Second Uncle had borrowed some when he was in trouble, but he'd never asked for it back. Second Brother was worried, but their uncle was such a shadowy figure, it was hard to know how to help him.

Mum would probably say it's all Grandpa's fault. When she was alive, Mum was always complaining, "*I slaved away day and night for your grandfather, for hardly any pay, and meanwhile he was showering your second uncle with money. Let me tell you, with all the money he lavished on that man, we could have bought a holiday villa. Your grandpa was very thrifty. He could never bear to spend money on himself, except for going to watch Cantonese opera. He had quite a bit saved up. In the seventies, the pork seller next door was moving away, and he really wanted to take over the lease to expand the kopitiam, but there was no one to help him out. Your grandma had just died, and I was already ill. How could I have looked after two premises when I was in such poor health? In the end, he had to let it go. If your dad and second uncle had done as they were told, if your grandpa had put his money into the business rather than throwing it away on them, we wouldn't be living in a government flat now, we'd be in a bungalow. Your grandpa didn't just stop at spoiling his own sons, he did the same with his grandsons too. Every single man: your father, your second uncle, your eldest brother, even your second brother. All big-headed because of him. He's supposed to be the head of the household, but he ruined the family. Imagine selling the business after all those years, putting so many people out of work. Terrible!*"

Right up to her death, Mum complained about Grandpa almost every day. Maybe this actually was Grandpa's fault, but so what? Yu Sau looks at him now, on the living room sofa. He's scrawny as a bundle of twigs, his face is waxy yellow, and his head droops forward as his withered hand effortfully comes up to scratch his face, before dropping back onto his thigh like a felled branch. Grandpa is old, and might not be much longer for this world. What's the point blaming or hating him? She remembers him grumbling that all the strength had gone out of his left arm (this was back when he still spoke to her, rather than staring into space all the time like now). He broke a couple of glasses while pouring himself a drink of water, and when he was brushing his teeth, the dentures in his other hand would drop to the floor. She thinks of what Maria said the day before. How could he have gripped her hand so tightly, in his enfeebled state? The way he is now makes her think of her father. Is this what Dad looked like, just before he died? Mum seldom mentioned her late husband when Yu Sau was taking care of her. Did she still hate him during his final illness? Yu Sau's antipathy to her dad might be due to her mother's influence. Seeing him lead an idle life after his business failed, and hearing her mother's constant complaints, she'd naturally grown to look down on him. That's why she suggested putting him in a home. Now she thinks of it, Dad was very loving towards her when she was a little girl. She started missing him while caring for Mum, remembering how he would carry her schoolbag when she was in primary school, how he held her on the carousel at the funfair. She has a faint memory of his giant face pressed against her little one. The recollection leaves her feeling guilty, because she never paid him much attention after growing up. For all she knows, the reason he never took a job after his business shut down, might have been that no one would hire him. Has she ever tried understanding his situation? She saw what was on the surface, but what about the pain inside? Yu Sau delves back in time, collecting the fragmentary memories of the time she spent with her dad as a kid. The more she gathers, the deeper her guilt. When she gave up her freedom to come take care of her mother and grandfather, perhaps she was in part trying to pay off her debt to her father. Taking care of a sick person is a draining business. Only after doing this for her mother did she understand Mum's frustration at having to care for Dad. Mum might have taken her suggestion to put Dad in a home, but when she got cancer herself, she kept blaming herself and saying this was retribution. Yu Sau comforted her again and again, saying illness was illness, and had nothing to do with divine justice. Besides, she'd been unwell herself, and taking care of a stroke patient couldn't have been easy. She'd done her best. Yet her mother couldn't put down this burden, but kept fretting over what she'd done to Dad. There's nothing immoral about sending someone to a facility when you can't take care of them yourself, Yu Sau frequently reminded her. Now, though, the question of whether to put Grandpa in a home torments her day and night. She has to work, and Maria's given her notice, so there may be no other choice. And yet, she's finding it extremely difficult to come to a decision.

3. GRANDPA WANTS TO COME HOME

KAH ONN ACCOMPANIES YU SAU AS SHE VISITS ONE OLD folks' home after another, until she finally finds a place she's satisfied with. Even so, she can't help feeling guilty, as if she's doing something she shouldn't.

A week before Maria's departure, Yu Sau sends Grandpa to the home. She tells him he's not well, and needs to spend some time in hospital. He can come back when he's better. As usual, Grandpa remains silent, his face wooden. She has no way of telling what he's thinking or feeling, whether he's willing to go or not, whether he's sad or angry. Perhaps it's better this way. She tells herself she hasn't lied. Every word was true, apart from substituting "hospital" for "retirement home". She tells herself she'll bring Grandpa back to the flat as soon as she finds a dependable helper. That never happens, though. Is she too busy at work, or just not trying hard enough? She isn't sure. Maria leaves, and her replacement never materialises.

Grandpa starts speaking again at the home, though not very often. Whenever Yu Sau goes to see him, he'll ask when he can come home. He complains that the beds are full of bedbugs, and he's itching all over. Yu Sau examines his arms and calves. She can see the scabs where he scratched too hard, but no sign of any insect bites. (The nurse says Grandpa has hives, that's why his skin is itching.) Next, Grandpa complains that the home is full of ghosts, flitting around his bed and preventing him from sleeping. (The manager says Grandpa often mutters to himself at night, and even if they give him sleeping pills, he goes on talking in his sleep. His roommates complain that he's noisy, though unlike Maria, no one has yet reported him producing animal-like howls or clutching their arms with superhuman strength.) At least Grandpa seems livelier here, and no longer sits staring into space. When Yu Sau and Kah Onn come to visit, he'll even talk to them, albeit only to ask if he can come home, because Kit is waiting for him. Who is Kit? Yu Sau has no idea, and assumes it's more of his nonsense. It starts getting to her that Grandpa keeps asking to return, and at every visit, she tells him soothingly that he can come back soon, as soon as he's better.

Yu Sau sincerely does want to bring him back home, yet after Maria leaves, she's somehow unable to find another domestic helper.

*

ANOTHER MONTH PASSES. ON ONE VISIT, GRANDPA FINALLY stops asking Yu Sau to come home, but only because he's stopped speaking altogether. His silence has resumed. Yu Sau doesn't mention bringing him home (no need to bring that up when he hasn't asked the question), but otherwise asks the usual things: what has he been eating? Is the food good? Has he been sleeping well? Does he still itch at night? After that, there's only small talk left. When Kah Onn goes with her, he adds a word or two, or reaches out to touch Grandpa's hand, but he too is reduced to the same questions: how's the food, how are you sleeping, how's your itching? They can still see scabs on his skinny face and arms from where he's been scratching, but he won't talk about it, just gazes vaguely at them, mouth firmly shut, staring at something non-existent in the distance. He looks like a philosopher, lost in thought. An elderly, frail philosopher.

Grandpa spends Christmas and Chinese New Year at the home.

Yu Sau has never thought of Chinese New Year as having any particular significance. Even the month before, when tangerines and new year snacks start appearing in the supermarkets, and the usual cheesy songs start blaring over the speakers, she still thinks of it as just another public holiday: two days off work, that's all. It doesn't seem any more of a special occasion than Christmas.

This year's a little different, because she has Kah Onn now. She visits Kah Onn's family, and his mother even gives Yu Sau a red packet, which helps her get into the new year spirit. She's also sadder than usual, thinking of Grandpa at the home. On the first day, she and Kah Onn pay him a visit. As usual, he's sitting up slumped in bed, silent as a statue. Yu Sau sits on the edge of the bed and holds his emaciated hand, remembering how, as a little girl, she'd dress up in her new clothes, kowtowing to wish him a happy new year: *We wish Grandpa good health, may all his wishes come true!* She and her brothers would kneel before him, chanting in unison. Grandpa would nod and smile happily, call them good children, and give them each a red packet. The day before, the kopitiam assistants would have spring-cleaned the place and closed up by afternoon, off home for their own new year celebrations, and the shop stayed shut till the fourth day of the new year. On the day itself, she and her brothers would pay respects to their elders first thing in the morning, then after breakfast, they'd go down to the kopitiam with Grandpa. From the other side of the closed doors, they'd hear the constant bang-bang of firecrackers, and children shouting gleefully. Her brothers would join in the fun with the next-door kids, while she'd sit in the airwell by herself, playing with mini-bangers. Everyone in the neighbourhood would come visiting, so she and her brothers collected quite a few red packets. The big round table in the kopitiam would be laden with soft drinks and sweets. Best of all, she was allowed to drink as many soft drinks as she liked. Her favourites were Green Spot, Sinalco and Coca-Cola. These days, she doesn't see the first two around any more, and Coca-Cola comes in cans, not bottles. On the fifteenth day, Uncle Kam would go up to the second floor and hang a long string of firecrackers from the window, which would bang away merrily. The whole street was filled with these deafening sounds, and shreds of red paper were everywhere, like fallen flowers.

We wish Grandpa good health, may all his wishes come true! Yu Sau and Kah Onn loudly call out, standing by his bed. His eyes are dull, and because he doesn't have his false teeth in, his lips have folded in over his gums. "*Grandpa, I brought you some eight treasures porridge. It's delicious!*" She ladles some out into a bowl, and holds a spoonful up to his mouth, which remains shut. His face doesn't change: eyes wide open, crooked lips somewhere between a frown and a sneer. Yu Sau puts down the porridge and stares at her stubborn grandpa in helpless rage. After a while, she pours it back into the Thermos, packs her things away, and walks out of the hospital. Her new year is not particularly happy.

On the fourth day, the manager of the retirement home calls Yu Sau to say Grandpa hasn't eaten anything for a few days now. She rushes over, sits on the edge of the bed, and coaxes him to have some food. Like before, he refuses to open his mouth, just stares at her in silence. Yu Sau holds up a plate and brings a spoonful to his lips. All of a sudden, his hand shoots out and grabs hold of her arm. His eyes flash ferociously, and he's babbling away in a language she doesn't understand. She cries out, and struggles to pull herself free from his hand, which is gripping her like an eagle's claws. Food spills all over the bed.

YOU'RE DEAD

You hear the faint sound of rain, and almost feel the light drizzle, so very soft. Each drop all but evaporates the instant it touches your skin. A slight dampness, but the water has no weight at all. It's dark but not pitch black. A mist of fine rain hangs before you. Through it you can make out a dirt road and groves of trees like phantoms. You are walking through a gloomy forest. This is a desolate place, so quiet you feel yourself losing your bearings. You think there's someone walking in the distance. You don't know where you are. Nothing about this is familiar.

You call out to the person in front of you.

No answer.

The figure wavers, but no one seems to hear your cries.

You've experienced something like this before, maybe in a dream. Yes, a dream you had repeatedly, that's why you remember it. You were immersed in the dark sea, and before that in your big sister's house. How did you end up underwater? (Big sister? Do you even have a big sister? But you did in the dream, which you'd had several times. You remember that clearly.) And in this dream, you don't drown but float to the surface. The sky is dark. You're exhausted, but not in any pain. Now you remember: before you fell into the sea, Japanese soldiers were shooting at you from behind. All around you are corpses, floating face down. Their clothes are soaked in blood. Lucky you, the bullets missed. You kick and discover that the water's actually not deep, and you can easily touch the bottom. You look back to the shore, which lies silent. The soldiers are gone. You push aside the dead bodies and wade up onto the beach. Then you arrived at a forest, like the one you're in now. How did the dream end? Why are you re-living it? It keeps drizzling, a constant pitter-patter of raindrops landing lightly on you.

Now you're in an old wooden hut. It's full of people, but doesn't feel cramped or noisy. All you can hear is a murmuring in your ear, quiet as the wind gusting through gravel. This feels familiar too. Is it also part of the same dream? Or another one? Are you, in fact, dreaming? Have you been here before?

You can't remember.

You've forgotten how far you walked, where you came from, how you suddenly ended up here.

You recognise Tat Yan in the crowd. You haven't seen him for a long time, but he looks exactly the same.

"*So you've arrived,*" he says dully.

"*Where have you been, all this time? You disappeared after the inspection,*" you say.

"*Where?*" His face is blank. "*I don't know. Inspection? What inspection?*"

"*Don't you remember? That morning we both went to the inspection point, but you never came back. Your sister and I were worried sick.*"

"*I think I saw my sis,*" he says, still not showing any emotion.

"*When did you see her? Was it recently?*"

"*I don't remember. I think not long ago. I walked into a hut and saw her. Maybe this one. Do you remember where you were?*"

"*In hospital. They say I'm ill, but I don't feel sick. I think they want to get rid of me, so they've left me there. Why am I there? When will I be discharged?*"

You're muttering to yourself in confusion now. You have no idea why you're suddenly here. How did you arrive? Why here? All you're certain of is that they didn't want you. Who are "they"? Your mind is all jumbled up.

"*You do know that you're dead?*" Tat Yan says.

"*Dead? I'm dead?*" Somehow, you don't feel shocked at the news.

"*You're dead, that's why you're here. I'm dead too, so you can see me. And my sister?*"

"*Dead a long time.*"

"*Maybe I saw her here. I can't really remember.*"

"*Am I really dead?*"

"*Yes.*"

"*Will I meet Ah Yoke?*"

"*You'll see her, but I don't know when. Maybe soon. Maybe you'll have to wait.*"

"*And Kit? Have you seen him?*"

"*Who is Kit?*"

"*My little brother Kit. I just saw him, he said we'd meet today. Maybe he meant here?*"

PART TWO

YU SAU

ELDEST BROTHER IN COSTUME

AFTER GRANDPA'S DEATH, YU SAU FINDS HIS AND GRANDMA'S wedding picture amongst his possessions. They look younger than she's ever seen them. She hasn't seen many photos of Grandpa, let alone Grandma. Going through her mum's belongings after she passed, she found a family photo: her parents, young; Eldest Brother and Second Brother as teenagers, her as a child; Grandpa and Grandma in their fifties, looking nothing like the young couple in the wedding picture, Grandpa especially. In the bridal shot, Grandma's face is a little stiff, no hint of a smile, as if she's reluctant to be in the picture. Her pale cheongsam is a little plain, but she looks elegant and refined. Grandpa is debonair in his suit. Yu Sau had no idea Grandpa was such a handsome devil. It's strange, her father and uncle both resemble him, but neither is as good-looking as the man in the picture. It's her eldest brother Kim Chau who has Grandpa's charisma, combined with Mum's delicate features (even when her face grew thin from the cancer, you could see the graceful woman she'd been). Yu Sau is moved to see Grandpa as a dashing young chap, a completely different person from the elderly white-haired man with skin like a plucked chicken. Which is the real him?

Grandma died when Yu Sau was still a little girl, so she only has blurry memories of a woman who didn't speak very much and often looked gloomy because of her illness (asthma, possibly?) but she was kind, and generally gave way to Grandpa rather than arguing with him. Now, Yu Sau looks at the photo and thinks she sees stubbornness in her face, not the meek woman she remembers. Was Grandma's quietness actually a silent protest? As for Grandpa, even though Mum repeatedly said he spoilt his sons and grandsons, she remembers him frowning all the time, not the easy-going, pleasant man in the photo. This attractive version of Grandpa does not exist in her mind. The people in the picture feel like strangers, but they are indeed her grandparents.

While going through Grandpa's Cantonese opera scores, Yu Sau finds a half-photograph of Grandma as a young woman. Unlike in her wedding photo, she is smiling, sitting very straight in a chair, in a light-coloured patterned blouse and trousers. There's a hint of sadness in her exquisite brow. The picture was stuck between the pages like a bookmark, and has clearly been torn in half. What was on the other half? Was it a person, and if so, who? If it was Grandpa, why was he removed? Who did this? Yu Sau is puzzled for a few seconds, before her next discovery distracts her: a photo of Eldest Brother in costume, raffishly handsome. She can't stop staring at him. He must have had quite a few fans, she thinks to herself. Grandpa used to say how famous Kim Chau was, and it looks like this wasn't just empty bragging. Even if Eldest Brother is still alive, she thinks sadly, he'd be old by now. What does he look like? How would a former star on stage deal with ageing?

But no, she realises, he's only twelve years older than her. That would put him in his forties, not old at all. He probably is still alive, and still good-looking. Everyone keeps saying how much she looks like him. Does she really? She holds up the picture next to a mirror, and thinks she can see a resemblance in the upper halves of their faces. If she ever played a male role, perhaps they'd look alike. She stares at her reflection, and sees the confusion in her eyes. When she's old, will she look completely different, like Grandpa? Of course she will. When that happens, will that woman with the silver hair and liver-spotted face really be her? The same person once loved by Kah Onn and her British ex? If she fears her appearance changing and can't accept looking older, how will anyone else? The thought saddens her. Now she understands why beautiful movie stars choose to kill themselves at the height of their radiance: that's how they want to be remembered, leaving no other version of themselves. She draws closer to the mirror, and stares raptly at her features.

She once dreamt she was striding boldly across the stage in an opera costume as the audience cried out, "*Bravo, Kim Chau!*" She looks back and forth between her face and Eldest Brother's, and the resemblance seems stronger each time. She feels an abrupt desire (perhaps this is her being shallow) to give a performance someday, in a resplendent robe like Eldest Brother, even though she's never had any interest in Cantonese opera. When she heard Eldest Brother singing as a little girl, it was fine but she didn't particularly enjoy it. Then her father decided she should attend an English school, and she found herself surrounded by English books, songs and films. Fortunately, her family was Mandarin- and Cantonese-speaking, so she retained some of the language, but rarely encountered Chinese literature, music or films. As for Cantonese opera, she only has a vague recollection of hearing Yam Kim Fai, Bak Sheut Sin and Fong Yim Fen on Rediffusion. Although she can still hum the tunes, only a couple of titles have remained in her mind: *Love Put the Couple in Their Graves* and *Fragrant Dew on a Red Blossom*. She can't name a single one of Eldest Brother's arias, though.

Seeing these pictures of Grandpa and Eldest Brother as young men has put Yu Sau in a bit of a panic, and she starts to worry about losing her looks. But actually, there's something even more precious that's been slipping away from her, and though she never noticed or cared before, now she feels the pity of it: her Cantonese. She was fluent as a child, or at least better than now, able to hold a conversation. After Grandma's death, her parents only spoke Mandarin to her, while she and her friends talked in English. Grandpa was the only person she still used Cantonese with, but as far back as she can remember, he never said much to her. All in all, since Grandma's passing, she's hardly had any opportunities to use her Cantonese. After secondary school, she mostly spoke English during her year at the trading firm, and of course used nothing else while at university in Britain. Back in Singapore, she spoke in English to her flatmates Geok Leng and Sandy, or sometimes in Mandarin to Geok Leng, but never Cantonese. When local television and radio stopped broadcasting Chinese dialects in the mid-eighties, she no longer heard any Cantonese. As a child, there'd at least been Hong Kong movies and serials, but these were now dubbed in Mandarin. There were occasional dialect news broadcasts on the radio, but she only watched the TV news. Yu Sau finds this ridiculous: local arthouse cinemas and TV channels are always showing French, German, Spanish and Italian films, but she's never seen one in a Chinese dialect (she has heard of rare screenings, but never been able to catch one). She's considered bilingual but her mother tongue, Cantonese, has withered away. Only when she moved back home to look after her mother and grandpa did this dormant language awaken after almost two decades' hibernation. She still has no confidence in her abilities, though, and can only speak hesitantly, always afraid she isn't expressing herself correctly.

Grandpa left behind a number of Cantonese scores. She flips through them now, but doesn't recognise many of the densely-printed Chinese characters. They do remind her of the tunes she heard on Rediffusion and from Grandpa's lips. She feels a stirring of interest for Cantonese opera, and makes a special trip to People's Park Complex for some CDs, but can only remember a few singers' names: Hung Sin Nui, Fong Yim Fen, Ng Kwun Lai, Yam Kim Fai, Bak Sheut Sin. Where should she start? The proprietor suggests Yam and Bak's four famous shows: *Princess Cheung Ping, Reincarnation of Red Plum, The Purple Hairpin,* and *Nightmare at Peony Pavilion.* She brings them home and plays them in her spare time. To start with, she's just trying to revisit the childhood feeling of listening to Rediffusion with her family, but grows to enjoy them for their own sake. She often brings out the picture of Eldest Brother in costume, and imagines herself on stage singing like him or Yam Kim Fai. She dreams again of the stage, but this time she isn't strutting her stuff as the audience cheers. Instead, she's made up and in costume, waiting anxiously in her wings to make her entrance, but wakes up before her cue.

YU SAU AND KAH ONN, PART ONE

1. HIS JEALOUSY

Yu Sau often got annoyed when she first started dating Kah Onn. Because he'd had his heart broken before, he was constantly imagining she'd fallen in love with another man. After almost two years together, she thinks he ought to have more faith in her, but he's still darting at shadows. Whenever she says anything complimentary about another guy, he gets all worked up and picks a fight with her. Eventually, he apologises, and she forgives him as usual. Kah Onn's groundless jealousy is frustrating, but she always convinces herself to overlook his nonsense on the grounds that it proves how much he loves her.

Apart from his insecurity and self-centredness, Kah Onn isn't a bad boyfriend. He's helped her deal with the aftermath of Grandpa's death; if not for him, Geok Leng and Sandy, Yu Sau doesn't know how she would have coped. After several arguments, Yu Sau learns how to live with Kah Onn. Unless it's necessary for work, she avoids dining alone with other men, and is careful not to praise them in front of him. For the most part, they now get on well, and even when they quarrel, Kah Onn is so quick to apologise that it always blows over.

When Yu Sau and Kah Onn start talking about marriage, Geok Leng reminds her to talk his jealousy issues through with him first.

"Otherwise, once you're his wife, he'll keep an even tighter hold on you," she says, sounding like a big sister.

Sandy jokes, "What if she does that and he still gets jealous all the time? Should she divorce him right away?"

"That's why you should only marry him if you're sure,"

snaps Geok Leng, glaring at Sandy.

Geok Leng often speaks to the other women in her department as if they're her little sisters. Some, like Sandy, find this annoying, even as they admire her strength and ability to cope with the unexpected. Geok Leng is a complicated woman who fought hard to get where she is today. She lost her father at ten and her mother at fifteen, but through sheer determination managed to raise her three little brothers and sisters. Two of them even got university degrees, while Geok Leng herself held a job all through secondary school, and got a management diploma. Yu Sau has a lot of respect for her, and doesn't mind being occasionally lectured. Sandy is the youngest of the three flatmates, and has an open, carefree personality. She is sometimes a little ditzy, which can make her hard to talk to. Right now, though, her joke does make sense. Yu Sau herself thinks Kah Onn's jealousy is no big deal. Surely once they're married and their togetherness is officially confirmed, he'll stop being so suspicious.

2. YOUR MUM ASKED WHEN WE'RE GETTING MARRIED

A NEW SHOPPING CENTRE IS HIRING A FINANCE MANAGER, and Yu Sau encourages Kah Onn to apply, as he's had a similar job before. She thinks he might have better prospects there (plus another reason she doesn't tell him: he sticks to her too closely at work, and keeps coming over to her department when he has nothing better to do; she'd like this to stop). He does as she suggests, and gets hired.

Now that Kah Onn's working somewhere else, he doesn't see Yu Sau as often, but still phones several times a day to ask what she's up to. Who did she have lunch with? What did she eat? Yu Sau calls him too, to show that she cares. Sandy jokes that they're joined at the hip. Kah Onn calls far too often at first, which is annoying, but he tapers off as he gets used to the new job.

It's definitely good that Kah Onn is working somewhere else. Now that they don't spend as much time together, they argue much less frequently.

"A couple that see too much of each other will end up quarrelling," she explains to Kah Onn. "We'll be more affectionate now we meet less often."

"Does that mean we'll be arguing from morning till night when we're married and living together?"

Kah Onn might have been teasing, but Yu Sau actually is a little anxious about this. She wishes Kah Onn would grow up. Even so, he doesn't seem that enthusiastic about getting married.

"Your mum asked when we're getting married, and I told her I was putting pressure on you," she grumbles to Kah Onn. "You refuse to use a condom, and I'm always worried I counted wrongly. Do you want me to end up as a pregnant bride?"

"Your big belly would look good in a wedding dress," Kah Onn chuckles.

"That's not funny." She frowns at him.

Kah Onn's excuse is that he hasn't settled into his new job yet, so he isn't ready to get married and have kids right now. His salary is higher than before, but his boss is difficult to deal with and there's a lot of pressure. Yu Sau thinks he's being selfish, and not considering her needs.

"Of course a higher salary comes with more pressure. No such thing as a well-paid, relaxing job. I'm not getting any younger. If we wait too long, it will be bad for me and the baby," she says.

Frustrating as this is, she understands the pressure that he's under. When he first started working there, he'd seem distracted when he was with her, always running off to speak on his mobile phone. Another annoying thing: he used to be very good about showing up to dates, but now he often calls to take a rain check because something urgent has come up at work.

Today, for instance, he was supposed to meet her at the Mandarin Orchard for dinner, and then a movie at Lido. He calls late in the afternoon to say there are some things he needs to take care of, and they might have to make it lunch tomorrow instead. This isn't the first or second time he's done this, and she yells at him, "You need to quit. Find a new job, or I'll find a new boyfriend."

She soon regrets having been so harsh, though she's still angry. In the end, she and Geok Leng decide to have dinner at Shangri-La instead.

3. ISN'T THAT KAH ONN'S CAR?

GEOK LENG PARKS, BUT BEFORE THEY CAN GET OUT, SHE points. "Look! Isn't that Kah Onn's car?"

Yu Sau thinks she can make out someone else in there, maybe a woman. "Let's stay in the car. I want to see who he's with," she says. She stares agitatedly at Kah Onn's car, as if she's a police officer on a stake-out. Soon, a long-haired woman in her twenties gets out of the passenger seat. Yu Sau's face gets hot, and her heart beats faster. A moment later, the driver's side door opens. Kah Onn steps out, shuts the door, and walks over smiling to take the woman's hand. She leans her whole body into his, and he lets go of her hand to stroke her bare shoulder. Yu Sau's heart thumps furiously, and her face is greenish. Her breath speeds up so much she thinks she might suffocate. Her face clenches, and she can't stop her jaw from twitching. It takes a great deal of effort to force out the words, "Let's go."

Geok Leng drives out of the car park.

Yu Sau's eyes are wide with rage as she scrabbles for her mobile. She calls Kah Onn, but his phone is off. She clutches her phone, furiously gnawing on her lower lip.

"Let's go get some dinner," says Geok Leng.

Yu Sau hugs herself, not speaking. Her chest is rising and falling rapidly.

Geok Leng drives them to a restaurant in another building.

Yu Sau drifts after her like an empty husk and sits down. Her mind are muddled, and her body is numb. She only takes a couple of bites of her salad. She keeps putting down her cutlery and picking up her phone, just to glare at it. Finally, she flings it on the table. Geok Leng knows she's having a hard time, and doesn't say anything, just sits there as Yu Sau drinks a glass of red wine, then drives her home.

They reach the car park outside Yu Sau's place. Geok Leng gets out with her and looks at her pale face with concern.

"I'm fine, don't worry. You should go home," says Yu Sau.

Geok Leng hugs her, pats her on the back, and tells her to take care of herself. Then she gets back into the car.

As she watches Geok Leng drive away, Yu Sau begins to weep. She finishes crying, dries her tears with a Kleenex, and takes a deep breath. Only then does she press the button for the lift. On the way up, her thoughts are still disordered. When did this start? How could he do this to me? Back in her flat, she can't stop her mind whirling with resentment. She tries calling a few times, but Kah Onn's phone remains off. She didn't get a good look at the other woman's face, but the image of Kah Onn holding her intimately is burnt into Yu Sau's mind. Liar! Cheat! Bastard! She does nothing all evening but pace around the flat and call his phone, lost in rage and anxiety.

After midnight, she collapses into bed, still fully dressed.

Her phone rings. Kah Onn tells her he's just leaving the office now, and didn't answer her calls earlier because he'd turned his phone off for a meeting, and forgot to turn it back on again. These lies just make her angrier, and she starts shouting. At first he stutters and tries to talk his way out of it, claiming she was just a female colleague he'd taken out to dinner to thank her for staying back late and helping him with his work. They went back to the office afterwards, he insists.

Yu Sau tells him what she saw in the car park, and he has nothing to say. He listens as she screams at him, then sadly admits that yes, that woman is the ex-girlfriend he's told her about. She happened to be working at his new company, but he didn't know until he started there. She's just gotten divorced, and her father has cancer, so she's in a low mood and needs company. He's just giving her moral support, and nothing else.

"Really, I'm not lying," he says. "We didn't do anything."

"Stop giving me these crappy stories, you bastard! This isn't a soap opera!" she roars.

"You have to believe me!"

"How can I believe you? Liar!"

"Yes, I still like her a bit. We were together so many years, of course I still have some feelings for her," he says. "But we didn't do anything, because I love you even more."

"Did you say that to her too?" Yu Sau says frostily.

"What do I have to do to make you believe me?"

"Quit your job."

"All right, I'll give my notice tomorrow."

"No use. She's your ex, you'll still be connected to her."

"Then what should I do?"

Yu Sau can hear him sobbing.

He shouldn't have got back in touch with that woman, he shouldn't have taken this job in the first place. Yu Sau is still furious, but doesn't say what she's thinking. Instead, she snarls, "We're not going to the Mandarin tomorrow. I never want to see you again. You bastard! Pig!"

Before she hangs up, she hears Kah Onn plaintively asking,

"What do you want me to do?"

Her phone keeps ringing. She doesn't take her eyes off it, as if it's a small animal that might lunge at her face at any moment. When it finally stops, she continues staring, until her vision grows blurry. The flat is remarkably still, so quiet she can hear her tears falling.

YU SAU

YOU DID THE RIGHT THING.
BETTER TO GET IT OVER WITH

KAH ONN CALLS MANY MORE TIMES, BUT YU SAU DOESN'T answer. He knocks on her door, but she won't let him in. (He has keys, but she changed the locks after deciding to break up with him.) He stands outside her office waiting for her, but she refuses to see him. Eventually, the calls stop, and so do the visits.

After some time, she starts to miss him.

Yu Sau has never imagined her anger could grow so strong, or that she could be this determined. Has she made a mistake? Maybe there really isn't anything going on between him and that woman. She ought to give him a chance. Maybe he really has left that woman. Why did she have to push things over the brink? She's not going to seek Kah Onn out, but she starts to wonder whether she should let him in if he ever tries contacting her again. Yes, then she'd forgive him. She starts waiting for Kah Onn to call or knock on her door, but he never does. He won't be back. Now she's miserable, and often sits staring into space, lost in bitter memories (Kah Onn standing on an aluminium ladder changing a light bulb for her; Kah Onn getting sprayed in the face while trying to fix her plumbing; Kah Onn carefully helping Grandpa out of the back seat of his car into a wheelchair; Kah Onn accompanying her to the funeral home, helping her greet her friends and colleagues as they arrived) as well as fantasies of the life they could have shared (Kah Onn taking over the housework when she gets pregnant; Kah Onn changing diapers and bathing their child; Kah Onn and her driving to school to pick up their child).

These images float into her mind when she's at her loneliest, leaving her sobbing, hurt, unable to sleep, with knots in her stomach.

It feels like the foundation of her life has been snatched away. She's unable to focus in the office, and at home can only stare at the walls or ceiling like a dead fish, lacking the energy to do anything else. And Kah Onn? Is he suffering as much as her?

"No way!" says Geok Leng forcefully. "He's enjoying life with that woman right now."

"I believe he still loves me," Yu Sau sighs.

"But he loves that woman more. You did the right thing. Better to get it over with. That woman's his ex. If you weaken and take him back, you'll just suffer again." Geok Leng's tone is cut-and-dried.

Yu Sau is usually a decisive person, but she seems to have lost all sense of will when it comes to this business of Kah Onn. She feels lost and confused all the time. "You should take driving lessons," says Geok Leng in her big sister voice. "Even I have a car. You have an overseas degree and a high position in the company, so you should have one too. If you'd learnt to drive in the first place, you wouldn't have needed to get lifts from Kah Onn, and that bastard would never have tricked you into a relationship."

It's not fair to say Kah Onn tricked her. He really did help Yu Sau take care of Grandpa. Yu Sau thinks Geok Leng is being hard on him.

"It's probably too late to start learning, at my age," she says.

"What age? I'm a year older than you, and Sandy's clumsy as hell. We both got our licences, there's no reason you couldn't get yours too."

Yu Sau takes her suggestion and signs up for some lessons. She works hard, and sure enough, by the time she passes her driving test, her emotional state has more or less recovered its equilibrium.

YU SAU AND KAH ONN, PART TWO

1. PLEASE GIVE ME ANOTHER CHANCE!

After work, Yu Sau heads to the car park in her building.

Kah Onn is waiting for her. He's lost a lot of weight, and his shirt hangs off him. He looks stricken. Rushing over, he sobs that he loves her, he can't live without her. Yu Sau pulls back in disgust because he stinks of cigarette smoke, and keeps walking to her car. He runs after her, grabs her hand, and wheedles, "I quit my job, I won't go near her again. Please give me another chance!"

She tries to shake him off, screaming, "Let go of me!"

But he won't remove his hand.

"You're hurting me," she cries. Although she still looks angry, her voice is a little quieter.

To be honest, Yu Sau's heart softened as soon as she set eyes on him. This is why, when his grip slackens, she doesn't withdraw her hand right away, but allows herself to be led to his car.

"I'll give you a lift home," he says.

"I have my car here." She turns to look at it.

"Don't worry, I'll drive you to work tomorrow morning." He opens the door.

In the car, Kah Onn tells her how much he loves her, how he missed her, how he suffered without her. His voice is choked with passion. Yu Sau keeps her arms folded across her chest, and doesn't say a word. The car reeks of smoke. On the radio, a man and woman giggle as they discuss something or other. She imagines they are making fun of Kah Onn.

She stares at the traffic through the windscreen, her mind

blank. When they reach her block, she opens the door and hurries towards the lift. Kah Onn catches up and tries to take her hand, but she pulls away.

He takes her hand again while they wait for the lift. A Malay woman comes to stand next to them and says hi. Not wanting to quarrel in front of her neighbour, Yu Sau leaves her hand in his, but makes sure there's a gap between their bodies. The woman's floor is first, and as soon as she's out of the lift, Kah Onn tries to hug Yu Sau, but she pushes him away hard and glares at him, still in silence. He continues holding her hand, and she lets him, until they get to her front door.

"Let go of me!" Keeping her face expressionless and her voice calm, she says, "You can go now."

He meets her gaze and states firmly, "I'm coming in with you."

The stalemate continues for a while, until Yu Sau reaches into her handbag for her keys.

They walk into the flat almost side by side. Kah Onn shuts the door behind them, then pulls her into his embrace. She struggles free and slaps him. He holds a hand to his stinging cheek and stares at her in anguish. She bursts into tears.

He comes over and holds her tight. "Forgive me, forgive me," he murmurs, nibbling on her earlobe, kissing her hard, investigating her body. She tries to fend him off to start with, but her resistance gradually melts away. Pressing her body close to his, she can't stop crying.

2. AS IF NOTHING AT ALL HAD HAPPENED

AFTER YU SAU AND KAH ONN GET BACK TOGETHER, HE ALL but moves in with her, only going back to his place once or twice a week. He drives her to work each day, sometimes in his car, sometimes in hers. With her colleagues, who are also his former colleagues, particularly Geok Leng and Sandy, he laughs and chats as before, as if nothing at all had happened. After work, he picks her up and takes her out for dinner, or to the supermarket. At the weekend, they go to the market for groceries, and in the evening they snuggle on the sofa watching TV like a married couple. Kah Onn really did hand in his notice and leave that woman, but hasn't found a new job. In fact, he's been unemployed for a whole year. According to him, he was so depressed when Yu Sau left him that he couldn't make himself look for work. He starts actively searching now, though, and within a couple of months, he has a new position at a finance company.

Yu Sau and Kah Onn start talking about marriage again.

"I'm not getting any younger, and I want a baby. The older you get, the more dangerous it is to get pregnant, and there might be something wrong with the baby," she says, unloading her anxieties onto him.

He tells her again and again that he's still finding his feet in this new job.

It's true that he hasn't been there long, and hasn't been confirmed yet.

"But I have a stable job!" she says.

"I don't want to live off my wife," he says.

3. KAH ONN'S HEART ISN'T IN IT

WHETHER BECAUSE YU SAU KEEPS HARPING ON MARRIAGE OR because of work stress, when it comes to sex these days, Kah Onn's heart isn't in it. He either can't get it up, or he climaxes too soon. This upsets him so much, he starts avoiding intimacy altogether. When they first got back together, he was extremely keen, and because they were living together, it happened almost every night. Since then, the frequency has decreased, and he's spending fewer nights at her place. He tells her his mother is elderly and not very well, so he can't just abandon her. A month goes by in which he hardly spends any nights at her place, just meets her for dinner after work, then brings her home. Even then, he doesn't stay long, but leaves after watching a bit of TV.

"When did you become such a good son?"

Yu Sau suspects he's just using his mother as an excuse, and can't help feeling frustrated. When she loses her temper, Kah Onn has no choice but to keep her company, but he seems distracted, and they never go beyond a bit of kissing and groping; he isn't able to take the next step. She knows he's upset and consoles him patiently, telling him it doesn't matter, it's just a psychological issue, and if he can just relax, everything will be back to normal in no time. She tells him that women care most about affection, and sex isn't as important to them. Besides, he's perfectly healthy, and if he just stops being so tense, his body will sort itself out. She has faith in him. Even so, she would like to know what the problem is, and almost urges him to see a psychiatrist, but worries that would hurt his pride. The words keep coming to her lips, but she's never able to say them out loud.

4. WE'LL REGISTER OUR MARRIAGE AFTER DEEPAVALI

Yu Sau tells Kah Onn that if this job is too tough on him, he should find another one, rather than continue to wreck his body and mind. All he says is: let's see. There are times when she can't help suspecting that he's lost interest in her because of another woman. She doesn't want to believe this, but whenever he leaves her flat, she feels the impulse to call him at home to check if he really is keeping his mum company. In fact, she did this once, phoning him two hours after they said goodbye. The phone rang quite a few times before he answered, saying he'd been asleep, what did she want? His voice was bleary, like he'd just woken up. Yu Sau hadn't come up with a pretext, and was so flustered she blurted out something that sounded like nonsense even to herself. She wished she'd never made that call. Kah Onn must surely have realised she was checking up on him, but he didn't mention it at all the next day.

She hasn't done anything like that since.

Yu Sau still doesn't know what the problem is, but she believes it's not another woman. He is always saying he loves her, and treats her well, with much more patience and tenderness than before. Kah Onn always had a hot temper, and whenever she got angry with him, he'd shout back at her with just as much heat and volume. Now, he just takes it mutely, and lets her have her way in everything. He may not stay over many nights, but whenever he has a day off, he almost always spends it with her.

Is he worried about his mother? She's a little deaf and her memory is going, but otherwise she's in good health. When Yu Sau's seen her, she's never complained about any discomfort.

She certainly can't marry a man who isn't interested in sex, especially if she wants to have a baby. She suggests that Kah Onn go see a doctor, and if nothing's wrong with him, they'll register their marriage right away. The ceremony can wait. Kah Onn keeps finding excuses to put this off. Naturally this is his male pride at work. She ignores that and forces him to make an appointment.

"Things will be busy at work for the next couple of weeks. Let's do it after Deepavali."

"Fine, we'll go see a doctor after Deepavali," she says firmly. "Afterwards we'll go to the ROM, and then we'll be a real couple and can live together properly."

"We live together now, and no one says anything, not these

days. You're too conservative."

"You hurry home every night. No one would think we were living together."

Kah Onn has nothing to say to that.

"I am conservative, anyway. As long as we register, even if I get pregnant after that, it's fine," says Yu Sau.

"It's fine anyway. No one cares, these day," he grumbles. "Why are you in such a rush to get pregnant? You'll lose your freedom once you have a kid."

"I want a child," she says.

5. NOW SHE UNDERSTANDS

THE NIGHT BEFORE HARI RAYA PUASA, A PUBLIC HOLIDAY, Yu Sau and Kah Onn watch TV after dinner. When Yu Sau reaches down to stroke his crotch, he actually responds for once: he pulls her into his arms and kisses her passionately, running his hands over her body.

Then they are naked in bed. "I knew you'd get over this! It was just a psychological block," says Yu Sau jubilantly.

"I don't need to see a doctor." Kah Onn is perspiring, lying on top of her and breathing hard.

The bedroom smells of semen. Yu Sau breathes it in deeply, rolls over, and kisses Kah Onn on his sweat-slick cheek.

"I'll go turn off the TV. When you're less busy at work, we'll go register," she says.

That night, Kah Onn doesn't go home to his mum. Yu Sau sleeps in his arms till morning.

The next day, Yu Sau reminds him to phone home. He calls twice before his mum answers, and chats briefly with her before hanging up. He doesn't explain why he wasn't home the night before, nor does he mention what time he'll be home. They go to a nearby hawker centre for breakfast, then back to the flat for more hanky-panky. Kah Onn offers to wash her car. (Yu Sau didn't get another domestic helper after Grandpa died, just a part-time cleaner. On public holidays, Kah Onn comes over and helps her with this and that, like mopping the floors or cleaning her car. This touches her, and makes her think he'll be a good husband.)

He goes down to the car park with a bucket of water, while Yu Sau sits on the sofa reading the paper. She thinks idly where they should go for lunch, and how to amuse themselves after that. Just as she's flipping to the entertainment section, she hears a mobile phone buzzing, not hers. Kah Onn's phone is on the coffee table, where he must have forgotten it. She picks it up and sees a text message from someone named Suzie. After a moment's hesitation, she opens it. Suzie wants to know where he was last night and why he didn't answer her calls, and reminds him that he's coming over to her place that night. The message ends with "kisses."

So he's still with her. They never actually broke up.

Trying to solve the puzzle, she dials his landline. No one answers, then a few rings later, his mobile phone goes off. Her number is on the screen. Now she understands: he diverted his calls. That explains why he wasn't worried about her calling him at home.

Liar! Bastard! Tears come to Yu Sau's eyes.

She is dizzy and unable to breathe from sadness and anger. Rather than rushing downstairs to confront Kah Onn, she clutches his phone tight, pacing the living room furiously, muttering to herself: bastard, cheat, bastard—

The instant Kah Onn steps through the door, Yu Sau flings the phone so it bounces off his forehead. Before he can react, she is upon him, slapping him hard across the face. He takes a few steps back, but before he can steady himself, a vase comes flying at him. Liar! Bastard! Yu Sau's fists whirr at him as she screams hysterically. She chases him out, and tosses his clothes after him. Like an animal in a cage, she is full of pent up fury, and doesn't know what to do but roar and sob.

She walks around the living room, hands clenched into fists. Only when a shard slices into her foot does she realise the floor is covered with pieces of shattered glass. She limps into the bathroom and washes the wound, then applies antiseptic and a plaster. Now in slippers, she walks unsteadily into the kitchen for a broom to clear up the mess, weeping the whole time. A perfectly good vase, broken just like that. The thought saddens her, and she cries even more pathetically. The hand she slapped Kah Onn with begins to throb, and she presses the darkening palm as she sobs. Why did she hurt herself like that? Bruising her hand, breaking her beloved vase, cutting her foot. Kah Onn's face will be swollen from her slap, and hopefully the vase left a bump on his head. Serves him right! Bastard, liar!

As she finishes sweeping up the glass, Kah Onn's face pops up in her mind, only his boyish features are now twisted with cunning. A hateful face. She digs up all their photos and rips them in two, tossing the halves with him into the bin. Then she collapses exhausted onto the sofa. He must have gone to that woman's place. They're entwined together while Yu Sau sits alone in an empty flat, raging to herself. Don't cry, she tells herself. Be strong. You're not to cry. She goes into the bedroom and lies down, staring out into the living room. Don't cry, she orders herself, but tears are streaming down her nose and past the corners of her mouth. She lies there for a while, she doesn't know how long, then starts to feel hungry, but doesn't want to get up, and anyway there's nothing in the fridge. She doesn't want to get changed and go out, so she lies there drowsily until the light begins to fade. Sunset. All of a sudden, she remembers what she found while going through Grandpa's stuff: a picture of Grandma ripped in two. Now she understands. Someone was on the other half, and he got torn away in anger. She doesn't know who it was, only that it can't be Grandpa.

Her phone rings. It's Geok Leng.

"Kah Onn says you kicked him out."

"Yes," she says dully.

"Can I come over?"

"Don't bother. I'm hungry. I need to get food."

"I'll have dinner with you. How about that?"

"I'm very hungry. I've already changed. I'm going out now."

She turns the phone off.

*

ONCE AGAIN, YU SAU EXPERIENCES EVERYTHING SHE WENT through when she split up with Kah Onn the first time. He calls, she doesn't answer. He sends texts and e-mails, downloads Leslie Cheung songs for her, begs her to forgive him, to give him yet another chance. She ignores all of this, changes the locks, and her phone number too. Logically, this break-up should hurt more than the last one, but she doesn't stay at home sobbing and staring into space this time. In fact, she's afraid to be at home at all. Almost every day, she goes for dinner with Geok Leng and Sandy after work. They go shopping and have facials. She buys many outfits and shoes, and replaces all her pillowcases and sheets. Hanging out with her friends doesn't help her depression; even when she's with them, she feels sad, confused and distracted. Her stomach hurts and she can't sleep, but lies in bed with her eyes open till dawn. Sometimes she thinks she can hear Grandpa pacing around the living room and muttering to himself. Suddenly she misses him enormously, and wishes she could see him.

"*Grandpa, he hurt me,*" she mumbles, staring wide-eyed into the emptiness before her.

In order to calm her tangled mind, Yu Sau starts jogging in the nearby park early each morning, but it's too easy to get lost in her memories while running by herself, which makes her feel even lonelier. The lack of sleep isn't helping. Unable to concentrate on her surroundings, she crashes into someone else, sending his glasses flying. She gives up jogging after that.

Sandy notices that how fragile and dejected she looks, and tells her she looks as morose as the heroine of *True Love*. She suggests Yu Sau take some time off and go travelling. Geok Leng agrees that she needs a break.

"I can take some leave and come with you," Sandy offers.

Yu Sau says there's no need. "I'll visit my brother in Hong Kong."

She misses Second Brother. She hasn't been to Hong Kong in a while, not since Grandpa died. She was very close to Second Brother as a child, and would tell him all her sorrows. Now that Grandpa's gone, Second Brother is the only family she has. She should do a better job of staying in touch with him.

YU SAU AND KIM MING

1. HE LISTENS ATTENTIVELY TO HER

KIM MING TAKES A FEW DAYS OFF WHEN YU SAU COMES TO visit. He brings her to Repulse Bay, Stanley, Ocean Park, and other tourist spots. Yu Sau's seen them all before. She's really here to do what she did as a little girl: tell Second Brother all her sorrows. Of course, Sandy or Geok Leng could also provide a listening ear, but she wants to talk to someone she trusts absolutely. Not that she doesn't trust her friends, but this has to be someone outside her immediate circle, like a therapist. Hence Second Brother. He's not a part of her daily life, she trusts him, and he's willing to listen.

As they rest their weary feet at a restaurant on The Peak, they talk about their childhood. She recalls how he pierced holes in flattened bottle caps and threaded a string through them to make a yo-yo. He used to do a magic trick in which he held a matchbox in the palm of his hand, then with a flick transformed it into a playing card, then back again. She tells Kim Ming about the little gadgets he made to amuse her. He listens with interest, then says all he remembers is that she used to bother him all the time, and everything else has slipped his mind. Yu Sau says it wasn't just toys he gave her, he also made up stories. That's why she liked spending time with him and not Eldest Brother, who didn't have the patience. "You remember all that? It was years ago," says Kim Ming. "I didn't invent anything, those were all from books." Next, they move on to the friends and neighbours they had as kids. Kim Ming gets emotional; he lost touch with his Singapore social circle after leaving the country. Yu Sau says it was the same with her. And so they start talking about friendship and love.

She asks why he's still not married. Does he have a girlfriend?

Kim Ming seems unprepared for this question. He stares through the restaurant window at the mist for some time, then spreads his hands and says simply, "I used to, and now I don't."

"So you've loved and lost?"

He smiles, but instead of answering, asks, "When are you and Kah Onn getting married?"

"We just broke up." She hesitates, looking at him as if to gauge his reaction, but he just grunts softly in acknowledgement. "That's why I came to Hong Kong. To tell you."

Actually, she's been meaning for the last few days to tell Kim Ming about her and Kah Onn, but couldn't get the words out. She misses the feeling she had as a kid of being able to tell him everything. He'd always listen attentively, and when she was done, would stroke her hair, put an arm round her shoulders, and say comforting things. He listens just as attentively now, but she's grown up, and hasn't spent much time with him. He feels much less familiar, and what she has to tell him is grown-up business, a romantic relationship. That's why she's been stalling. Would she have the courage to tell Second Brother about her amorous encounters? Can she control her emotions? She makes herself calm down before speaking, and tells him everything in as level a voice as possible. She stammers a bit out of nerves, but her voice steadies as she goes on. She even gets a little glib, as if this is something that happened to a friend, or the plot of a movie. Nothing to do with her.

Kim Ming looks at her, taking an occasional sip of coffee, listening in silence. Yu Sau feels back to her childhood self, only this time Second Brother doesn't try to comfort her or give her any suggestions. Not that she wants his advice, all she needs is to spew her feelings and frustrations at someone she can trust. She's not a kid, she understands that nothing Second Brother says will help. We have to deal with our own emotional problems, and no one else can solve them for us. Even so, she longs to feel his arm around her shoulders, ruffling her hair. At the very least he could take her hand or pat her arm.

Instead, he just listens without saying or doing anything. She's an adult woman, and Second Brother is a man who's had a traditional Chinese education. He wouldn't normally touch a young woman's body, not even his little sister whom he used to adore so much. It's okay. She doesn't need him to comfort her. She doesn't need him to say or do anything, just sit quietly and let her say everything she has to say.

2. YAU MA TEI

THE NEXT DAY, KIM MING BRINGS YU SAU TO YAU MA TEI after dinner for a stroll. As they turn into Public Square Street, they pass a row of bric-a-brac stalls. Yu Sau notices some of them are selling sex toys, and marvels at how liberal Hong Kong is, especially as it's often a young woman behind the counter. Second Brother seems embarrassed, and hurries along as if they're piles of smelly rubbish. Yu Sau wonders how close he actually was to his ex-girlfriend. He never mentions her, and refuses to answer any more of Yu Sau's questions. She ought to show him more concern. Maybe he also needs someone to spill his guts to! Women find it easy to tell other women their problems, but what about men? Kah Onn once told her that no man would ever bare his heart to another man, not even his best friend. But what about to a woman? Say his own little sister? Will Second Brother tell her what's troubling him?

Past the sex toys is a row of fortune tellers. Some of them are young woman, which again is something Yu Sau's rarely seen in Singapore. Across from the last few stalls are three buskers. Each stands at a microphone, with an electric keyboard for accompaniment. They're all singing Cantonese pop songs, and the woman closest to the street has the loudest speakers, drowning out the two middle-aged men, who nonetheless continue warbling. It sounds like they're mumbling to themselves. Yu Sau hasn't seen many people singing in the street like this. She and Kim Ming watch them for a while before moving on. Near the main road, she hears Cantonese opera. "That's Yung Shue Tau," says Kim Ming.

They walk in that direction, and see an old man and woman singing at microphones. Next to them are others clacking wooden boards, tapping a yangqin and sawing at an erhu, crashing cymbals and beating drums. A miniature orchestra. The musicians are elderly, like the singers, who don't seem to have enough air in their lungs. The opera stand is near a bus stop, but none of the people waiting there so much as glance at them. Yu Sau feels a twinge of sadness, and drops a twenty dollar coin into the plastic box by the mics. They listen a while longer. Yu Sau suddenly thinks of Eldest Brother. Did he ever sing here? No, he wouldn't have sunk so low. "Do you know where Eldest Brother is?" she asks Kim Ming. He smiles grimly and shakes his head, eyes fixed on the gleaming neon signs in front of them, the sky tinted purple by all that light. How could he know? Yu Sau wonders why she bothered asking. Her two brothers exist in different worlds. Even if Eldest Brother were in Hong Kong, he wouldn't know where Second Brother was.

3. FROM CHINA TO HONG KONG

ALTHOUGH YU SAU OFTEN CALLS SECOND BROTHER AND visits him in Hong Kong, she knows very little about his life right after leaving Singapore. This is partly because her visits are usually fleeting, but mostly because Second Brother doesn't like talking about that part of his life. Even when she brings it up, he just says a few non-committal things. Maybe she hasn't asked the right questions.

This evening, as they walk from Tsim Sha Tsui East to Jordan, they pass a little park on Cox's Road. Yu Sau suggests taking a break, and they settle themselves on a bench. Smiling, she says, "I told you about my love life the other day, but you still haven't told me about yours. Do you have a girlfriend? I want to know about my future sister-in-law."

Kim Ming shakes his head. "My finances are too shaky for a girlfriend."

"You really don't have one?" Yu Sau widens her eyes.

"I don't," he insists.

She'd like to know more about his ex, but senses that he'd rather not talk about his emotions, so doesn't ask any more. Instead, she demands to know about his life in China. He shakes his head again. "That time you came to visit me with Mum and Dad, didn't I tell you everything?"

It's true, he did, but Yu Sau was only fifteen or sixteen then, and a lot of things went over her head.

"I didn't understand, and anyway it was so long ago, I've forgotten most of it." She watches him as his brows crinkle and he lowers his head in thought.

"Yes, it's been a long time. I don't remember what I told you back then, and actually, my memory of that time has started to fade. I lived such a pampered life as a leftist in Singapore. When I first got to China, I wasn't used to hard labour. A few days of hoeing ripped open the skin on my palms. I was in a lot of pain." He holds up his hands and glances at her, ready to embark on his story.

"When I first came home to China, I was dispatched to the Overseas Chinese Farm. This was in the mountain zone, where no one wore glasses. In fact, the villagers had never seen a pair, so a four-eyes like me was some sort of monster to them. They looked at me strangely to start with, and sometimes I caught them whispering and laughing at me. The farm was terraces on the side of a hill, for growing tea. In the winter, we had to carry water up the hill for the plants. Each trip took several hours. I was a bookish little weakling, and could barely move the buckets on level ground. Getting them uphill almost killed me." He looks ashamed, as if he'd done something wrong.

"After you left for China, Mum always said you were *skinny as a twig*, and worried you wouldn't be able to take it. When we first came to see you in Hong Kong, you were practically a different person. More well-built. Grandpa even said you were finally grown up. You're still in pretty good shape. No beer belly," Yu Sau says.

"It's all from back then." Second Brother looks down at his flat stomach, smacking it proudly like a martial artist. "In the hills, we faced typhoons, floods, or burst water tanks. I was on the rescue team. Whenever anything went wrong, I dealt with the dead and injured. There was a Singaporean girl who was so unhappy she killed herself by drinking insecticide. To be honest, our comrades in Singapore couldn't possibly have imagined how bitter our lives were." He heaves a heartfelt sigh. "The people I used to organise with found it hard to understand what we were going through. That's why they thought those of us who left China for Hong Kong were traitors." He pauses, looking at Yu Sau. "You know, Auntie might have killed herself from the psychological pressure. When Uncle was shot dead by Communists in the jungle, she blamed herself for coming to Hong Kong. And maybe it was her fault. They probably thought if you believed in socialism, it was your duty to stay in the fatherland and be a socialist. Why live a capitalist life in a British colony instead? But they lived in Singapore, and because they loved the fatherland, their brains were full of revolutionary fervour. They hadn't actually experienced revolution, hadn't seen big-character posters or violent struggle. They didn't know what socialist China was really like. Besides, they were different people. What did Auntie's actions have to do with Uncle? What kind of logic is that?" Second Brother seems agitated, but quickly calms down, and continues in a more even tone. "I was sent to the Overseas Chinese farm. This was during the Cultural Revolution, when we descended into complete lawlessness. We were too busy denouncing each other to work or study. I'd already seen signs of this when I joined the organisation as a teenager in Singapore. Back in the fatherland, it was the same thing, but worse. I was so tired of it. I refused to join any factions, and when the struggle reached the farm, I pretended to be ill and hid in a friend's house in Santou. I was on medical leave, so the state continued issuing me ration coupons. As an overseas Chinese, I was allowed thirty kilogrammes of rice each month. The locals only got twenty-odd kilos. When the struggle was over, I returned to the farm, but then I got denounced anyway. They started with my clothes. Us overseas Chinese generally had better quality, more fashionable clothing. Even if they were worn out and covered in patches, we still got criticised. Next, it was my family background. Grandpa owned a kopitiam and Dad was a businessman, so they were both considered capitalists. I was forced to criticise both of them, and then self-criticise."

"Is that why you left the Mainland?" Yu Sau asks.

"It wasn't that easy to get out, once you were in China," he sighs.

"Oh," she says blankly. She doesn't have a sense of Chinese politics; things like the Cultural Revolution and struggle sessions are unknown concepts to her. Even more baffling, if life was so harsh under Communism, why did Second Brother and Auntie believe in it? Is he still a Communist? She doesn't ask him that. Instead, she asks how he managed to get out, if it was so difficult.

"My job on the health team was to dispense medicine. It was easy to offend people."

"How so?"

"There were quotas on imported drugs, and the state put limits on our allocation, so naturally we had shortages. The Chinese place more importance on human connections than the rules. If you only did what you were supposed to, you'd make enemies. At the time, China had just opened diplomatic channels with America, and a few overseas Chinese were released. A cadre said to me that with a job like mine, I was sure to get denounced every minute of the day, and as an overseas Chinese, I should try to leave as soon as I could. So I put in an application for Hong Kong. This was a risk too. Before the Cultural Revolution, many overseas Chinese applied to leave, and those who didn't succeed ended up getting denounced and severely punished. I decided to take my chances, even though I knew I was burning a bridge. After handing my form in to Public Security, I didn't hear anything for a long time, then one day they suddenly notified me that I could leave. I had to be out of Canton within roughly twenty-four hours. At ten that night, the Public Security Bureau told me to go back to my unit and pack a small bag. I got in a lorry that drove overnight to Shenzhen, and by eight the next morning, I was in Hong Kong. The whole journey felt like a dream."

Kim Ming looks up at the condos across from the park, and sighs deeply at the sky. The streetlamps come on as the light fades, and flying insects flutter around their glow. Suddenly he exclaims, with as much excitement as if he's spotted a UFO, "Look, stars! You hardly ever see stars in Hong Kong." Yu Sau follows his gaze and sure enough, there are a few pinpricks of light.

"You didn't know anyone here, and didn't have a penny to your name. How did you survive?" Yu Sau asks curiously. She remembers he didn't write to the family until two years after his arrival in Hong Kong.

Kim Ming is silent for a while. "When I came here in '73, I had nothing on me except the two hundred Hong

Kong dollars we were issued by the government. My future was really uncertain. Luckily, I ran into someone from the Overseas Chinese farm who'd left before me, and he got me a job at a garment factory in Kwun Tong. I did that for a while, then moved on to a handbag factory. I earned fourteen dollars a day. Life was hard, though actually I was one of the lucky ones. There were women who couldn't find any work, and ended up selling themselves. I hardly ever ate meat in China, but it was the other way round here: vegetables were expensive, a dollar a plate, the same as rice with meat. I lived in a cage-home to start with, then a flophouse where we each got a little space partitioned with boards. Rent was forty or fifty a month. Actually, both cost about the same, but you were allowed to stay longer in the cage homes. I did this for six or seven years."

"When you first left China, why didn't you look for work at a Chinese goods firm?"

"I tried, but they weren't hiring anyone who'd just come from the Mainland."

Yu Sau is startled by this. She'd assumed coming from China would be an advantage.

Kim Ming quickly corrects himself. "No, that's not true, Mainlanders could get hired if they had a guarantor. But I didn't. Eventually, in 1978, I found one, and got a position in Yue Hwa. Starting pay was four hundred, and I worked twelve hours a day. Now that I was in a China-owned firm, I had to fall in with their way of doing things. I smoked Chinese cigarettes and read the state-owned newspapers, Ta Kung Pao and Wen Wei Po. Later, I transferred to Chung Tai, a small Chinese company. My pay went up to eight hundred. I saved some money, and when China opened its borders, I started doing business on the Mainland, buying raw materials in Hong Kong and importing them to Guangzhou to be processed into traditional medicine."

"I never thought I'd have a businessman for a brother."

"That's how I managed to buy the flat in To Kwa Wan."

Yu Sau has been to the flat. It's only a little over three hundred square feet, but as the saying goes, the sparrow may be small, yet has a full set of organs. The place consists of a tiny kitchen, a bathroom, and a living room containing a table, two chairs, and a cupboard with an old TV set perched on top of it. There are also two inner rooms: a bedroom, and a study filled with cardboard boxes, as well as a desk, a chair, and a sparsely-stocked bookcase. Now Yu Sau understands why she mostly saw Chinese medicine books. Other than that, his library is comprised of English-learning books: grammar, conversation, business letters, and a thick dictionary. Hong Kong is a British colony, like Singapore was, and even with the Handover imminent, English is still very important. Second Brother must be learning the language in the hopes of getting a better job. "Actually, I'm very lazy, and I don't open those books as often as I should," he'd said to her then. "That's why my English still isn't any good."

Did Second Brother buy the flat with the thought of getting married? Why is he still single? Yu Sau didn't ask when she went to his flat, partly because she wasn't there even long enough to sit down. He'd seemed uncomfortable having her there. She's visited twice, and both times he's said how cramped and messy the place was, then hurried her out after less than twenty minutes. Or maybe the first time was a bit longer: like an estate agent, Kim Ming led her around the flat, then after she'd seen every room, took her to the cafe downstairs for tea.

"Are you still running your traditional medicine business in Guangzhou?" Yu Sau asks.

"I stopped long ago. It costs a lot more to do business in China these days. A million yuan might not be enough."

"I see."

He grimaces. "Actually, there was a woman once. Mum and Dad knew about this, Grandpa too. I met her at Yue Hwa. We were together for four years. Practically married."

"Oh!" Here, at last, is Second Brother's love story.

"But then she fell in love with another man." He pauses, rubbing his hands together as if trying to get a stain off his fingers. "He was a manager at a western firm. That hurt me a lot, but I didn't blame her. Everyone wants to lead a more comfortable life. What woman would willingly marry a poor devil? Being poor but happy only happens in films. In real life, water isn't enough to fill your belly, no matter how much in love you are. Money is very important."

"Maybe it wasn't the money. It could be that the other guy loved her more, or she thought they were more compatible," Yu Sau interjects. She is thinking of Kah Onn, who perhaps found Suzie more suited to him. When a third person enters a relationship, someone's bound to get hurt.

"Maybe you're right," says Kim Ming slowly, his voice like a sigh. "Maybe my attitude made her feel insecure. I'd always just drifted along. You could charitably say I wasn't materialistic, but really it was lack of ambition. After that shock, I woke up and decided to go into business, and started earning real money. If I ever met another woman I liked, I should at least own a flat, so I could offer her a home. But once I had a flat, I wanted a car, and more money. I wanted to be a rich guy. I overworked myself and got so sick, I almost died. During my illness, my mind cleared. This is a place where money breeds money. No one makes a fortune just by doing business, no matter how hard you work, unless you're crooked. Like Michael Hui said, '*Look at the cows in the New Territories. You see any of them getting rich?*' A small businessman like me was just slaving away for the big capitalists. It was blind luck that they didn't eat me alive, and I was able to put some money away, enough for the To Kwa Wan flat. I could have worked myself to death and I wouldn't have made so much money. Not now, not ever. So why did I put myself through that? And—"

Kim Ming stops, sorting through his thoughts. Yu Sau notices his hands are no longer writhing together.

"Money is important, but—" He looks up at Yu Sau. "Real happiness doesn't come from money. That just buys you material pleasure, not spiritual joy, which you need to truly be happy. If it cost so much just to find someone to be with, then I'd rather be single." There's something profound behind his smile.

Yu Sau suspects he must have suffered extraordinarily in the course of his striving, because she can hear the sadness and isolation in his voice. She doesn't ask, and doesn't want to know. His present emotional state is more important to her. "You really don't want to find a partner? Aren't you lonely?"

"I'm helping out a friend who owns a tenement bookshop. The pay is bad, but I have a lot of freedom. I'm old now. Who's going to want someone my age who's earning so little? I've resigned myself to being a bachelor."

"You don't look old at all," says Yu Sau.

He is silent for a while, looking a little uneasy. Finally, he sighs and stands up. "It's late. We should go."

Yu Sau glances at her watch; it's not even ten o'clock. Perhaps this was the wrong time and place to have brought up the subject. The sky is dark, and the streetlamps feel dimmer now. Couples are boldly making out in the hazy light, and her old-fashioned brother might not feel comfortable witnessing this. Yu Sau doesn't mind, but she stands up too.

"All right," she says.

Kim Ming brings Yu Sau back to her hotel. The bright neon lights, rowdy crowds and rumbling buses seem to perk Kim Ming up, erasing the earlier awkwardness. He starts telling Yu Sau more about his early days in Hong Kong. "I was most afraid of losing my job. It wasn't just that you never knew when you were going to find more work, you also didn't dare let your landlord know, otherwise he might evict you. So even when I was unemployed, I'd still pretend to go to work, and just roam the streets or nap in the park, until going-home time." Kim Ming thinks back to his arrival here in '73, a time of boom and bust for Hong Kong's stock market, while the oil crisis and global downturn were slowing down the local economy. Quite a few people were out of work, and he was very fortunate to find a job so soon. "In Hong Kong," he now says to Yu Sau, "as long as you're not afraid to take a few hard knocks, there are always jobs to be had."

They pass by a newspaper stand outside a hotel. Kim Ming stops to look at the colourful array of magazines and papers. Yu Sau notices that quite a few of them are pornographic. Kim Ming says hi to the owner and buys the *New Evening Post*. He says to Yu Sau, "In '75, there was an employment crisis in Hong Kong, and I was out of work. In the end, I still found something." He gestures at the newspaper stand. "I sold papers. I had to be here at five every morning, to fold the papers and put them in place. I worked till noon. There were more newspapers back then, more than ten titles, left and right wing, fifty cents each. My stand was outside the temple in Wong Tai Sin. I got to see the Queen when she visited there." He flashes a rare, playful grin.

They continue walking towards her hotel. Kim Ming smacks the newspaper, folded into a neat rectangle, against his right hand. "You can lose a job at any time. In the eighties, the economy was doing better, and I still got fired. I ended up at McDonald's for a month. Not even behind the counter, I was a cleaner. The chain wasn't open twenty-four hours back then, so my shift started at 11pm and went on till dawn. I cleaned the floor, wiped the tables and chairs, and scrubbed the stovetops, so everything was ready for the day shift to start at seven."

Of course, Kim Ming wasn't able to pick up odd jobs during every stretch of unemployment. He might sound light-hearted recounting it for Yu Sau now, but these were anxious times for him. He once went a whole six months without work. He started skipping lunch to save money, and by the end, was eating only one meal a day: breakfast. The road ahead looked bleak. He'd always paid his rent promptly, but now began to avoid his landlady. He wasn't completely broke, but his tiny savings wouldn't last long, and he didn't know when another job would come his way. Spending money on rent might mean not eating at all. Luckily, something turned up eventually, and he'd only owed half a month's rent in the end, but every day of that half month felt like a year. He'd had to sneak in and out of his flat, heart in his mouth, scared he would run into the landlady. His room was near the front door, and he never came or went without first opening the door a little and peering through the crack to see if she was in the living room. If the coast was clear, he'd fling the door open and quickly slip out. Actually, he did bump into her a couple of times, and she never pressed him for the money he owed. All that shame and fear was only in his head.

4. STUBBORN AND WILFUL

PHONE CALLS AND VISITS NOTWITHSTANDING, YU SAU ISN'T as close to Second Brother as when she was a little girl, because they were separated for a while. He feels less a brother, more a friend she doesn't see very often. At least this visit lasts a little longer, so she gets to spend more time with him. The childhood sense of togetherness returns a little, that feeling of having a sibling.

Yu Sau realises that she and her brothers actually have similar personalities: stubborn and wilful. Has this affected her relationships with her friends and colleagues? Not that she's noticed, but these traits are probably why she never got on with her parents, not since she was a young girl. How deeply did she hurt them? There's no way to find out now. What she does know is why both her brothers and her aunt suffered greatly: they had dreams and ideals which they stubbornly, wilfully pursued. That's why, even though Second Brother and Auntie knew how tough life would be in Mainland China, they still went out of idealism. There's a gap between ideals and reality, and perhaps they understood this, but found the gap wider than they could possibly have imagined. And so they went through hell.

Eldest Brother's dream was to be a Cantonese opera star. He got his wish for a while, but his happiness was short-lived. After Lily Teo's marriage, his life became harder. How hard? Yu Sau doesn't know. She's the luckiest of them all: just as stubborn and wilful, but without dreams of her own, she's turned out pragmatic, asking no more than regular happiness, the same as any other woman. Because she has no ideals, her life is light, lacking any weight at all. Better that than moving through life with the burden of ideals weighing her down. True, Kah Onn's betrayal hurt her, but that was pain she could bear, nothing compared to what Second Brother and Auntie went through. Perhaps this would be a sort of ballast, helping her to grow up. (What she'd thought was old age, might actually be maturity.) As a woman, Auntie might have suffered even more in China than Second Brother. Having survived that, why did she kill herself in Hong Kong? Did she really love Uncle that much? Yu Sau would never commit suicide over a man. She's too afraid of death. Dying means losing everything you have: your friends, your family (she still has Second Brother and Eldest Brother, assuming he's still alive). Did Auntie think of her family as she killed herself? Of Grandpa, Mum, Dad, Second Uncle, Eldest Brother, Second Brother, and Yu Sau? What went through her mind as she swallowed those sleeping pills? Did she take them one by one, or gulp them all down at once? Did she feel regret afterwards? What if she did? What did she think about after taking the pills but before she got drowsy?

Suicide is the culmination of despair, and Auntie must have had no hope left to do what she did. Yu Sau thinks Auntie killed herself not only because of her husband's death, but also because her ideals had been extinguished.

Yu Sau thinks sadly of the people in her family who've tried to leave: herself, Auntie, Eldest Brother, Second Brother (she forgets Second Uncle, who is practically a stranger to her). What's going on here? Is something wrong with this family? Mum used to sigh that she didn't know what their ancestors had done wrong, to make their family so unlike a family. What was it, then? Was it Grandpa who'd sinned? Where did this legacy of stubbornness and wilfulness come from? Grandpa? Grandma? Auntie and Second Brother were forced to leave, but Yu Sau and Eldest Brother did so out of choice. Yu Sau used to loathe her family, especially her constantly quarrelling parents, her mother's meanness, the way she scolded her in front of others. She remembers how Mum would call her a waste of space, insisting she'd learnt nothing but shit from her studies, that her mum would have been better off giving birth to a piece of char siew than a daughter like her.

These remarks about shit and char siew drove a wedge between them. She said to her mother, "*I didn't ask to be born. If I had a choice, I wouldn't want to be your daughter either.*"

Her mum retorted, "*If you don't want to, why not just go and die?*"

Yu Sau was furious. What kind of mother wishes death on her daughter? She was angry about those words for more than a decade afterwards.

When Yu Sau left home, she promised herself she'd never come back, and never see her mother's face again. Her heart only softened when her mother got breast cancer, and she found herself unable to keep hating the woman who'd given her life. Anyway, Yu Sau's temper was worse than her mother's. When she thought back to her childhood, her mother honestly hadn't treated her that badly. What was there to hate? The family now consists of her and Second Brother, split between Singapore and Hong Kong. Although, yes, there's Eldest Brother too, whom Yu Sau thinks is still alive. Where is he now?

YU SAU

1. LEARNING CANTONESE OPERA

TWO WEEKS LATER, YU SAU GOES BACK TO WORK.

Her colleagues tell her Kah Onn spent the fortnight waiting for her outside the building, but she never sees him. Even if she does, she tells herself, she'll ignore him. Her heart is dead to him, and she isn't going to fall for any more of his tricks. Geok Leng was right: this other woman has a prior claim. If Yu Sau were foolish enough to take him back, she'd lose out in the end.

Sandy happens to hear Yu Sau mention her interest in Cantonese opera, and lends her a couple of discs: Yam Kim Fai and Bak Sheut Sin's *Princess Cheung Ping*, and Connie Chan Po Chu's *A Sentimental Journey*. Yu Sau loves watching these, and begins to understand how Eldest Brother was so entranced by these performers. Now she recalls the costume Grandpa mentioned, and imagines herself dressed like Eldest Brother, in a young gentleman's robe, striding dashingly across the stage. She looks through the scores Grandpa left behind, and tries hard to remember the tunes he and Eldest Brother used to sing. In her spare time, she searches online for the black-and-white Cantonese opera films she watched as a child, and hums along to half-remembered tunes.

Yu Sau would love to get some formal training, but she's already in her thirties, and her Chinese is terrible. It may be a little late to learn a language as well as opera skills. When she mentions this, Sandy introduces her to her friend Siew Foong, who is training as a "flower role performer". Siew Foong says, "If you were planning to do this for a living, then of course you'd have to start with the basics, and thirty-something might be too old for that. But we're just doing it as a hobby. If you can pick up some stage-walking, poses, hand gestures and expressions, our teacher will take you through some excerpts, and within a year you'll be able to perform the 'Fragrant Sacrifice' from *Princess Cheung Ping.*" Yu Sau worries she might look like too much of an amateur. What's the use of going on stage if you haven't mastered the craft? She'd just embarrass herself. Seeing her hesitate, Siew Foong makes a decision for her: why not just take Cantonese singing lessons to start with? People do that up to their sixties, and it's never too late. "I study opera at the community centre near my place, but I also go to a clan association in Big Town for Cantonese singing lessons. Why don't you come along one of these evenings and give it a try?"

So Yu Sau goes along to the clan association with Siew Foong. When sees finds the dozen or so students in the classroom, she almost bursts out laughing. They're all in their sixties or seventies, and mostly women, with only a couple of men. Siew Foong, who looks about fifty, is the youngest. According to her, these elderly folk have been singing here a long time, some of them more than ten years. If this were a university, they'd have two or three PhDs apiece. Many of them are retired, and and like Siew Foong, they study singing in more than one place. Every couple of weeks, they hire some musicians to give a small concert, and occasionally rent a hall for a full performance.

They happen to be starting a new song. Siew Foong asks Yu Sau to join in, but she shakes her head and protests that she was English-educated, and her Chinese really isn't good enough. How is she meant to sing a Cantonese song with such patchy Cantonese? The teacher, a man in his fifties, overhears Yu Sau and tells her not to worry. Many of the people in this class went to English-medium schools, and some aren't even Cantonese, but they manage just fine. Siew Foong encourages her, "Just try one song, and see how it goes? If you feel you can't cope, you can quit. The teacher won't mind." Yu Sau is swayed. The teacher made a good point, and indeed she notices that the students are chatting amongst themselves before class in English as well as Cantonese. And so she signs up; her first lesson will be in the "level throat" voice.

Apart from Yu Sau, there are three or four beginners who've only been here a couple of months. There's only one class at the clan association, so they're together with the veterans who've been doing this more than a decade. Yu Sau struggles to pick up the tune, and has to come up with her own phonetic system to remember the Cantonese pronunciation. The other newcomers are probably having a tough time too, but at least their Cantonese is better than hers. Luckily, the teacher takes them through the lyrics before they start singing, reciting the words very slowly and getting the class to repeat the trickier phrases. He introduces them to some basic terms: what "two reeds" is, what the "wooden stick" percussion instrument is; the various styles of speaking, including wave talking, drum talking, verse talking, hero talking and lead talking, as well as ancient mouth, plain tone, white olive and so on. Naturally, those who've already been studying know these basic concepts inside out, and the teacher is probably just going over them for Yu Sau. She stumbles through this, and feels herself picking up all sorts of interesting facts.

The teacher sings the new piece through once, then the students do it to the accompaniment of his erhu. Yu Sau found it easy to follow along with the CD at home, but live music is a different matter altogether. She and the newer students keep going out of tune and mumbling. Luckily, the teacher is patient (as are her classmates) in correcting their mistakes, getting them to go over these difficult passages again. He reminds them to hit the right notes and keep up with the tempo, the fundamental requirements of Cantonese singing. Also, they must be steady when singing fast, tight when slow. And still Yu Sau keeps getting it wrong. Her Cantonese isn't there yet, and once the tempo picks up, her words collapse into nonsense syllables. When they go slowly, her pronunciation is off, like a scratched record.

2. BREAKING THE LONG WILLOW PAVILION, REMEMBER?

AFTER YU SAU STARTS TAKING CANTONESE MUSIC CLASSES, the lyrics she's just learnt swirl through her brain day and night. She sings under her breath as she drives, and sometimes even spits out a line or two of two reeds as she's walking along. Geok Leng jokes that she might be turning pro, but Yu Sau just laughs. How could anyone possibly make a living singing opera in Singapore today? Even Eldest Brother couldn't support himself, back in the day, and it must be much worse now. Geok Leng says, "You should go on stage if you have the chance. It won't just be me and Sandy in the audience, everyone from the office will come too." Yu Sau is touched, and thinks she actually does have some talent in this area, so perhaps in two or three years she will indeed get to perform. But to Geok Leng she says, "Amateurs like us take five or six years to reach any kind of standard, and I don't know if I'll stick around that long."

They spend about two months on each tune: a month to learn it, and another to perform it in turn individually. Yu Sau works hard, and her rhythm is not bad for a beginner, though she tends to go faster and faster out of nervousness, she needs to work on that, especially with grace notes, which frequently trip her up. After almost a year of lessons at the clan association, she gets a bad cold and stops for a month. When she's better, she drops by after work to sign up for the next session. Her classmates are presenting the song they've just learnt, and she stays to listen. A new student, a middle-aged man, is up on stage performing opposite a woman who sings falsetto. He looks a little familiar, but she can't remember where she's seen him before. He must have done this a lot; his rhythm and pitch are rock solid. Never mind Yu Sau, he's better than many of the students who've been taking lessons for several years.

After class, Yu Sau is heading for the exit when she sees this man making a beeline for her.

"Remember me?" he asks.

Yu Sau's brow crinkles as she studies his face.

"*Breaking the Long Willow Pavilion*, remember?" He grins.

Yu Sau shakes her head.

"How's your grandfather doing?" he asks.

"Oh!" She jabs her finger at him. "You're the guy who sang Cantonese opera by the river in Bishan Park." Looking down, she murmurs, "Grandpa passed away."

He hesitates for a moment, then introduces himself. "My name's Chan Siu Wah."

Yu Sau tells him her name, and adds that he sang very well.

"I almost didn't recognise you with your new hairstyle. You look more like your big brother now," says the man.

"You knew my brother?" She looks at him in surprise, unconsciously patting her short hair.

"Didn't your grandfather say Leong Kim Chau was your brother? He's the one who got me interested in Cantonese opera."

"Really?" Yu Sau is excited at the mention of Eldest Brother, and asks if they were close.

"I interviewed him at Rediffusion, and we became friends afterwards. He's very talented."

"It's a shame he never achieved his dreams," Yu Sau sighs.

"I lost touch with him later. I heard he left Singapore."

"Do you still live in Bishan?"

"Yes, still." The man nods.

They have been walking as they chatted, and soon reach the car park.

"Did you drive?" Yu Sau asks.

The man shakes his head and says he doesn't have a car. "Nor a license," he adds.

"I'll give you a lift home. It's on my way," says Yu Sau.

In the car, she tells the man, "Eldest Brother left home when I was very small, and I never saw him again."

"Leong Kim Chau used to play scholar-warrior parts for Rediffusion, and Lily Teo was our resident ingénue," the man says. "Then Lily married the troupe leader and they left Singapore for Canada, and the troupe disbanded."

"Eldest Brother went through a hard time. Other people in my family told me he tried joining other opera troupes, but it never worked out."

"There weren't many troupes in Singapore by then, only the clan associations and a couple of amateur groups. These were set up by enthusiasts, and didn't earn any money. In fact, you had to pay dues to be a member, and foot the expenses for every performance. Also, these cliques had people they wanted to push forward. If Kim Chau had joined, he might have got some junior parts, but not scholar-warrior roles."

"My mother said something similar. Things went downhill, my brother never recovered, and eventually gave up opera altogether. After he left home, my family lost track of him."

"He gave afternoon performances at a hotel," says the man. "Around that time, a female singer named Lau Cho Wan fell in love with him."

"How do you know?" Yu Sau turns to gape at him, then quickly looks back at the road.

"Kim Chau told me," says the man. "Maybe it was fate. We clicked when I interviewed him, and stayed in touch."

"Then what happened? Did he end up with this woman?" Yu Sau is curious about who her brother fell for after Lily's marriage.

"I think she really did care for him. I don't know what happened, maybe it was fate again, but in the end she married the owner of a record label."

The car stops at a red light, so Yu Sau is able to turn and smile at the man. "You seem to know a lot about my brother."

"He knows a lot about me too. Like I said, we were pretty good friends. I had a lot of time for your brother. His Chinese was excellent. When we were talking, he'd casually quote a line or two of Tang poetry. He was fond of Li Shangyin: 'We have no phoenix wings to soar together, but at least our hearts are linked.'"

"Eldest Brother left school after Sec Two," says Yu Sau.

"That's why I have a lot of respect for him." The man pauses, as if deciding whether to divulge more. "After Lau Cho Wan's marriage, Kim Chau started singing at a bar. I went to hear him often. He was different from other singers—instead of pop songs, he did opera arias like *The Red Candle's Tears*." He bursts into song: "*My body bends like a willow branch in the wind.*" Then he adds, "And also *Breaking the Long Willow Pavilion*."

"*Helpless before the heavens we part, what sorrow, what rage,*" sings Yu Sau, hands on the steering wheel, eyes on the road.

"Ah, you know it too?" The man stares at her, surprised.

"I didn't when I heard you sing it by the river in Bishan Park, but I do now." Yu Sau raises an eyebrow cockily.

"You sound a lot like Tsuih Lau Seen," he exclaims.

"I'm nowhere near as good as her, don't bluff me," Yu Sau protests, glancing at him. "There was another man who admired Eldest Brother a lot. I don't know if he ever mentioned him?"

"I don't remember him talking about any man in particular."

"So the name Lam Meng Hung doesn't mean anything to you?"

"He was the boss of Rediffusion, Lily Teo's husband," says the man.

3. ELDEST BROTHER AND MENG HUNG HAD DRUNK A LOT

AFTER YU SAU DROPS THE MAN OFF. AFTER THEIR conversation, the rest of her drive home is full of memories. She recalls something that had almost vanished from her mind: when she was twelve, the evening before Lily Teo's marriage to Lam Meng Hung, she went for a stroll with some classmates along Queen Elizabeth Walk. They nibbled at kacang putih and jabbered away like sparrows about the latest entertainment gossip from their showbiz mags, while the sunset spilled gorgeous light over the sea, and waves lapped against the bank.

There weren't many people on the esplanade, but Yu Sau noticed two men quarrelling heatedly at the far end of the park, and recognised them as Eldest Brother and Meng Hung. They were too far away to hear what the argument was about, so all she saw was Meng Hung coming close and putting his arm across Eldest Brother's shoulders, as if he was trying to explain something, but Eldest Brother flung the arm off and hurried away in agitation. Meng Hung froze for a second, then ran after him. She wasn't sure if her friends had caught sight of this little scene, but it didn't matter anyway, they'd never met her brother and would have no idea who he was.

She didn't tell her family what she'd witnessed. This incident has long lain buried in her memory, but for some reason is surfacing now. Meng Hung's face also pops into her mind. It's been a long time since she's thought about him. In fact, she's almost forgotten him, but when she was a little girl, she liked him a lot.

Meng Hung was Eldest Brother's classmate in secondary school, as well as his best friend and number one fan. He was in the audience almost every time Eldest Brother stepped on stage, from his very first performance. Meng Hung was the son of a hotel owner. In secondary school, he often came to their house, and would watch shows with Eldest Brother and Grandpa. Like Eldest Brother, he loved Cantonese opera, though he never trained as a singer. Even if he'd wanted to, his family would never have allowed him. He did well at school, and got into the Nantah Chinese faculty. After graduation, he helped his father manage the hotel.

Because Meng Hung admired Eldest Brother so much, when Eldest Brother started making a bit of a name for himself in the opera scene, Meng Hung often donated money to his troupe. That's when Eldest Brother started taking on scholar-warrior roles. He'd partnered with Lily Teo all this while, and their troupe was called Li Kim, a portmanteau of their names. According to Grandpa, audiences loved seeing them perform. After every performance, matrons and young ladies would cluster backstage, pressing herbal soups and other nourishing foods on them.

Yu Sau remembers how Meng Hung enjoyed teasing her whenever he came round, and how she'd pout at him. Meng Hung was tall and dashing, and witty too: her ideal man, and her first crush. She told herself that when she grew up, she'd marry someone just like him, or maybe Meng Hung himself, if he was willing to wait. Instead, he married Lily Teo, which was disappointing. How she envied Lily. This marriage was a shock to everyone, not just her, because they'd all thought Lily was dating Eldest Brother. How could she have been so shallow, to go for a rich man instead? Yu Sau was crushed and furious to discover that Lily was heartless and Meng Hung was a bad friend. Now, when she thinks back to the two men fighting at Queen Elizabeth Walk more than twenty years ago, her disappointment and rage have faded, but she still feels a sense of pity and loss. Two good friends, torn apart by a woman.

Yet the day of the wedding, it was as if they'd never argued. Yu Sau can still see it: Eldest Brother wishing Meng Hung a long and happy life with Lily, raising glass after glass to him. By the end of the evening, both Eldest Brother and Meng Hung had drunk a lot. Yu Sau watched them closely, and could tell Eldest Brother was still heartbroken. Even after all these years, she still feels for him. She remembers Meng Hung's eyes also glistening with tears, but maybe he was just drunk.

SIU WAH AND YU SAU

1. CHAN SIU WAH

WHEN HE WAS WORKING AS A PRESENTER AT REDIFFUSION, Chan Siu Wah was put in charge of a Cantonese Opera programme. He grew fond of this type of music, and after leaving the station, he'd sing a few lines now and then, though it was getting harder to hear Cantonese opera in Singapore, and he never trained formally. He only signed up for the clan association class by chance: a friend gave him a ticket to a local community group's show, and he recognised some of the performers as former Rediffusion employees, from the Cantonese opera team. The next day, he caught up with them over tea. They said that after Rediffusion stopped broadcasting in dialect and the drama group was disbanded, they'd joined an amateur troupe instead. They asked if he wanted to take part, but he felt that Cantonese opera, like other traditional music arts, had such a high degree of difficulty that it would take a long time to pick up. His interest lay in reading and writing, which he hoped to eventually take up professionally, and didn't have energy to spare to learn something else. Although he said no, his friends often asked him to come watch them perform. Finally, he decided it wouldn't take too much time to learn just the music, which is how he ended up at the clan association. He ran into Yu Sau, and it turned out she was there for the same reason: to learn singing, but not performance.

Even so, Siu Wah isn't sure how long he'll be able to do this, because he doesn't really have time to practice. Still, perhaps because of Yu Sau, he shows up promptly at eight o'clock every Tuesday, and never misses a class. Like Yu Sau, he lives in

Bishan, so she always gives him a lift home afterwards, which makes it much more convenient for him. Besides, they have things in common they can talk about: Cantonese opera and Kim Chau. Soon, they become quite close. Sometimes, they don't go home immediately after class, but linger for a chat at a nearby coffee shop.

2. LEONG YU SAU

AFTER SPLITTING UP WITH KAH ONN, YU SAU HASN'T SPENT much time with any men, not even her male colleagues. A couple of them asked her out on dates, but she said no. Going on dates leads inexorably to a relationship. When she was with Kah Onn, she was eager to get married. Now they've broken up and she's still hurting, she'd rather live quietly on her own for a while, rather than rushing back too quickly into the swamp of emotion. How long for? She doesn't know herself. Her once-a-week encounter with Siu Wah is the most contact she has with any man. They have things in common, but most importantly, she feels comfortable in his presence.

Siu Wah is humble. Unlike other men (including Kah Onn), he doesn't brag constantly about his accomplishments. Like Second Brother, he has the patience to listen when she talks. Kah Onn was much more self-centred, and would often interrupt her to state his own point of view. Only when she lost her temper would he shut up. The other thing she's noticed is that men always try to push for intimacy after they've spent a bit of time with you, but although she sees a lot of Siu Wah, he always keeps an appropriate distance, so she never feels awkward when she's with him. As they get to know each other, Yu Sau realises he's knowledgeable and cultured. For a former radio presenter, he's strangely introverted.

Yu Sau also finds out that Siu Wah has had his heart broken

before, and doesn't have a girlfriend at the moment.

His ex is Chang Mun Yee, a former Rediffusion colleague who has since become a TV actress. At the radio station, along with presenting, Siu Wah also wrote and performed dramas, with Mun Yee as his partner. She was very beautiful, and naturally wanted to move on from radio. She left Rediffusion and signed with the TV station. Soon after, she fell in love with her co-star while filming a serial.

"Did it hurt you that she fell for someone else?" Yu Sau asks.

"Of course it hurt. But I told myself she wasn't right for me, and I wasn't right for her." He shrugs. "I'm fine now. Time heals all wounds, and doesn't charge any medical bills."

"You're funny." She giggles.

Chang Mun Yee split up with the actor after half a year.

"Did she come back to you?" Yu Sau asks.

"She fell in love with the guy who played her boyfriend in her next serial."

Chang Mun Yee started to get famous in the early nineties. She was pretty, and audiences liked her refined persona. Yu Sau tells Siu Wah that she's seen Mun Yee's shows, and likes her acting. Who would have thought this elegant TV star would be so free with her affections?

"Actually, she's a very dedicated performer, and always throws herself wholeheartedly into whatever part she's playing. She was still new to the profession, though. Experienced actors know how to leave a role at work. TV serials have very long shoots, and after spending so much time in character, she couldn't extricate herself. She also spent a long time with her co-stars, and started to lose track of the difference between real life and the show. That's how she ended up loving these men," Siu Wah explains.

"Was she acting opposite you when she fell in love?"

"That's right, in a script I wrote." Siu Wah smiles grimly.

3. CHAN SIU WAH

THE REASON SIU WAH IS SO INTROVERTED, ACCORDING TO him, is self-doubt. He always feels he's not particularly good-looking or rich, and only ended up with a beautiful girlfriend like Chang Mun Yee out of sheer luck. Though, actually, maybe it was bad luck, because that meant their break-up was inevitable. After Mun Yee dumped him, he gave up on finding love. Now he sees Yu Sau once a week, the most time he's spent with any woman for quite a few years.

He feels happy when he's with Yu Sau, and after a couple of months, starts looking forward to their Tuesday classes. He always spends time with her afterwards, chatting over coffee then getting a ride home. The happiest day of his week. A few more months, and he can't get her out of his mind: her charming short hair, the confidence with which she speaks, her mischievous smile, her wide, attentive eyes when she listens to him talk. When he thinks of her, his heart fills with sweet joy, and he hopes to see her more often than on Tuesday evenings. If only he were brave enough to ask her out, or could think of a pretext so she won't think he's pursuing her.

He worries she might sense what he's thinking, because she told him her had been heart broken, and she didn't want to fall into the pit of emotion again. What did she mean by that? He grows cautious around her. They're getting on well, and he doesn't want to damage their friendship by behaving inappropriately. (He's sure his interest is inappropriate, because she'd never choose someone like him as a partner.) Yet he can't stop thinking about her. Finally, he comes up with a plan, and asks if she still does morning exercises in the nearby park, now that Grandpa's passed? She replies that it's been a long time since she went to the park. He says it's the same with him, but he gets tired easily due to lack of exercise, and so he's decided to start jogging on Saturday mornings. He reminds her that they're both cubicle rats who work with their brains and don't move their bodies as much as they should, which is unhealthy and will leave them prone to illness. Maybe she should exercise more. Why not head to the park when she has time?

It's true that Siu Wah hasn't been to the park in a while, but the Saturday after having this conversation with Yu Sau, he goes jogging with the unrealistic hope of bumping into her. Three Saturdays in a row, he has no luck. After class the following Tuesday, he makes a point of mentioning how much better he feels as a result of his Saturday morning runs. His mood is much improved, he says, and he's sleeping well at night.

He continues jogging by the river every Saturday morning, and Yu Sau continues not showing up. Another two weekends go by, and he starts to realise how ridiculous and unrealistic his fantasies were. He decides to give up the habit, but when Saturday morning comes round again, he pulls on his exercise clothes out of habit, and ends up by the river again. There's no sign of Yu Sau, of course, but the jogging is doing him good. As he told Yu Sau, he doesn't get tired as easily as before. He carries on with his weekly runs, though he no longer mentions them to Yu Sau. It's not bad that he gets to see her once a week, he thinks, and as they're never going to be together, he might as well try to stop being so crazy about her.

The next Saturday, he is on the return leg of his run when he sees her.

She is in a pure white sports outfit, revealing her lovely legs, breathing hard as she comes towards him. The faint sheen of sweat on her forehead and her glowing cheeks make her look especially young and attractive. He is so overjoyed, he thinks he can feel his heart leaping from his mouth, but takes care to act surprised when he says, "Fancy meeting you here!"

Yu Sau says she needed exercise, and decided to take his advice. That's good, he says right away, he hopes he'll run into her every Saturday morning. He jogs alongside her for a while, then they go to a nearby kopitiam for breakfast. Siu Wah now sees Yu Sau twice a week: at singing class, and during their Saturday morning jogs.

4. CHAN SIU WAH AND LEONG YU SAU

THERE ARE WEEKS WHEN SIU WAH AND YU SAU MEET EVEN more often.

Since breaking up with Kah Onn, Yu Sau has spent her weekends either alone or with Geok Leng and Sandy. Now she starts hanging out with Siu Wah too. One Sunday, she meets Siu Wah at an open-air cafe on Orchard Road. To start with, they discuss the song they are currently learning, "Sorrowful Parting at the Southern Tower". Siu Wah tells her the story: Liu Rushi and Chen Zilong said a sad farewell at the Southern Tower when she left to marry Qian Qianyi, a talented scholar twice her age. When the Qing army laid siege to their city, Liu Rushi suggested that they drown together, martyring themselves for their country. Qian Qianyi thought about and said, "I can't do it, the water's too cold." Liu Rushi tried to kill herself anyway, but Qian Qianyi pulled her back.

Siu Wah manages to make this story comical, and Yu Sau bursts out laughing. "I guess he surrendered to the Qing Dynasty?" she asks.

"Thanks to Liu Rushi's influence, he resigned from his ministerial position and went back to his hometown. The two of them then joined the resistance movement to restore the Ming."

Next, they discuss Tang Ti-sheng's four famous compositions: *Princess Cheung Ping, Reincarnation of Red*

Plum, *The Purple Hairpin*, and *Nightmare at Peony Pavilion*. Siu Wah is surprised at how well she knows them, and Yu Sau smiles as she explains that her love of Cantonese opera started with these four. She mentions that the pieces they're learning now are all by composers from China, but she actually prefers the ones from Hong Kong, and hopes their teacher will choose an aria like "Reunion of Sword and Hairpin" or "We Suddenly Meet Under This Willow Tree". Siu Wah thinks their teacher wouldn't be interested in these old tunes.

They change the subject again, and start talking about a Hong Kong movie that's currently playing, *Summer Snow*. They've both seen this, and Siu Wah says he likes Ann Hui's work a lot. Yu Sau says he must have seen *Song of the Exile*, and he says of course he has. As soon as the words leave his lips, she grows very quiet, and stares at the pedestrians streaming down the pavement. Someone has caught her attention.

She's spotted Kah Onn. He's in a lavender long-sleeved shirt and black trousers, and is walking towards them with a man about his age. Yu Sau freezes. How could this be happening? *Song of the Exile* was the first movie she saw with Kah Onn.

"You're looking well," says Kah Onn, waving as he walks towards her.

"You too," she answers.

"I left my job." He looks uneasy, rubbing his hands together as he gazes at her.

"Oh, did you?" she says simply. He smells faintly of cigarettes, just like he did when he first joined her firm, a few years back.

Did he leave that woman too? Yu Sau wonders. "This is Chan Siu Wah," she says. "We're learning Cantonese opera together."

Kah Onn politely shakes Siu Wah's hand.

Yu Sau is a bit shaken after Kah Onn leaves. Why did she say that about Siu Wah? Was she hinting that he's not her boyfriend? She is furious at herself for a moment, but quickly calms down.

"My ex," she tells Siu Wah. Her eyes drift to the crowds hurrying across the pedestrian crossing. "But that's all in the past." She mutters to herself, "In the past."

"I could tell," says Siu Wah.

"You could tell he's my ex?" Yu Sau looks at him, startled.

"No, that it's all in the past, in the past."

Yu Sau laughs. "How do you feel when you see your ex-girlfriend?"

"We've stayed in touch," he says.

"You still have feelings for each other?" Yu Sau's eyes widen.

"She likes calling me up to complain."

"What about?"

"If she's had a bad day at work, or if her relationship isn't going well."

"She complains about her relationship? Is she trying to get back together with you?"

"No, she knows I'm not right for her. I'm just a regular guy. She could never be in love with someone as ordinary as me."

"Weren't you together once?"

"We broke up because she realised how ordinary I am. I'm only fit to be her good friend, not her lover or husband. That's what she said. I'm not good enough to love, only to be her relationship counsellor."

Yu Sau narrows her eyes like a cat, and studies him. Abruptly, as if the thought has just occurred to her, she blurts out, "I listened to those skits you gave me. You're very funny and talented." She reaches into her handbag, pulls out his cassette tapes, and hands them back to him.

Siu Wah takes them. "Thank you. I wrote them in a hurry—I had a programming deadline."

"They're very good. I laughed a lot. They didn't feel rushed."

"I'm not too bad, I guess, just lazy. I've wasted a lot of time."

"I think you must be a good performer too. Have you

thought of doing some acting?"

"I'm too short and ordinary-looking," he says self-deprecatingly. "I mean, I'm plain. That's fine for radio, because listeners don't know what I look like, but I could never be a real actor."

"Don't be so hard on yourself. You're no stud, but you're not bad-looking either. And you're funny. Have you ever thought of doing stand-up?" Yu Sau leans over and pats his wrist, as if to encourage him. "Woody Allen isn't that handsome either."

"You mean I'm short and balding?" He ruffles the sparse hair at his temples. "Those are the only things I have in common with Woody Allen. Oh, and we both wear black-rimmed glasses."

"You're funny. Stop being down on yourself. You have talent, and you're a good singer."

"You have a point. I bet Woody Allen can't sing Cantonese opera."

5. CHAN SIU WAH

HE FEELS MORE AND MORE UNCERTAIN, AS HE SPENDS MORE time with Yu Sau. He's falling for her. How does Yu Sau feel? She likes him, undoubtedly. When they talk, she often pats him on the shoulder or tugs at his arm, and these moments of contact leave him even more besotted and perturbed. When she gets excited, her pale face flushes and her liquid eyes stare directly at him, and he longs to stroke her cheek or wrap his arms around her. Of course, that would be inappropriate, because he's not good enough for her. There are so many outstanding men around her, why would she pick an ordinary-looking, low-income guy to marry? He doesn't dare hope their friendship will ever move to the next level.

To be honest, he doesn't have much hope for his future

either. When his mum asks if he has a girlfriend yet, he gets annoyed. Although time is supposed to heal all wounds, he is still smarting from being dumped by Chang Mun Yee, and his self-confidence is shrinking by the day.

When he thinks back to his time at Rediffusion, he remembers being full of himself and very ambitious. He wanted to be a playwright, screenwriter and film director, and fantasised about becoming the next Neil Simon or Woody Allen. He even considered quitting his job and trying his luck in Hong Kong, where he knew many people in the film and TV industry through his work. One of his friends, an editor at a Hong Kong TV station, read some of his writing and asked if he'd like to come work there. Siu Wah had just started dating Mun Yee, though, and couldn't bear to give her up. Well, fine, but he should have been able to leave Singapore after breaking up with Mun Yee, right? He would have, except that's when his mum got ill. His father abandoned them when Siu Wah was a teenager, so he and his mum are dependent on each other. There's no way he could have left her at this juncture.

In fact, that wasn't the real reason, because even after his mum made a full recovery, he still didn't leave his job and move to Hong Kong. He simply didn't believe enough in himself, and couldn't bring himself to give up a familiar situation to start all over again elsewhere.

Nonetheless, he hadn't given up on his dreams. After leaving Rediffusion, he didn't look for another media job, but became an insurance salesman. This meant his income was less certain than before, but he had more time to write. The problem was what he actually did with this free time: nothing except fritter it away, lost in his fantasies. Not long ago, he took a good, hard look at his life: he's in his late thirties, and doesn't have much youth left to waste. As a result, he quit his insurance job, which had taken up too much of his time already. Besides, he's thin-skinned and impatient, which is precisely the wrong personality for this job that contributed nothing to his creative life, apart from paying his bills. Since it's completely unrealistic to dream of being a film-maker in Singapore, he gave up on that idea too, and set his sights on becoming an author instead. He threw himself into his writing, and took part in short story competitions locally and in Taiwan, some of which he even won. Now that he had a bit of a reputation, newspapers and magazines started asking him to write columns and book reviews.

Very few people in Singapore read Chinese books, and Chinese-language writers here mostly do it as a hobby. It's all but impossible to make a living, unless you get your books published in Hong Kong, Taiwan or Mainland China. Writing a novel is the best way to do that, and so he began one, hoping to finish it quickly so he could send it to overseas publishers.

Just as he was gritting his teeth stoically and getting on with his dreams, he met Yu Sau again. This was frustrating, as he really can't think of dating in his current financial situation. It's not just Yu Sau; starting a relationship with any woman at this point would be a bad idea.

And yet he can't stop thinking of Yu Sau. She seems to like him, but he doesn't know how she would react if he declared his love. She just broke up with her boyfriend. Siu Wah watched them closely when they ran into each other on Orchard Road. Kah Onn acted calm, but his body language revealed anxiety and sadness. He obviously still loves her deeply. Yu Sau said it was all in the past, but seemed dazed by the encounter. Is she really over him? She might not be sure herself. He doesn't dare to take this risk. Not only might Yu Sau still love Kah Onn, her education and earnings far surpass his, and she's very beautiful. Her office is full of much more eligible men. Anyone could see Siu Wah isn't right for her. For all he knows, someone in her office might already be courting her. He's been unlucky in love once, and doesn't want to suffer the same fate again. He'd just be the butt of the joke. He had a proper job before, and still Mun Yee left him. Now, he's a so-called writer trying to support himself with his manuscripts, in an even more precarious position. The longer he spends with Yu Sau, the stronger his feelings will grow, and eventually he'll no longer be able to extricate himself. If something were to happen (that is, if another man were to get together with her), it would be a heavy blow to him. He ought to do the smart thing and remove himself from the situation, before he gets too caught up in his infatuation.

In order to cool down his feelings, he steels his heart to stop seeing her, and finds excuses to say no when she asks him out. He even skips their Saturday morning runs. After a month of this, he realises he can't do it. He thinks of her non-stop and misses her unbearably, like withdrawal from an addiction. Why torture himself like this? And so he caves in and arranges to see her. Does Yu Sau have any idea how crazy he is about her?

6. LEONG YU SAU

The day after Yu Sau sees Kah Onn, she gets an email from him asking how she is, and wishing her happy birthday in advance.

Of course Kah Onn remembers her birthday. She doesn't mind him sending greetings, which is just being polite, but it doesn't thrill her. She doesn't want to get all wrapped up in Kah Onn again, so she just sends him back a couple of lines to say thank you. On her actual birthday, Kah Onn sends an enormous bunch of roses to her office. The card says he hopes she'll stay young and beautiful forever, and his time with her was the happiest in his life. Even though Kah Onn didn't bring the flowers in person, she feels embarrassed and uneasy. No matter what, she can't let herself be swayed by his honeyed words. When she emails him to say thanks for the flowers, she adds that she is soon getting married to her boyfriend Siu Wah.

Kah Onn replies to wish her well, but a couple of days later, she gets another email from him asking if Siu Wah was the guy she was with the other day? It would be such a shame if she married someone like that, says Kah Onn, not to mention a source of pain and humiliation for him. Siu Wah isn't good enough for her: he's plain-looking, or even downright ugly, and as far as Kah Onn knows, he doesn't have a real job or steady source of income. Yu Sau should think twice. He regrets what he did, and broke up with Suzie long ago. He wants Yu Sau to forgive him, and give him another chance. He promises not to make the same mistake again. He loves her so much that if she marries another man, he'll stay single for the rest of his life, and die alone.

Yu Sau knows how prone to jealousy Kah Onn is. He must be suffering a lot right now. She feels a little sorry for him, and when she remembers how loving they could be together, she must admit she still misses him. But then she thinks how many times he hurt her, and her anger swamps any lingering affection. His attacks on Siu Wah especially enrage her. Why did he make inquiries about Kah Onn's background? Who did he ask? Furious, she sends Kah Onn's email to Trash without a response, and deletes all his subsequent messages without even opening them.

Kah Onn gives up after seven or eight more emails. Yu Sau worries he'll try the same trick of waylaying her in the car park, and always walks out with a colleague, usually Geok Leng. A long time passes without any word from Kah Onn, so it seems he got the message.

She is a little worried about having told Kah Onn that she was getting married to Siu Wah. What if he talks about it, and the lie finds its way back to Siu Wah's ears? That would be awkward. But then, she reassures herself, Kah Onn isn't in contact with her colleagues any more, and they probably won't ever hear about it. Even if they do, so what? Who knows, maybe she actually will marry Siu Wah.

Would she ever marry Siu Wah?

She can't deny he left a good impression on her. They're pretty good friends, but maybe no more, which is probably how most people see them. She's known Siu Wah almost two years, and sees a lot of him, but they never touch in front of others. No one would mistake them for a couple. Siu Wah is not her ideal mate, but she spends more time with him than any other male friend. In fact, in or out of the office, she stays clear of men altogether, unless she is forced to for work.

Her colleague Henry likes her, and has asked her out several times, but she keeps saying no. Henry asks Sandy if she already has a boyfriend, and Sandy says she's not sure. In fact, she has wondered if Yu Sau wants to be with Siu Wah, but immediately told herself that couldn't be. She knows what Yu Sau looks for in a man, and Siu Wah's unattractive features and low income don't fit her requirements. He appears to have no skills other than writing and broadcasting, and survives on newspaper columns and freelancing for the radio station. That will only ever be enough to support himself, and he can forget about providing for a wife and kids. Yu Sau couldn't possibly be interested. She has high standards.

Still, Sandy can't help asking Yu Sau, "You're always with Siu Wah. Are you dating?"

"What do you think?" Yu Sau replies.

"You're not going to marry him, are you?" says Sandy doubtfully.

Yu Sau laughs. "It's hard to say. After all, I never thought you'd end up with Shing Yip."

Shing Yip is a teacher, and was Sandy's secondary school

classmate. A year ago, Sandy introduced him to Yu Sau and said he was after her, but she wasn't into bookworms. Despite that, she continued seeing him, and they started to seem like a couple. Yu Sau has met Shing Yip a few times. He has the same sort of black-rimmed glasses as Siu Wah, though he's probably even more short-sighted, and seems to wear only light-blue shirts. He doesn't talk much. A stereotypical nerd. It's hard to believe that lively, fun-loving Sandy would be with someone like him.

Ever since she lied to Kah Onn about marrying Siu Wah, Yu Sau has been seriously considering the possibility that he might be her life partner. In terms of looks and finances, he can't compete with Kah Onn. She no longer cares about that, though. She's an independent woman, and as long as her man isn't mooching off her, she isn't going to complain about his income. It's more important that he's honest and dependable than handsome and rich, and Siu Wah seems honest and dependable to her. He has other good points: he has a good sense of humour, and holds strong opinions without excluding others. (Kah Onn was well aware of his good looks, and was far too prone to being in love with himself and dominating every conversation.) Having worked in entertainment, Siu Wah knows a huge amount about both Chinese and international films. He's introduced her to many classic Mandarin and Cantonese movies, as well as Cantonese operas (including Yam Kim Fai's *Big Red Robe*) and important European films such Bergman's *Wild Strawberries*, Antonioni's *Blowup*, and Fellini's *8½*. Even though she was English-educated, this is her first time hearing about New Wave Cinema, Truffaut's *The 400 Blows* or Godard's *Breathless*. She's enchanted to learn new things from him. Yet even though they spend so much time together, he doesn't treat her as anything other than a good friend, and has never uttered a single affectionate word, not even a hint. She can sense that he likes her. Are Chinese-educated men not in the habit of telling women they love them? If he doesn't say anything, how is she supposed to know? When she was dating Kah Onn, he never said "I love you" either, but took the initiative and got intimate with her very quickly. His actions told her what he felt. Siu Wah hasn't done anything other than lightly touch her on the back when they're crossing the road. She gets frustrated and loses her temper at him. Siu Wah doesn't know why she's angry, but absorbs the tantrum and calls her a couple of days later to ask how she's feeling. His good nature makes her feel both confused and guilty.

She also wonders if Siu Wah might be gay. She's very confident in her own attractiveness, yet Siu Wah doesn't show any sign of desiring her or wanting to touch her. He doesn't ask her out often, and it's mostly her arranging to meet him for coffee. He doesn't seem particularly occupied or devoted to his work, but he disappears for an entire month, and when she asks him out, he claims he's busy, though he can't say what with. Doesn't he miss her? She certainly thinks of him a lot when too much time goes by without them meeting.

Does Siu Wah prefer men? He often talks about Eldest Brother, and his expression and tone of voice tell Yu Sau that he greatly admires Kim Chau. He frequently remarks on how much she looks like Eldest Brother, and says if she were ever to play a young male lead, she'd be just as dashing as him. Does Siu Wah only like her because of Eldest Brother?

Yu Sau quickly talks herself out of her fears. Siu Wah's definitely interested in women, because he's already been in love with one. He was with Chang Mun Yee, and she broke his heart. That means he's not gay. He doesn't seem gay, anyway. She's never seen him look at a man the way he looks at her. Yes, it's in his eyes. She can sense his love in the way he gazes at her. Did he ever stare at Eldest Brother like that? Surely not! He loves her. So why doesn't he show it? For example, he could hug her, or give her a little kiss. At least hold her hand, or put

his arm around her waist. Does she need to give him a hint?
Siu Wah said he has an inferiority complex. It's true, he does.

YU SAU AND SIU WAH

1. MEETING KAH ONN AGAIN

On Saturday evening, Yu Sau and Siu Wah stroll down Orchard Road. Siu Wah's hands are behind his back, and Yu Sau's clutch her handbag. She talks randomly about her week: her run-in with a road hog on the way to work, her lunchtime encounter with an old classmate she hadn't seen in years, and so on. She has a lot to say to Siu Wah. He mostly looks straight ahead, but turns to smile and nod at her every now and then. Although he looks very interested in her words, he is actually struggling to stay in the moment because his feelings for her are so overwhelming.

Outside Ngee Ann City, they stop to look at a human statue in a black hat and weird-looking long black robe, his face powdered white with a bright red nose and lips painted into an exaggerated smile. His eyes look enormous beneath fake eyelashes. Yu Sau and Siu Wah are fascinated.

"That can't be easy. He's not even blinking," says Siu Wah. Her eyes drift to her left, and there is Kah Onn.

He is separated from them by a few white people, probably tourists. He wears a date-red long-sleeved shirt, which suits his boyish face and draws out the colour in his lips. The last time she ran into him with Siu Wah, she emerged a little shaken, but now she feels nothing at all. He barely seems worth bothering with. Hoping to get away without him seeing them, she lightly tugs Siu Wah's arm and says, "Let's go."

Unfortunately, she's too late. No sooner has she taken Siu Wah's hand and started walking away, when she hears Kah Onn calling her name. As she turns around, she instinctively draws closer to Siu Wah and leans into him.

213

Kah Onn is grinning as he comes over with his friends. "Out for a walk?" he says, his voice a little stiff.

"Uh-huh." Yu Sau nods and smiles politely. She sees Kah Onn's eyes flicker over to Siu Wah, and clutches his hand more tightly. Her upper body tilts like the leaning tower of Pisa, coming to rest against his shoulder.

Kah Onn hesitates for a moment, then reaches out a hand to Siu Wah. "Congratulations," he says. His smile looks forced.

Siu Wah seems confused as he shakes Kah Onn's hand.

"I'm leaving for Shanghai for work next week. All the best for your wedding." He waves at Yu Sau and Siu Wah, then he and his friends disappear into the crowds.

Siu Wah has no idea what Kah Onn was talking about, but still beams happily at Yu Sau.

"My ex. You've seen him before," Yu Sau explains. "After we met last time, he kept pestering me, so I told him you were my fiancé and we were getting married soon." She ducks her head, but he can still see her blush.

Siu Wah grunts in acknowledgement, and his arm remains around her shoulders. Yu Sau's heart is a jumble of emotions. What must Siu Wah think of her, that she would tell such a lie to Kah Onn? Could he ever be her fiancé for real? Is Kah Onn really moving to Shanghai, or is this another trick? Or maybe it's true. In any case, he seems to have accepted that they won't be getting back together again. How come they've bumped into him twice on Orchard Road? Is that really a coincidence? Because it's convenient, she often came her after work with Geok Leng, Sandy or Kah Onn. Has he been lying in wait because he knows she spends a lot of her free time here? But how is that possible, on such a long street? No, Kah Onn might be jealous, but he's not an obsessive. Anyway, they should avoid Orchard Road from now on. Complicated feelings swirl inside her. Her unease over Kah Onn has more or less evaporated, but now she feels a bit sad and lost. Maybe she and Siu Wah should hang out in kopitiams instead. They'll never meet Kah Onn there, he didn't like those places. The first time Siu Wah brought her to a kopitiam for lunch, he said he was worried she wouldn't like the noise and heat, because he thought of her as someone who preferred restaurants and cafés. She smiled and said her grandpa owned a kopitiam, so she practically grew up in one. In fact, when she first came back from England, she still mostly went to kopitiams. When did she start spending more time in fancier places? Was it when she started working in finance and hanging out with Geok Leng and Sandy?

"Let's go to the kopitiam in Small Town. I feel like chicken rice for dinner," she says to Siu Wah.

"Sure."

"Let's walk."

"Okay."

Siu Wah is silent after that. They walk for a bit, and Yu Sau realises she isn't speaking either, just leaning against him. She can feel the warmth of his shoulder.

They stroll along slowly, not talking. Although people are jostling past them on the crowded street, Yu Sau's mind is blank, apart from the image of the man dressed like a clown, standing perfectly still, not even blinking. Everything seems to quieten down. The cars and crowds vanish. It's so still, she feels as if she can hear the crisp clicking of her heels on the pavement, her own heartbeat, and maybe Siu Wah's too. The twilight is beginning to fade, and without her noticing, the streetlamps and neon signs have come on. They've wandered quite far down the road by now, and are at the little park opposite the Istana.

There are only a few people here. Her face grows hot, and her heart thumps violently. She stops walking and looks up at Siu Wah. He stares back at her, a little stunned, looking into her liquid eyes, her faintly flushed cheeks, her slightly open mouth. Her face draws closer. The tips of their noses are almost touching. His lips are very close to hers. He hears a low sound like a moan in her throat, and realises his hands are on her waist.

"Hold me," she murmurs.

He reaches out to wrap his arms around her, and after a moment's uncertainty, starts running his hands over her bare shoulders, her back, her neck. His cheek rubs against hers.

"Kiss me, kiss me—" Her eyes are shut and she is breathing hard. Her body presses close to his. Even with their clothes between them, he can feel her warm, soft breasts, and something urgent stirs in his chest. Very gently, he presses his mouth to hers.

Almost two years after their first encounter, they share their first kiss.

Yu Sau lets out a shaky breath. Siu Wah looks at her anxiously, not knowing what this means.

"Do you love me?" She looks up at him.

"Yes, of course!" he hastily answers, looking at her besottedly, greedily. He folds her into his arms again.

"Because I let you kiss me?"

"No, I've loved you almost as long as I've known you."

"Why didn't you say anything?"

"I was afraid you'd turn me down."

Yu Sau smiles at him and throws her arms around his neck. "Kiss me again," she says.

2. DREAMS ARE FINE, BUT MONEY IS ESSENTIAL

NOW THAT SIU WAH HAS CONFESSED HIS LOVE FOR YU SAU, the first order of business is to give up his dreams of becoming a writer. He decides to look for an office job, and finds one at a company that publishes popular magazines.

He struggles a little with accepting this job. He had such huge ambitions, not only to be an author, but a playwright as well. He read that Neil Simon spent three years on his first script, producing more than twenty drafts, until he finally made it to Broadway. That play was a hit: it ran for 678 performances, and made him famous. Siu Wah has a great idea for a play. If he could just spend three or four years developing it, like Neil Simon, he is sure it would do well, assuming he could ever get it staged. Of course, no play would ever receive 678 performances in Singapore, but he can aim for 20. These days, getting 20 performances of a Chinese play is considered a big success. Up to now, this has been his dream. People say love is blind, but as far as Siu Wah is concerned, love has opened his eyes to reality. He understands that when poverty comes in the front door, love flees through a window. And so he rouses himself from his beautiful dream. Even ignoring the fact that the Chinese-language theatre scene is in a slump, even if he really did spend three or four years writing an excellent script, who would ever produce it? Local theatre companies keep complaining that there's a shortage of good plays, but in the end they only commission people they know, or else perform overseas work in translation. No matter how well you write, no company would use a script by someone outside their circle.

As for writing a novel, his other dream, he sets that aside too. Who would publish it? And even if he gets it published, so what? Would anyone read it? Could he support himself by selling four or five hundred copies? After telling Yu Sau he loves her, he starts taking a closer look at his dreams, and the more he thinks about this, the more depressed he gets.

Dreams are fine, but money is essential. That's a quote from Lu Xun. In the end, Siu Wah counts himself lucky to have found a nine-to-five job.

3. WHY ARE YOU IN SUCH A HURRY TO GET MARRIED? IS IT YOUR HORMONES?

Yu Sau tells her friends that she has decided to marry Siu Wah. Sandy doesn't seem surprised, even though she'd previously said she didn't believe this would ever happen. Geok Leng is a little suspicious, and asks Yu Sau, "Are you sure about this?"

"I've thought about this a lot," says Yu Sau. "I'm not that young any more. If I don't get married soon, I'll be left on the shelf."

"I'm older than you, and still single. I don't think I've been left on the shelf. Why are you in such a hurry to get married? Is it your hormones?" says Geok Leng.

"Maybe. Anyway it's better to have kids young."

"In any case, Siu Wah is a good man," says Sandy.

"I think so too," Geok Leng agrees.

Once they realise that Yu Sau is serious, they start praising Siu Wah.

"One good thing about marrying someone like Siu Wah," Yu Sau jokes. "He doesn't have money or good looks, so he'll behave himself."

"And you can bond over Cantonese opera," says Sandy.

"We've stopped going to the clan association," says Yu Sau. "I just sing at home in my spare time. It's a shame we both sing 'level throat', so we can't duet. I want to change to another voice part. Hey, when are you and Shing Yip getting married? Have your hormones kicked in?"

"We have no common interests, and our personalities are so different. I think we should take a break and see what happens." Sandy shrugs.

Some time later, Geok Leng tells Yu Sau that Sandy hasn't just taken a break from Shing Yip, she's gone out and found a new boyfriend.

4. THE BOOKCASES ARE STILL QUITE STURDY, BUT WHO WILL HE GIVE THEM TO?

SIU WAH'S MUM SAYS GETTING MARRIED IS A VERY important decision, and he should think it over carefully. Yu Sau is beautiful, as well as better-educated and higher-earning than him. Won't that be stressful? Siu Wah reassures his mother: Yu Sau doesn't mind him being less accomplished, and he doesn't either. His mother can only trust him.

True, Yu Sau doesn't seem like a haughty women. When Siu Wah first brought her home to meet his mother, she was so polite, always saying Auntie this and Auntie that. Of course, after they're married, she'll have to call her "Mum." Yu Sau suggested they all live together after the wedding, but Siu Wah and his mother live in a three-room HDB flat, just two bedrooms and a living room. Yu Sau has a five-room place, with an additional bedroom and dining room. Should Siu Wah rent out his flat, and have his mum move in with them? But Siu Wah's mother doesn't want to leave her familiar surroundings and neighbours. The real reason, though, is that it's easy for Yu Sau to treat her nicely when they only see each other occasionally; living together as mother- and daughter-in-law might be much more fractious. After much thought, she decides she'd rather be on her own. If Yu Sau and Siu Wah have a baby, she tells them, she'll definitely come help with the childcare. Siu Wah is uneasy about his aged mother living on her own, but she insists on staying put, and there's no changing her mind, so he arranges to rent his former bedroom to a Malaysian couple they know. This way, his mum will have people around her, and they'll have a bit of extra income.

What worries Siu Wah most is his book collection. Since he started buying them in secondary school, he has amassed enough to fill several bookcases: two big ones in the living room, and three more in his bedroom. He reads all kinds of books. Not just film, theatre and literature, but also volumes of philosophy, history, art and music. He might not have as many as a real collector, but there are enough to be a problem if he wants to rent out his room. He can't just move everything to Yu Sau's flat, can he? When he mentioned it to her, she didn't object to his library moving to her home (soon to be their home), but she reminded him to leave some space for when they have a baby.

Siu Wah knows children need a lot of space, and so he starts to cull his collection ruthlessly, keeping only the books on film and theatre, plus some famous classics (of course he's not getting rid of *Dream of the Red Chamber* or *Anna Karenina*). Everything else goes to a second-hand bookshop in Bras Basah Complex: literature from China, Taiwan and Hong Kong, aesthetic theory, philosophy (including Tang Chun-i, Mou Zongsan, Ch'ien Mu, and Bertrand Russell's *A History of Western Philosophy*), Chinese studies (more than ten works of classical sinology in modern editions, published by San Min and Commercial Press), history (not just Chinese and world history, but also the histories of literature, music and art).

When he reluctantly gets rid of the first batch of books, he feels depressed. It's not that he's hardly offered any money, but rather because he may never be able to replace some of these. Yet his heartache is rather ironic. When these books were on his shelves, he rarely touched them, and some he never even got round to opening. An unread book is just so much scrap paper; it might as well not exist. It doesn't matter whether or not it's on the shelf, so why be so sad to sell it? After another two or three trips to the second-hand shop, he starts to feel differently. His heart is steel, without the faintest twinge of sorrow or regret. He is as unmoved as if these were boxes of waste paper. But is he really unmoved? No one but Siu Wah himself could know that. One thing is certain: he can never patronise this shop again, for fear of seeing his own abandoned books for sale.

After he gets rid of the final box of unwanted books, the empty shelves make the room look much larger. He walks around one last time, and just before he closes the door, glances back the way a hotel guest might take a final look at the room he spent a few nights in. The bookcases are still quite sturdy, but who will he give them to, if the new tenant doesn't want them? He doesn't know a single person who enjoys reading.

Siu Wah sorts out the books he wants to bring to his new home, just four boxes, about one bookcase. Yu Sau won't think that's too many, will she? He has decided to stop buying books from now on. That won't be difficult: if he can stop dreaming about becoming a playwright or author, then he won't want any books. After all, he and Yu Sau might have more than one child, and children need so much more space as they get bigger.

5. HER HEART CONTINUES TO CHURN WITH UNEASE

EVEN AFTER YU SAU DECIDES TO MARRY SIU WAH, HER HEART continues to churn with unease. She keeps asking herself if she made the right choice. It's only been a year; how well does she know Siu Wah? And he her? In the past, when Kah Onn said he loved her, she worried he was just heartbroken, in a hurry to find someone to fill his emptiness and heal his wounds. And her? She broke up with Kah Onn less than a year ago, and in that time she's fallen in love with Siu Wah and accepted his proposal. Is that too much of a rush? No, she tells herself, she's different from Kah Onn. She's a woman, and if she wants to have children, she can't wait too long to get married. This thought makes her hate Kah Onn for his selfishness and irresponsibility. He only wanted to possess her and satisfy his desires, but not to marry her. She wasted so much time and emotion on him.

Still, she decided to marry Siu Wah very quickly. How long will this last? Love requires understanding. Do they understand each other well enough? She firmly believes that Siu Wah is an honest, dutiful man who won't betray her. It's herself she worries about. She isn't sure she loves Siu Wah. Perhaps she only admires his talent and character. Does she really know him? Marriages don't necessarily fail through affairs or divorce. So many couples start out from a basis of familiarity but insufficient understanding, and end up as bitter enemies, torturing each other into old age.

Now that Siu Wah has a stable job at a publishing house, she's noticed he doesn't look as carefree as before, but frequently seems tired and distracted. When she asks if work is weighing on him, he laughs and says he's gotten too used to freedom, but hopefully he'll adapt to this nine-to-five life soon. In any case, this proves how much he loves her, to give up freelancing just for her.

6. HAVE YOU GIVEN UP ON YOUR DREAMS?

After Siu Wah moves his books to Yu Sau's flat, she often finds him staring blankly at the bookcase. She knows he sold most of his collection to a second-hand shop, and asks if there were some he misses. He shakes his head and says it's fine, he wouldn't have read them again anyway.

When she sees him at the bookcase again, she gets concerned and asks what he's thinking.

"It's strange that I kept this one." He pulls out *Moby-Dick*. "It's supposed to be a great novel, but I only read a couple of pages right after I bought it. I've had it almost ten years, and haven't touched it since then." He smiles wryly as he flicks through it.

Before he can return it to the shelf, Yu Sau takes it from him. "I'll read it when I have time," she says. "Shame this is a Chinese translation, I'm not sure I'll understand all of it."

As she puts the book back, Siu Wah reaches for another one. "This is Chen Yinke's *The Biography of Liu Rushi*. I'm not advanced enough to read this. If we hadn't been learning 'Sorrowful Parting at the Southern Tower', I'd have got rid of it long ago."

"Don't, you'll need it for research when you write your Cantonese opera about Liu Rushi." Yu Sau grabs his hands, as if she's actually afraid he might throw it away right now.

"You're joking, aren't you? I'm nowhere near knowledgeable enough to make sense of this book, and barely understand Cantonese opera. *Are you mistaking me for Tang Ti-sheng?*" He turns and grins at her.

"You told me you wanted to be an author. You wanted to write a play and a novel."

"Let's talk about that another time."

"Have you given up on your dreams?" she asks.

"In this country, they were fantasies, not dreams. So what if I've given them up, as long as we can live together happily?"

Yu Sau is moved by this, but also a little sad. "You're so talented. It's a pity," she says.

LEONG KIM MING

1. ALMOST ALL THE FAMILIAR BUILDINGS AND STREET MARKETS ARE GONE

IN THE SIXTIES, KIM MING WAS EXILED FOR HIS LEFTIST activities. He was worried about getting stopped at the airport coming back into Singapore, and didn't return even after gaining Hong Kong citizenship. Now Yu Sau is getting married, and he decides to come back for the wedding.

Thirty years after his departure, Kim Ming steps back into the country of his birth. Queueing at immigration, he feels a complicated mix of anxiety and uncertainty. In the end, there are no problems at all. His unfounded fears now feel ridiculous and misguided. Of course, he also didn't come back because he didn't like the political regime, but he regrets not making the trip for his parents' and grandpa's funerals.

Kim Ming walks out, wheeling his suitcase behind him, and spots Yu Sau in the crowd. She introduces Siu Wah, and they go for lunch at an airport restaurant before heading back to Siu Wah's flat. Yu Sau explains that they're not moving in together until after the wedding. She'll be busy with work and the final details of the ceremony over the next few days, so she won't have time to keep him company. It'll be better if he stays with Siu Wah, who has taken leave and can look after him.

"You'll have to share a bed with Siu Wah, though."

"That's fine!" Kim Ming says.

"No, I'll sleep on the living room sofa," says Siu Wah.

Apart from a couple of days when he has to help Yu Sau with wedding stuff, Siu Wah takes Kim Ming out sightseeing every day after breakfast. In the evenings and at the weekend, Yu Sau drives him around too. On the ride from the airport, Kim

Ming notices that his hometown has completely transformed, and now resembles Hong Kong: a modern city crammed with skyscrapers. There are even fewer older buildings than in Hong Kong. On his drives with Yu Sau and Siu Wah, he receives an intense, complex series of impressions. The place where he grew up looks completely different. Almost all the familiar buildings and street markets are gone, replaced by strange new constructions. When he walks around, he feels like a tourist in a foreign land, rather than someone returning home. Before setting off for Singapore, he dug up some old friends' addresses and phone numbers. Now that he's here, he can't find a single one of them. Their homes have been torn down, and even the roads have different names. As for the phone numbers, forget it. Not one of them works.

2. WE AREN'T USED TO PROTESTING. WE JUST SUFFER, COMPLAIN, AND THEN FORGET

AT THEIR FLAT, SIU WAH AND HIS MOTHER TALK TO KIM Ming about the old Singapore. This is how Kim Ming finds out that the stone lions on Merdeka Bridge, Kallang Embankment and Kallang Park are all gone. The National Theatre has been demolished too.

"Those were symbols of our nation-building. How could they be torn down?" he says, sad and angry.

"According to the government, it's for development." Siu Wah smiles bitterly.

"For the sake of development, they'll wipe away our memories of nation-building?" The question isn't directed at Siu Wah, of course, but at the government "developing" Singapore on behalf of its people. "Kallang Park was built in the name of development too. When the PAP won the 1959 election, Ong Eng Guan announced that they were turning

Kallang Airport into a park and children's playground," Kim Ming tells Siu Wah.

"Ong Eng Guan?" Siu Wah looks confused.

"*I know! He was the MP for Hong Lim,*" says Siu Wah's mother.

"That's right, Auntie. Good memory. He was also the first elected mayor of Singapore!" Kim Ming says, as Siu Wah's mother beams. Siu Wah is a little embarrassed, and awkwardly explains that he doesn't pay much attention to politics. Kim Ming says if young Singaporeans like Siu Wah don't know or can't remember who Ong Eng Guan was, then many other pioneering figures will surely disappear from history, vanishing like the buildings they put up.

"He was the Minister for National Development," Kim Ming adds, as more memories return to him. In 1959, when he was about ten, Auntie Yeuk Lan took part in the construction of Kallang Embankment. One morning in late July, she put on her overalls, picked up her tools, and enthusiastically went off to join the thousand or so volunteers gathered at the Padang. They marched to the site and got to work. It was the same every Sunday and public holiday from then on. In fact, more and more people took part each time. And now, the government has torn it down on a whim, wasting all this passion and effort.

Kim Ming says to Siu Wah, "In 1963, right after the National Theatre was built, Singapore organised a Southeast Asia Cultural Festival there. I saw artistes from Phoenix and Great Wall performing there, including my idols Shi Hui and Fu Qi. Have you heard of them?"

"Yes, of course! And also Hsia Moon, Sisi Chen, Bao Fong, Wang Xiaoyan, Tseng Chang, Ping Fang..." Without pausing for breath, Siu Wah names a string of performers from these two studios. "I'm quite familiar with movie actors," he adds, a little shame-faced.

"I was just fourteen years old then," Kim Ming continues.

"I was so excited! When did they tear down the National Theatre?"

"I think it was around 1986," Siu Wah says, glancing uncertainly at his mother.

"*I don't remember!*" She smiles and shakes her head.

"Did you know? The National Theatre was built with donations from citizens. One dollar a brick. I was still a schoolboy, but I donated too. At least one brick. Now they've torn it down, did they keep the bricks?" Kim Ming asks.

"Probably not." Siu Wah looks bemused, and a little foolish. He can't tell if Kim Ming is serious or joking. Did they keep the bricks? How would he know?

"Did anyone protest?" Kim Ming asks.

Siu Wah hesitates. "I don't think so. We aren't used to protesting. We just suffer, complain, and then forget."

"Oh." Kim Ming's rage quickly subsides. He's no longer angry, just disappointed and alienated. He once loved this place, but now it's unfamiliar to him. He feels like a foreigner criticising a country that has nothing to do with him. He's uneasy, and apologetic for his presence.

Even so, Kim Ming is delighted to be here for his little sister's wedding. At the banquet, he represents the bride's family on stage, standing with Yu Sau to offer the guests a toast. He calls out *yam seng* from deep in his throat, until tears come to his eyes. He remembers how Yu Sau would pester him and whine when she was a little girl. And here she is in her wedding finery, standing next to him. She's beautiful. What a pity Eldest Brother isn't here.

He drinks a lot that night, more than he's ever drunk in his life.

YU SAU

1. SECOND UNCLE IS DEAD

It's almost midnight when Yu Sau and Siu Wah return from their ten-day honeymoon in Europe. Yu Sau has a voicemail from Kim Ming: Second Uncle is dead. it's shocking news, but she feels no more than she would if an old friend she hadn't seen for a long time were to pass. She can't have been close to him, if she feels so unaffected now. When she tells Siu Wah her uncle is dead, her voice is flat, as if she's mentioning a newspaper obituary of some has-been celebrity. She and Siu Wah unpack, set aside the dirty clothes to wash later, have a shower, brew some camomile tea, and go through their mail. Afterwards, she calls Kim Ming.

Kim Ming sounds sad on the phone. He tells Yu Sau that he got a phone call from a woman in Guangzhou, who told him Second Uncle had had a heart attack a month ago, and was dead before they could get him to hospital.

"Why did it take her so long to call you?" she asks, suspicious. "Was she Second Uncle's wife, our Second Aunt?"

"I didn't ask. I mean, I didn't ask why she took so long to call. And I don't think she's our Second Aunt. She told me to call her Miss Huang, and said she was Second Uncle's friend. She found my number going through his stuff. I thought it was strange: if she wasn't very close to Second Uncle, how did she end up sorting out his possessions? I asked how I could get hold of her, but she said there was no point, she was moving in a couple of days. She read out the address I gave Second Uncle, to make sure I still lived there. Second Uncle didn't leave much, just some personal documents: his identity card, passport, university cert, plus some photos and letters. She's sending them all to me, though so far they haven't arrived yet."

"That's a strange phone call." Yu Sau is still doubtful. "We still don't know who this Miss Huang is, and she didn't give you any information other than that Second Uncle's dead. Is he really dead? We don't know. Do you believe her? If he really did pass away, do you think he'd have left nothing at all except some personal documents?"

"I think she may have been the woman Second Uncle was living with, but she didn't want to say that because they weren't married. Or maybe she's keeping her identity secret because she has some kind of shady past. Anyway, she had no reason to deceive me. She spent money on that long distance call, and what did she get out of it? If she'd killed him or stolen his possessions, she wouldn't have called at all. I think she felt it was her duty. Maybe it helped her set her heart at rest."

They start sharing their memories of Second Uncle. As they reminisce, Yu Sau starts feeling a sense of loss. She wasn't close to Second Uncle, and her impression of him is hazy. All she can recall is that he was very particular about his clothes, and seldom spent time at home. He never helped out at the kopitiam. When she was a child, the whole family would eat lunch and dinner with the servers at the shop, and as her mum said, he only put in an appearance when it was time to eat. Mum hadn't liked Second Uncle. She said he aimed too high, and took too many short cuts. After he came back from studying in America and went into business, he paid even more attention to his wardrobe. Sometimes he came to see Grandpa all dapper in a long-sleeved shirt and tie, but Mum said he was being pretentious, and all he'd learnt in that fancy university was how to fill his diaper with crap. (Yes, *crap*, that's what she said, she really was that harsh on him.) He was always borrowing money from Grandpa, and sometimes from Dad too. He never paid them back.

Yu Sau has a sudden thought: Grandpa lived till almost

ninety, and never had any serious health problems. Why have all his children died of strokes or heart disease? Auntie killed herself, so that doesn't count, but Second Uncle would have been around sixty-six, and her father was just sixty when he died, both short-lived by comparison. She sighs and says to Kim Ming that they both have their parents' genes, and might get the same illnesses. Knowing that Kim Ming is a bachelor, she reminds him to eat properly and take care of his health.

After the phone call, Yu Sau is sad for a while. Second Uncle's death still feels unresolved, but at least someone told Second Brother. What about Eldest Brother? If something happens to him, who's going to tell them? She misses him, and hopes very much that he's still alive.

2. MARRIED LIFE

EVEN AS A NEWLY-WED, YU SAU FINDS HERSELF OCCASIONALLY thinking of Kah Onn and remembering their time together. This isn't because married life with Siu Wah is unhappy in any way, only that she was with Kah Onn for so long, it isn't easy to forget.

Kah Onn was very different from Siu Wah. He was much more passionate in bed. Maybe that was just lust, not love, but it clings to her mind. She is sure Kah Onn still misses her, given how jealous and possessive he is, which makes her think of him even more. She knows she's very important to him, but then so was his ex, which was the problem. Before breaking up for the first time, Yu Sau and Kah Onn were inseparable, practically living together. She probably understood him better than she does Siu Wah, whom she's only just married. Of course, that was just an illusion (she tells herself it's an illusion), and they split up in the end. Yu Sau feels a little guilty thinking about Kah Onn. She is Siu Wah's wife now, and shouldn't have other men on her mind. She definitely shouldn't be comparing Siu Wan and Kah Onn.

And yet, for a long time into her marriage, Yu Sau finds herself plagued by the same questions that unsettled her before. Did she rush into this? She's known Siu Wah for much less time than she knew Kah Onn, and didn't get as close to him before they were married. Does she know him well enough? There's no doubt that Siu Wah is a good man, and he loves her. But is that enough? It's not easy for two people with different upbringings to get together. You need to live with someone for quite some time before you learn all their foibles and habits. Before moving in with Siu Wah, she thought he was a good conversationalist: not only was he knowledgeable about theatre and film, he listened attentively when she spoke, rather than being over-eager to interrupt and share his opinion like Kah Onn, who would then change the subject to something he was interested in. Kah Onn was very rigid in his opinions, and so the two of them would frequently get into arguments for no reason. Siu Wah is a good listener, and hardly ever disagrees with her. He's the sort of person it's easy to unburden yourself to, and Yu Sau is surprised at how many things she told him, soon after they met, that she'd never shared with anyone before. For example, she'd only seen him a few times when she came clean about her awful relationship with her mother. It's only after the wedding that she starts noticing he's actually quite detached, and isn't particularly interested in many people or things. His easy-going nature and willingness to give in to her starts to seem irresolute, as if he has no opinions of his own. When she offers him a choice, he always answers that he doesn't mind, and she ends up making most of the decisions. What's more, he never tells her afterwards whether or not he likes what she chose.

Siu Wah doesn't enjoy socialising. She doesn't know whether it's out of low self-esteem or introversion, but he's never keen to hang out with her colleagues, and keeps finding excuses not to join in their gatherings. (He's skipped so many, she knows they are just excuses.) Even when she manages to drag him along, he sits quietly in a corner, outside the circle of conversation. Now and then he'll say something vague, but it's obvious that he's not really present. Before they got married, Siu Wah would often say he had an inferiority complex, but she never believed him. How could someone so talented, with so many radio scripts to his name, be down on himself? Now that she's actually living with him, she can see what he means. A big part of this might be his lack of higher education. He only studied up to secondary school, and was Chinese-educated. His English grammar isn't great; he's always using the wrong tense or mixing up words. Yu Sau doesn't mind this (although she can't help wondering how he learnt so much about western film and literature, with such poor English) and doesn't think her friends do either. They know he's Chinese-ed, and their Mandarin is much worse than his English, so they'd never make fun of him. Yet he acts all sensitive when she corrects his grammar mistakes, which she finds frustrating.

Siu Wah's easy-going nature extends to his wardrobe. He goes around in the same old white or blue shirts and black trousers, After the wedding, she buys him a few more colourful outfits, but he says he feels more comfortable in his usual clothes. Sometimes he actually looks dishevelled, and goes out with his collar twisted or his shirt buttoned up wrong. His pockets are stained with ink from when he forgets to put the caps back on his ballpoint pens. (Why didn't she notice any of this before they were married? Has he only become so slapdash now? Was he like this when he worked at the radio station? Or did he change after leaving that job?) When he's with her colleagues, everything about him feels wrong: his clothes, his words, his point of view. He doesn't fit in. Luckily, her unhappiness over this hasn't affected their marriage so far.

After she gets over her anger, Yu Sau continues to believe she'll change him for the better. His taste in clothes, for example, is slowly getting less staid. Eventually, he'll adjust to sharing a social life with her.

3. SECOND UNCLE'S POSSESSIONS

KIM MING CALLS AGAIN. MISS HUANG SENT OVER A large envelope with Second Uncle's identity documents, school certificates, business contracts and so on, as well as photographs of him and his friends, many of whom are women. Miss Huang probably isn't in any of them, because she seems determined to keep her identity secret, and would have removed any pictures she appeared in. That said, even if one of these women was her, Kim Ming would have no way of knowing which one.

Second Uncle's possessions don't hold much meaning for Kim Ming, now that he's passed away. There are a couple of items that pique his curiosity, though: two photographs and a letter from an older man named Leong Siu Tak.

The photos were taken at different times; one is dated 1987, the other 1993. Both of these, and the letter, are stuffed into an envelope: recorded delivery, returned from Singapore to Guangzhou, with a 1987 postmark. It's addressed to Mr Leong Ping Hung, that is, Grandpa, at the kopitiam he used to own. Kim Ming thinks it was returned to sender because the kopitiam had been torn down. The letter asks how Grandpa is doing, and says the writer no longer appears on stage, having been injured during the Cultural Revolution. He is sad that Ah Yoke (that must be Grandma) has passed away, sends his condolences, and urges Grandpa to take good care of himself. They're all getting on, and don't have much time left on earth, so he hopes they can let go of the past. He mentions that he saw Grandpa and Ah Yoke's son Kung Woo (that is, Second Uncle) and was very happy to find him so accomplished, with a successful business on the Mainland. He heard from Kung Woo that Grandpa's eldest son, Kung Man (Yu Sau and Kim Ming's father) was doing well in Singapore, and was happy for Grandpa. Leong Siu Tak married late, and his wife died a few years ago. They never had any children, and now he was hoping to take Second Uncle as his godson. Grandpa's brother Kit and sister Sai, he adds, died during the Japanese invasion of China.

Yu Sau and Kim Ming aren't surprised that Mr Leong Siu Tak was a fan of Second Uncle. He was always such a smooth talker, and could flatter you outrageously without turning a hair. Old people and women he didn't know him well were easily taken in by this.

"Every time we spoke on the phone, he'd tell me he'd just concluded a multi-million dollar deal, and the money was coming in any day now. I never believed him, but didn't have the heart to argue," says Kim Ming.

"Why not?" asks Yu Sau.

"He told so many lies, I was afraid he'd started believing them himself. He depended on those lies to go on living. It would have been cruel to expose him."

Yu Sau and Kim Ming guess that Leong Siu Tak must be Tak Chai, the opera singer Grandpa often mentioned, the new Siu Kai. That photograph from 1987 must be the first time he met Second Uncle, and Second Uncle probably looked him up because Grandpa asked him to.

"But Second Uncle left Singapore in the seventies. Why did it take him until 1987 to find Grandpa's old friend? If he'd done it in the seventies or early eighties, Grandpa might have been able to renew his friendship with Tak Chai. Now they'll have to meet in the afterlife," Yu Sau sighs.

"So when Second Uncle visited him again in 1993, the old

man gave him both photographs and the letter, hoping he'd pass them on to Grandpa. But of course, Grandpa was already dead," says Kim Ming. "I did tell Second Uncle when Grandpa died, but he never mentioned having seen Grandpa's old friend."

"Why does he say to forget the past? What happened?" Yu Sau asks.

Kim Ming has no idea.

And they still don't know who Miss Huang is.

But that's how the world is, you're never going to understand everything. Second Brother says, "Maybe they weren't as close as we're imagining. Maybe she and Second Uncle were just friends. It's very good of her to take care of his affairs and send us his stuff."

4. OF COURSE I HAVE GIRLFRIENDS, BUT I STILL HAVEN'T FOUND THE RIGHT WOMAN

IN THE SECOND YEAR OF THEIR MARRIAGE, YU SAU GETS pregnant. She worries that something will be wrong with the child because of her age, and takes every possible precaution. Unexpectedly, this is when Siu Wah snaps out of his distracted approach to life, and grows cautious too, taking exceptionally good care of her. They don't have a domestic helper, so he does the bulk of the housework, and makes sure Yu Sau has everything she needs. He patiently puts up with her tantrums, soothes her, and tries to cheer her up. Most touchingly, he gets up at the crack of dawn every day to make her a delicious breakfast, and when there's time, he rides with her in the taxi to work or to see the doctor.

After a visit to the obstetrician, Siu Wah helps her and her enormous bump down a slope. They are about to cross the road to the taxi stand when they see Kah Onn coming towards them. He is paler than before, and has put on quite a bit of weight.

"Yu Sau!" calls Kah Onn. He turns around and follows them across the road.

"You're going to be a mother," he says, glancing at her belly and beaming warmly.

"Yes." She smiles at him.

"How are you?" says Siu Wah.

"Same old, same old." He shrugs.

"Are you still in Shanghai?" Siu Wah asks.

"Yes, I'm heading back there next week."

"Married?" Yu Sau asks.

Kah Onn shakes his head.

"Are your standards too high? A man like you surely has plenty of girlfriends," Yu Sau teases, leaning against Siu Wah.

"Of course I have girlfriends, but I still haven't found the right woman."

Yu Sau feels a jolt through her heart. She smiles meaningfully at Kah Onn, then looks sidelong at Siu Wah, who is still grinning foolishly.

"Is your mother well?" asks Yu Sau.

"Very well. When I'm not in Singapore, my little sister takes care of her."

"Tell her I said hi," says Yu Sau.

They chat a little longer, then go their separate ways.

KIM CHAU

AH, SHE REALLY DID RECOGNISE ME

He stops his trolley to collect a departing customer's used plates and cutlery. Just as he finishes clearing the table, a woman of about forty sits down. He notices her studying him a little doubtfully, and steals a closer look out of the corner of his eye. His heart thuds. Where has he seen her before? She watches him as he wipes the table, looking like she wants to say something. He ransacks his memory. Could she be a former fan? But no, it's been more than two decades, surely none of them remember him. He quickly finishes cleaning the table. As he turns away, she says a quiet thank you, which sends another tremor through him. Her voice is familiar too. Who is she? He can't resist stealing another look, and that's when he realises: she looks a lot like his sister, Yu Sau. Isn't she supposed to be in England? No, he has to remind himself, that was more than twenty years ago. She was so unhappy back then. She didn't like their family, especially their parents. Has she come back? It's been more than twenty years, of course she's come back. She'd be about the age of this woman. He pushes his trolley to another table and clears the crockery there. As he works, he keeps glancing back at the woman. Yes, it's Yu Sau. She was a teenager when he left home, but he recognises her features in this middle-aged woman. Her voice is the same too. It's her. Something wells up inside him. He's getting old and confused. How could he have forgotten his own sister?

When he came back to Singapore, he knew the day would come when he'd run into someone from his family. He thought he was prepared for this, but now that it's actually happened, he's all over the place. He remembers Grandpa. How odd, of all the people in his family, the first one to come to mind is the one he least wants to think of. Grandpa must be dead by now. What about his parents? And his little brother Kim Ming? His heart is a jumble of feelings, his brain a muddle of thoughts. He can't focus, and his hands shake so much he almost smashes a plate.

He pushes the trolley farther away and observes the woman from a distance. There's no mistake, this is definitely his little sister Yu Sau. Her face has changed a little, transforming her into a mature woman, but her expressions are the same as when she was young. The way she dabs at her lips with tissue paper when she's finished eating, the way she picks up the handbag from the back of her chair, the way she stands and turns to face him. He's afraid to meet her eye, and pretends to be busy stacking plates on the trolley as he pushes it away.

When he looks back at where she was standing, there's no one there. Did she recognise him? It was Kim Ming who always played with her when she was a child, not him. He's suffered a lot over the years, and that's aged him. She might not have known it was him, especially in this green T-shirt, this cleaner's uniform that strips away his individuality. He looks like just another old person clearing tables. He has a sudden urge to run after her, but doesn't.

He is standing there, letting this nonsense flow through his head, when she appears again on the crowded pavement. She must have turned around and come back. "Ah, she really did recognise me," he thinks. Before she can come in, he hurries to the men's bathroom.

From his hiding place, he hears one of the servers, Ah Lian.

"You mean Laifa?" Ah Lian is quiet for a while (probably looking around for him), then she says, "Maybe he's in the toilet."

He is Laifa. After coming back to Singapore, that's the name he used while job-hunting. He stays in the gents for quite a while, only coming out when he's waited long enough for the woman who might be his sister to have left.

YU SAU, SIU WAH, KIM CHAU

MY BODY BENDS LIKE A WILLOW BRANCH
IN THE WIND

Yu Sau tells Siu Wah about the man she saw clearing tables in the kopitiam.

"He looked a lot like Eldest Brother," she says. "But his hair was all grey, and his face was covered in wrinkles. Eldest Brother isn't that old. I wasn't sure it was him, so I didn't dare ask. As soon as I walked out, I realised I didn't want to let this go. So what if I might be wrong? I turned around and went back in, but he wasn't there. I spoke to a woman who said he was called Laifa." She frowns. "It probably wasn't him. Eldest Brother's ten years older than me, but this man looked around sixty. I don't think it was him. He used to play scholar-warrior roles. Such a dashing man. How could he stoop to this kind of work? But this Laifa really did look like Eldest Brother."

Siu Wah suspects Laifa is Kim Chau. If he wasn't there when Yu Sau went back inside, that means he doesn't want to be found.

"He just looked so old. All that white hair, and so scrawny. He can't be Eldest Brother." Yu Sau can't accept that the handsome figure she remembers could become so shrivelled and elderly.

"Tell me which kopitiam, and I'll go see. I know what he looks like, and I'm not a family member. Maybe he'll be willing to talk to me," says Siu Wah.

A couple of days later, Siu Wah heads to the kopitiam Yu Sau named for lunch. When the middle-aged woman at the next table finishes eating, the cleaner in a green T-shirt comes by with his trolley to clear her plate. He's a man of about sixty,

240

short and thin with white hair, his triangular face covered in wrinkles. A sparse moustache sprouts like weeds on his upper lip. He doesn't look like Kim Chau in any way. It's been a long time since Siu Wah set eyes on Kim Chau, but that clean-cut youth surely didn't end up getting so bedraggled?

Siu Wah goes back and describes the man to Yu Sau, who is dubious. This sounds like a different person altogether. Although the man she saw was frailer and more faded than the Eldest Brother she remembers, his features remained recognisable. Crucially, the person she saw didn't have a moustache. In order to be certain, Yu Sau and Siu Wah go back to the kopitiam together. Sure enough, the man Siu Wah described is there, but the one who looks like Eldest Brother is nowhere to be seen. She asks at the counter where she can find Laifa, and the girl says Laifa doesn't work there any more.

Yu Sau and Siu Wah are disappointed. Kim Chau must have quit his job in order to avoid Yu Sau, which makes her even more certain it was him. If he's hiding from her, though, she's not going to see him again. The thought fills her with sadness.

About a month later, Siu Wah goes back to that kopitiam for lunch. He sees a different man in a green T-shirt clearing tables. This one also has white hair, but his features are better-defined. The years have carved deep lines into his face, but his good looks are still visible underneath. This might be the first person Yu Sau saw.

Siu Wah continues studying him, closely observing those long, elegant fingers, the eyes and nose that are so similar to Yu Sau's. Now he's certain, and calls out, "*Brother Chau!*"

The man doesn't seem to hear, and continues clearing the table. Siu Wah tries again, louder this time. The man shoots him a sidelong glance and says impatiently, "Drink orders to the waitress." With that, he wheels his trolley to the next table. Siu Wah refuses to let it go. As the man starts walking away, Siu Wah quietly sings, "*My body bends like a willow branch in* the wind, tossed back and forth helplessly."

The man halts in his tracks and shakes his head. He stares at Siu Wah for some time, then chuckles. "Where did you learn that crap? So sentimental!"

Overjoyed, Siu Wah shoots back, "Brother Chau, I was afraid you wouldn't recognise me!"

"Siu Wah, you could be turned to ash and I'd know who you were."

Kim Chau pushes his trolley over and stands next to him.

Siu Wah excitedly explains that Yu Sau told him she'd seen a man who looked like her eldest brother, but when she went back to the kopitiam, he'd vanished. "She and I came back later to see if it really was you, but another man was clearing the tables. I thought I'd never get to see you, but here you are!"

Kim Chau admits it was him that Yu Sau saw, and he knew it was her, but didn't dare face her looking the way he does now. This kopitiam is part of a chain, he explains, and he wasn't deliberately staying away, his boss happened to send him to another branch. Then a cleaner here quit, so he was transferred back. He's conflicted about this, but wants to see Yu Sau. Instead, he's found Siu Wah, and is surprised to learn he knows Yu Sau too.

"It's fate," Siu Wah laughs. "Yu Sau's my wife. I'm your brother-in-law. Come by our flat after your shift. I'm sure she'll be delighted to see you."

Kim Chau hesitates, but Siu Wah tells him again how much Yu Sau has missed him, and finally manages to persuade him. "Not today, though," says Kim Chau. "I don't finish till late. How about Tuesday? I get Tuesdays off."

KIM CHAU

TALKING ABOUT THE PAST

Sɪᴜ Wᴀʜ ᴀʟsᴏ ᴀʀʀᴀɴɢᴇs ᴛᴏ sᴇᴇ Kɪᴍ Cʜᴀᴜ ғᴏʀ ᴅɪɴɴᴇʀ, just the two of them, before Tuesday.

Around closing time, Siu Wah turns up at the kopitiam. When his shift is done, Kim Chau changes out of his uniform, and they leave together. Siu Wah takes him to another kopitiam two streets away, one where he likes the food.

On the way, they pass a housing estate in which a temporary platform has been set up on a field. Several workers walk around the empty stage; one of them, apparently the supervisor, is pointing here and there, explaining something to them. It's almost Mid-Autumn, and they must be preparing for a getai. He wonders when they stopped performing Cantonese opera at Mid-Autumn, but doesn't ask. Siu Wah might not know the answer anyway. They cross the road and continue past a row of shops, and at the very end is the kopitiam.

Siu Wah orders two bottles of beer and some dishes: kung pao chicken, deep-fried ribs, kailan in garlic sauce.

"More than twenty years since we last shared a drink," says Siu Wah. *"Remember where we used to go back then?"*

"The Apollo Hotel," says Kim Chau. *"We'd have beer and coffee, all the way till dawn."*

They were young then, and didn't know what it meant to be tired. At least three or four times a week, they stayed up drinking all night at the Apollo Hotel's coffee house. More than twenty years ago. Siu Wah must think he's an old man now. Siu Wah's changed too. It's not just that he's aged and his hair has thinned, he seems like a completely different person. Siu Wah's a little younger, but must still be pushing fifty. He hardly has any wrinkles, but exhaustion is written all over his face, and the drive he had two decades ago has evaporated.

"How many plays have you written?" he asks.

"Not a single one."

"How about novels?"

"Writing novels in Singapore? I'd have starved to death by now."

"What do you do, then?"

"I edit lifestyle magazines for a commercial publisher. I just work hard and do my job. No more chasing dreams."

Kim Chau says nothing. The kopitiam's TV set is screening a Taiwanese soap opera: two women screaming at each other. Against their cacophony, he hears Siu Wah mumbling, almost to himself, *"I've changed. Now that I have a wife and son, it's my duty to be a good husband and father."*

Now it becomes clear: it's not time that aged Siu Wah, but the pain of giving up his dreams. He understands what his friend is saying. In a place like Singapore, chasing your dreams can only lead you over a cliff. He lowers his head in thought, while Siu Wah looks up and raises his glass. *"Cheers! Let's drink to seeing each other after more than twenty years."*

They eat and drink, chatting idly about local issues: how things are getting more and more expensive, or how immigrants these days come from so many different countries. When they get onto the old days hanging out at the Apollo Hotel, Kim Chau asks Siu Wah about their former colleagues at Rediffusion, and mutual friends in the showbiz world. Naturally, Chang Mun Yee's name comes up. Siu Wah tells him they split up, then she became a TV actress and married a Hong Kong businessmen. He hasn't stayed in touch with the rest of his former colleagues. When Kim Chau gave afternoon performances in the hotel lounge, Siu Wah used to come and support him, but he doesn't want to talk about that now. Instead, Siu Wah mentions that Lau Cho Wan is divorced.

"Not long after that, her ex-husband had a heart attack and died," he adds.

Lau Cho Wan? The name smites his heart. A woman he once loved, and he's all but forgotten her. What's she doing now? Maybe she's a grandmother. *"How did you find out?"*

Siu Wah says all this happened more than ten years ago. Lau Cho Wan was still singing then, and he read about it in the entertainment pages of the newspaper.

They get through three bottles of beer. Siu Wah is as much of a lightweight as before, or maybe he's gotten worse, and is tipsy after just one bottle. Kim Chau has the bulk of it, but remains completely sober. He built up quite a tolerance to alcohol after his time in the Hong Kong music scene. It's strange that Siu Wah hasn't asked about Hong Kong. Or maybe he can guess, from Kim Chau's current job and appearance, just how things went in Hong Kong. Even so, he's a little annoyed that Siu Wah doesn't ask. What does he mean by that? Is Siu Wah afraid of hurting his pride? He doesn't need anyone's pity.

"Why don't you ask me about Hong Kong?" he almost blurts out.

In the end, though, he keeps his mouth shut.

REUNION

WHATEVER YOU DO, DON'T LET HIM GO INTO OPERA WHEN HE GROWS UP

On Tuesday evening, Siu Wah brings Kim Chau home after work.

The front door opens. Standing there are Yu Sau, their child, and their Indonesian maid.

"*Eldest Brother!*" Yu Sau cries out, her voice full of emotion. She turns to the little boy next to her and says in Cantonese, "*Call uncle!*"

"*Uncle.*" The kid has just gotten home from kindergarten, and is still in his uniform of grass-green checks. He stares shyly at Kim Chau, his voice tentative.

"*Good boy. He speaks Cantonese!*" Kim Chau ruffles his hair. "*These days, most Singaporean children don't know any dialects.*"

"*I'm making a special effort to teach him! He's called Kwok Sau. Kwok as in 'country', Sau as in 'cultivated',*" Yu Sau says.

Kim Chau studies Kwok Sau's face. "He looks like you," he says to Yu Sau.

She beams. "*That means he looks like you too. Everyone says how much I look like my eldest brother.*" She turns back to the child. "*Kwok Sau, when you're grown up, you'll be as handsome as uncle, then you can be a scholar-warrior too!*"

Kim Chau is silent for a while, then says very solemnly, "*Whatever you do, don't let him go into opera when he grows up.*"

Yu Sau is momentarily embarrassed by his earnestness, but then cheers up again. It's so good to see Eldest Brother. She ushers him to the living room sofa. The helper sets out some snacks on the coffee table, then retreats to the kitchen. Out of excitement, Yu Sau can't stop babbling at Kim Chau, as if she needs to tell him two decades' worth of family news right this minute. She talks about studying in England, coming back to Singapore for work, moving back home to look after their ailing mother and grandfather, as well as Second Brother's life in China and Hong Kong. Their parents, grandpa, and aunt died, and now their uncle too.

"Second Brother is able to travel back to Singapore these days. He came for my wedding!" Yu Sau shows him photos from the day, and he flips through the album. When he comes to one of Kim Ming, he frowns. *"Is this Ming? I almost didn't recognise him."*

"I wish I'd found you sooner. Then you could have come to my wedding, and met Second Brother too," says Yu Sau sadly.

Whether because she's nervous or because she isn't used to being around Kim Chau, Yu Sau feels a little awkward speaking Cantonese. Her Cantonese improved a lot thanks to the singing class, but they stopped going before the wedding, and now Kwok Sau is here she doesn't even have time to listen to her recordings. She and Siu Wah usually speak Mandarin to each other, and apart from teaching her son some basic Cantonese, she hasn't had much contact with the language for years now. Her Cantonese was never strong, and this is a real effort. Nonetheless, she continues using it with Kim Chau.

Yu Sau wants to know what happened to Kim Chau after he left home, but he's unwilling to talk too much about it. All he'll say is that he sang at a Singaporean hotel lounge for a while, then moved to Hong Kong to perform opera, while also performing at a nightclub. That's all. More than two decades away from home, and he sums it up in under five minutes. Yu Sau asks how he ended up working at a nightclub, and he says simply he hurt his back performing on Cheung Chau Island, and couldn't do opera for quite a long time. He needed to earn money somehow, so when his friends told him about an opening at a nightclub, he went for it. After all, he'd already appeared in hotel lounges in Singapore. Yu Sau is excited to learn he's performed on Cheung Chau. She tells him jubilantly that she's heard many old hands have been there, such as Yam Kim Fai, Bak Sheut Sin, Sun Ma Sze Tsang and Law Ban Chiu. Why didn't he go back there once his back was better? Kim Chau smiles and says no one offered him the chance. She senses that he doesn't want to talk about opera, and doesn't ask any more questions.

After dinner, Yu Sau animatedly shows Kim Chau the photos Grandpa left behind: Grandpa and Grandma as a young couple, Kim Chau on stage in a show. Kim Chau glances at them, but seems just as indifferent and remote as when he was talking about his own past.

"*Before Grandpa died, he kept saying you had an opera costume of his. Is that true?*" Yu Sau finally asks the question she's been holding in for a long time.

"*Mum threw it away,*" he says simply.

As she says goodbye to Kim Chau, Yu Sau urges him to move in with them. "You could sleep in the study," she says, but he declines.

"*My place is close to the kopitiam, it's easier for me to get to work from there,*" he says.

"*It must be hard on you, having to work in a kopitiam,*" says Yu Sau.

"*I didn't even finish secondary school. I'm a real shit sword. What else can I do?*"

Yu Sau stares blankly at him. Knowing she hasn't understood, Siu Wah explains that *shit sword* is a slang expression for someone with neither physical strength nor education (because you can't use it, and it smells terrible—"smell" in Cantonese sounds like "learning"), who isn't fit for any work. The pun is intricate, and now that Yu Sau gets it, she can't help laughing. Even so, she finds it heartbreaking that Eldest Brother is so down on himself.

Realising that Yu Sau is having trouble following his Cantonese, Kim Chau switches to Mandarin. "I left school after Secondary Two. That doesn't count for very much. Another cleaner at my kopitiam even made it as far as Pre-U. We're Chinese-educated. We can't speak English and don't know how to use computers. What else can we do except clear plates in a kopitiam? At least that's better than scrubbing toilets or sweeping floors."

"But you're different. You sing opera, you were a famous scholar-warrior performer. With your experience, you could go to a clan association or community centre to teach Cantonese opera." Yu Sau sounds a little upset, as if she's angry with someone: maybe with Kim Chau, or with whoever left him so beaten down and defeated, or with the whole of society.

"Famous? I didn't even know how to perform." Yu Sau's agitation making him raise his voice too. He remembers how he was mocked in Hong Kong. Someone heard that he'd been a scholar-warrior in Singapore, and said behind his back, *"Him, a scholar-warrior? He can't even walk on stage! Strides around like he's kicking a football."* Kim Chau was crushed when these words made their way back to him. One of the seniors tried to comfort him by telling him this performer had a grudge because he'd been treated badly while performing in Singapore, so Kim Chau shouldn't take this to heart. Yet it was hard to ignore this, and Kim Chau began to wonder if he had any talent for performing at all. What talent did he have, then? *"Shit sword,"* those were his mother's words. She'd always said he wasn't very strong, and refused to work hard at school, so he was destined to become a shit sword.

"Besides, no one wants to learn Cantonese opera these days," he says to Yu Sau.

"They do. Siu Wah and I met at a Cantonese opera class at

a clan association," says Yu Sau, switching to Mandarin and glancing at Siu Wah. Her Cantonese really is rusty. When she gets worked up or needs to argue, she has to switch to English or Mandarin.

"Are you two still learning?" Kim Chau asks.

"We stopped when Kwok Sau arrived," says Siu Wah.

"So you've stopped classes?"

"I was planning to start again next month. Why don't you come meet our teacher?" says Yu Sau.

"I can't teach. I haven't sung in so long, I've forgotten all my technique." Kim Chau shakes his head, still sounding unsettled.

KIM CHAU

LOOK IN YOUR HEART AND ASK YOURSELF:
ARE YOU LETTING DOWN MASTER WAH GONG?

HE LEAVES YU SAU'S FLAT AND RETURNS TO HIS LITTLE rented room, where he sits on the edge of his bed, sunk in thought.

He bends and reaches under his bed to pull out a red suitcase. Squatting down, he touches its surface, getting dust on his fingertips. He claps his hands to clean them, and stares at the suitcase for quite a while before turning the dials of the combination lock. He stops after just two digits, shoves it back under the bed, and returns to his perch. The suitcase contains two or three of the costumes he wore on stage whilst performing in Hong Kong. To open it would be to re-open his memories of this part of his life, a time that he remembers as mostly unhappy. Why would he want to touch it? Out of nostalgia? Or is it his hunger for the limelight that makes him long to return to his time on stage?

When did he ever get to play a lead role in Hong Kong? He smiles bitterly at the thought. It's not like he didn't have any more opportunities after he sprained his back, but he wasn't willing to take on any more small supporting parts, preferring to sing at Tsim Sha Tsui nightclubs, or even the open-air stalls on Temple Street. These unsavoury locations didn't feel welcoming either, but he kept reassuring himself that sooner or later, he'd find a patron who understood his talent. When that happened, he'd be able to put on his fine robes again and return to the limelight. He kept his head down, gritted his teeth, and soldiered on with a forced smile. The longed-for patron failed to materialise, and eventually he gave up and withdrew from the world. He smoked, he drank, he stayed up all night, wrecking himself and his voice. Sometimes he'd recall roles he'd played and try to sing a few lines, only to find the lyrics had left his mind. His memory was deteriorating. Sometimes, halfway through a song he'd sung a hundred times before, he'd be unable to remember the rest of the words, and the audience would boo him. Friends offered him parts, but he turned them all down. He claimed to have lost interest, but the truth was he'd lost all confidence in his abilities. When Yu Sau suggested he could teach opera, it felt like she was mocking him. He once saw a film in Hong Kong called *The Dutiful Daughter*, in which a stern teacher, played by Liang Tsi-Pak, berates his disciple (played by Lam Kar-Sing), "*People like you are ruining Cantonese opera. You've been in a few shows, you know a bit about the craft, and you think you're something special? What can you actually do? You think you're already fit to be a teacher? You'll just produce half-full buckets, like what you are now. Look in your heart and ask yourself: are you letting down Master Wah Gong?*"

Kim Chau had never thought of himself as letting down Master Wah Gong, the deity of Cantonese opera, but when he heard himself being scolded and ridiculed backstage, he didn't just curse his lack of skill, he also blamed his mentor, who'd only cared about making a living, and took in students even though his own abilities were inadequate. In order to continue earning his fees, the teacher constantly praised Kim Chau in front of Grandpa, filling the boy with hot air so he went around preening himself. Now he remembers first being taken on as a pupil. His mentor led him to Master Wah Gong's altar to offer incense. Then he kowtowed to the mentor and served him tea, but unlike in the traditional mentor-pupil relationship, he didn't have to be an unpaid servant. Instead, Grandpa paid his teacher a fee each month (Kim Chau still isn't sure exactly how much), until Kim Chau left to set up his own troupe with Lily Teo.

Was his mentor really a half-full bucket? Kim Chau has tried to consider this question impartially, acknowledging how much he learnt during their time together. He must admit that while his mentor might not have fulfilled all his duties, Kim Chau wasn't the best pupil either. Over the years, he's come to accept that his failure can only be blamed on his own lack of hard work. He's seen many young performers do the same thing, taking on the big stances before they've even mastered the seven stars or pulling the mountain. He was in too much of a hurry, and set his sights too high. In his rush to be famous, he set up an opera troupe with Lily Teo before his skills were up to scratch, setting himself up as a scholar-warrior lead. After the troupe disbanded, he appeared in a few other shows in Singapore, and was well-received. He made a bit of a name for himself. As soon as he stepped on stage, he would get entrance applause, and sometimes young women in the audience would even call out his name. The other performers were amateurs from the clan association, and couldn't compete with him in any regard: voice, gesture, or movement. This puffed up his ego, but the clan association only promoted their own people, and favoured a scholar-warrior performer within their ranks. Even though Kim Chau didn't think much of this man's abilities, he was the one who got all the lead roles, while Kim Chau was relegated to smaller parts. He resented this unfairness, and didn't get on with the clan association people anyway, so he quit after a few shows. It was only when he got to Hong Kong and saw what true excellence looked like, that he realised how inadequate his own abilities were. He was a half-full bucket. Even so, there was enough in his half bucket for him to struggle on in the Hong Kong scene for a while.

"Me, teach? I would never be so irresponsible," he mutters to himself, staring at the erhu on the wall and caught between warring emotions. It's a long time before he is able to calm

down. He walks over to take the erhu off its shelf, tunes it, and plays a few notes. Quietly, he sings, *"With 'The Autumn Tomb' as her swan song, pity the seventh month's fallen blossoms."* He wants to carry on, but it's late and he might disturb the neighbours. With a sigh, he stops. Gazing at the erhu, he sings acapella in a voice so low, he could be whispering sweet nothings to the musical instrument. *"Her voice fades, the moon is glorious above. My tears of pity scatter in the autumn wind."*

While training as a singer, he studied the erhu under the troupe's musician Uncle Chan, who also taught him quite a few other things: how to sing southern-voice, wooden fish, dragon boat, as well as seven clear words and rolling flowers. His singing technique improved a great deal thanks to Uncle Chan, who filled in all the gaps his mentor left. It's been a long time since he touched the erhu, even though he brought the instrument all the way to Hong Kong. His living quarters there were even more cramped than now, and he hardly ever practised. Since moving back to Singapore, he's been even less inclined to play. He's beset with despair, his dreams turned to ashes, and he's desperately tired of opera and singing. Did he ever truly love it? Or did he just enjoy the attention? Did his thirst for fame lead him down the wrong path? All those years on stage were a waste of time. He isn't good enough to earn a living from his craft. It's been a long time since he sung anything, but for some reason, he has a strong urge to play the erhu tonight. Is it because of what Yu Sau said?

"Today old backstage friends weep by a new grave. Can the dead hear them? May the spirits accept my humble gift: poor wine and fresh flowers." Despite his worsening memory, the lyrics of "The Seventh Month's Fallen Blossoms" come to him in their entirety. He gazes at his erhu, which listens as he sorrowfully warbles his way through the song, hot tears running down his cheeks.

COSTUME

1. SO YOU'RE LEONG KIM CHAU'S SISTER

Yu Sau and Siu Wah frequently visit the kopitiam where Kim Chau works. Whenever she sees her big brother clearing dishes and wiping tables, Yu Sau feels a pang of pity. She knows he'd rather not be doing this, but has no choice if he wants to pay his rent and eat. He must resent this job. She remembers how she and Kim Ming had to help out at Grandpa's kopitiam, and it was only the favourite grandson, Eldest Brother, who wasn't made to greet customers, serve drinks and wash dishes. Grandpa never asked him to, and he never volunteered. Now, in middle age, he's picking up after others. Is this retribution, or is he punishing himself? How long has he been working here? Has he tried looking for another job? What about teaching Cantonese opera?

Yu Sau starts attending classes at the clan association again. She hopes to introduce Eldest Brother to her teacher. Siu Wah doesn't join her because he's working part time at the radio station, and is often on shift during their lessons.

She gets to class early one day. The teacher hasn't arrived yet, but there are already several students waiting. One of them, Fong, trots over when she sees Yu Sau come in, grabs her by the arm, and murmurs in English, "So you're Leong Kim Chau's sister."

Startled, Yu Sau asks, "How did you know?"

Fong smiles mysteriously. "I'll tell you later. Are you free after class? Let's get a snack."

Later, they go to a dessert restaurant. There, Fong says, "I used to be a big fan of Leong Kim Chau and Lily Teo."

Yu Sau quickly works out that this must mean Fong is at

least sixty, even though she looks much younger, maybe early fifties.

"We all thought those two were the perfect couple, and they'd be sure to get married." Fong sighs. "Who'd have thought Lily would end up marrying the boss of her opera troupe, what's his name, something Hung. Apparently he was good friends with your brother. Lily Teo and her husband migrated to Canada. Your brother appeared in a few more shows, then he disappeared. He looked and sang a bit like Lam Kar Sing. Such a shame that he suddenly stopped. A few of us stayed in touch with Lily Teo. Her husband recently passed away." (This news gives Yu Sau a twinge.) "She came back to Singapore and wanted very much to see your brother, but didn't know where he was. She asked after everyone in your family: your grandfather, your mum, your dad, your uncle, then finally your other brother and you. When she said your name, I didn't make the connection right away, but when she mentioned you looked a bit like Kim Chau, I realised it might be you. No wonder I thought you were familiar when you first started coming to class. I kept thinking you reminded me of someone, but could never work out who."

2. SO GRANDPA WAS RIGHT, THE COSTUME STILL EXISTS

FONG ARRANGES FOR LILY TEO TO MEET YU SAU IN A HONG Kong-style restaurant at Bishan Junction 8. Lily is astonished at how much Yu Sau looks like her brother, even more than when she was a little girl. She seems filled with emotion as she tells Yu Sau how much she'd love to see Kim Chau. For her part, Yu Sau feels like she's seeing a stranger. Lily's curly hair is short and still jet black, her blue cheongsam trim and elegant, and her thin black-rimmed glasses make her look like a schoolteacher. She looks no more than fifty, not at all like an old woman of sixty. It is only after quite a while that Yu Sau can discern in her features the ingénue she saw so often as a little girl.

Yu Sau used to adore Lily. She remembers how, in the living room of their old house, Lily would teach her some simple steps: little hops, elegant steps, flower hands. This was just for fun, and because she never practised, Yu Sau had forgotten all of them by the time she grew up. At the crack of dawn, Yu Sau and Eldest Brother rode Meng Hung's car to Fort Canning for throat-voice practice. She had no idea what they were shouting about, only knowing they kept reaching higher and higher notes. Now she understands this was Cantonese opera, probably the ho-ce-luk scale. But then she recalls Lily's act of betrayal, and the warm feelings brought on by nostalgia quickly cool. That's why, to start out with, she is unwilling to bring her to see Eldest Brother, going so far as to claim she didn't know where he was. When Lily insists, Yu Sau thinks, haven't you hurt him enough? Why do you need to see him? Lily says she absolutely has to, and Yu Sau has no choice but to tell the truth: Eldest Brother probably isn't keen to see her.

"Why is this so important to you?" asks Yu Sau frostily.

"Kim Chau gave Meng Hung a costume for safekeeping. I want to give it back in person."

Yu Sau's immediate thought is: So Grandpa was right, the costume still exists. Suddenly excited, she is forced to cover up the lie she told Lily earlier. *"Eldest Brother doesn't like seeing his old friends, but I'll see if he'll make an exception for you."*

3. *WHO'D HAVE IMAGINED I'D BE MORE HEARTBROKEN THAN JIA BAOYU*

Yu Sau wasn't actually lying when she told Lily that Kim Chau doesn't like seeing his old friends. Worried that he might still not have forgiven Lily, she thinks about it a long time before deciding that the best course of action is to simply bring Lily to his lodgings with no warning.

She remembers that he has Tuesdays off, and will probably be at home. She takes the day off, and knocks on the door of his flat that afternoon, with Lily standing beside her. Her heart thumps with worry. What is Eldest Brother isn't in? What if he is, but gets angry?

When the landlord opens the door, she hears someone inside singing Cantonese opera to the accompaniment of an erhu. She lets out a sigh of relief: at least he's here. She wonders for a moment who's playing the erhu, then recalls that it's Eldest Brother's instrument.

The landlord ushers her and Lily into the flat. Eldest Brother is singing a sorrowful tune:

Heartbroken verses, heartbroken lyrics. How can I bear to keep reading?
Blame the beauty for her cruelty, spurning the ardent youth at her feet.
When will this debt of longing be repaid? This bitterness is hard to endure.
How thin must I grow through grief? Already my tears have flowed a thousand times.
The blossoms are sorrowful, the swallows homeless. Such desolation and sadness.
I mourn fruitlessly for the Red Chamber.
Who'd have imagined I'd be more heartbroken than Jia Baoyu?

"Laifa's in his room," says the landlord in his Teochew-accented Mandarin. "He's been hiding in there singing a lot recently. I don't speak Cantonese, but it sounds like the same song every day."

Fong gave Yu Sau a CD of old Cantonese arias, and she recognises the tune Eldest Brother is now singing: Sit Kok Sin's *Jade Pear Spirit*. She's glad he hasn't given up on opera altogether. Was that because of her encouragement? In any case, she's thrilled to hear his voice, a little hoarse with an undercurrent of melancholy. He must have sounded much better before, she thinks sadly. And who was the woman who hurt him so badly? Yu Sau shoots Lily a sidelong look, but Lily's eyes are fixed on the closed door, her expression solemn. Yu Sau is close enough to see that Lily, who'd once seemed such a paragon of beauty, is getting old too. There are deep lines at the corners of her eyes, the pale skin of her face is slackening, and her jowls are beginning to droop. Yu Sau still hates her a little. If not for her, Eldest Brother wouldn't have ended up like this. Trying to disguise her rage, Yu Sau sighs. From behind her, the landlord calls out, "Laifa, visitors!"

The singing and erhu stop abruptly.

"Laifa?" Lily repeats the unfamiliar name, giving Yu Sau a puzzled look.

Yu Sau looks around the flat. There are three bedrooms, and the other two have their doors open. The landlord's room is next to Eldest Brother's, but all she can see from where she's standing is a corner of the bed. In the third room, behind her, two boys are playing a computer game, filling her ears with excited squeals and the *rat-tat-tat* of the sound effects. The landlord sits in a living room armchair, reading a newspaper. When they first got here, his wife emerged from the kitchen to say hello, then retreated again. There's a small dining table near the kitchen entrance. A low hum is coming from beyond that, probably a washing machine.

Yu Sau and Lily stand outside Eldest Brother's door for quite a while, but it remains stubbornly shut, forbidding as a wall of ice.

"*Kim Chau, it's me, Lily,*" says Lily in a low, gentle voice, tapping at the door. No response.

"*Kim Chau!*" she calls again, and finally the door opens.

Kim Chau's frail, aged face appears before them. The years have carved wrinkles into him, but cannot obscure the handsome features that, back in the day, captivated so many young women, Lily included. This face was once elegant as a jade cameo, and it pains Lily to see it so withered. She loved him more than Meng Hung, but what good was that? She dropped so many hints, but he did nothing. He treated her well, but only seemed to like her as a close friend, or maybe a little sister. He never showed any sign of desiring her, never mind getting married. And so she chose Meng Hung. Why hadn't Kim Chau been interested in her? It was only a long time later that she worked it out.

Kim Chau stands in the doorway, looking silently at them.

"*Can we come in?*" says Yu Sau. He says nothing, just pulls the door open and steps aside. His room is simply furnished: a wooden shelf by the door holding stacks of clothes and towels, and a variety of unidentifiable jars and bottles. Farther in is the bed, its sheets and pillowcases yellowing. Scattered across it are music scores and an erhu. Next to the bed are a chair and small wooden table, on which is a hot water dispenser and a porcelain cup. A faded blue checked shirt and black trousers hang over the back of the chair.

"*You have no idea how hard it's been to track you down,*" says Lily. Without waiting to be invited, she sits on the edge of the bed. Yu Sau takes the chair, first folding the shirt and trousers and putting them on the table.

Kim Chau shuts the door.

"*Meng Hung said I should come and see you,*" says Lily.

"*What for?*" he asks. His voice is low and a little unclear, as if he's choking something back.

"*He wanted your forgiveness.*"

A long silence. Finally, Kim Chau says, "*Why didn't he come himself?*" He looks calm, but the quiet fury in his voice is palpable.

"*He's gone.*" She pauses for a moment. "*Two years ago. Pancreatic cancer.*" Kim Chau doesn't react, apart from lowering his eyes and shutting his mouth. Lily is quiet too, then suddenly remembers the plastic bag she's holding. Letting out a strange cry, she opens it and pulls out a white cloth pouch. "*I've been back to Singapore quite a few times in the last two years, and each time I asked all our old friends if they knew where you were. I spoke to our percussion mentor, and he was the one who told me you were back in the country, though he didn't have your address. Luckily, I'd stayed in touch with some of our fans. One of them, Ho Yueh Fong, was taking singing lessons with Yu Sau. I asked Yu Sau to bring me to you.*"

Kim Chau turns to look at Yu Sau, his face blank. She can't tell if he's angry, but instinctively avoids his eyes.

Lily has been untying the cloth pouch as she speaks. Now she pulls it open to reveal a long blue robe. "*He said I had to return this to you, no matter what.*"

Kim Chau hesitates, then reaches out a trembling hand to take the opera costume from her. He stares at it for a long while, gently stroking the fabric, then slowly unfolds it. The colour is faded, and it's moth-bitten in quite a few places. He walks over to the bed. Lily shifts aside, thinking he wants to sit next to her, but he doesn't. Instead, he spreads the robe out on the bed and stares at it, then in a few agile moves, folds it into a neat rectangle. This goes over his arm, and he retreats to the doorway, stroking it with his other hand as if it were a little cat.

This is the first time Yu Sau has really paid attention to her brother's fingers. They are long and delicate, and she suddenly thinks he could play female parts. Has he ever done this?

Kim Chau doesn't notice Yu Sau watching him. He is lost in memory.

He was still in school. He'd brought home such a terrible report card that his mum, in a rage, had flung the opera costume his grandfather gave him into the bin. When she wasn't looking, he quietly retrieved it and sprinted over to Meng Hung's place, begging him breathlessly to keep it safe. Meng Hung held his hands tight, looked him dead in the eye, and said with great certainty, *"Don't worry. I'll definitely take care of this for you."* Overcome with emotion, Kim Chau had burst into tears. Forgetting it was Meng Hung holding him, he'd leaned forward into his embrace. Standing there, he'd felt Meng Hung's broad, sturdy chest. A warm hand gently caressed his back. Meng Hung said something in his ear, but he was weeping too hard to hear.

They later became a lot more intimate, but it was that first moment of contact he found hardest to forget. *"Why don't we start over again?"* He can still hear Meng Hung's voice. This was in 1997, when he was eking out a difficult existence in Hong Kong as a costume and propmaster, and it was clear he would never tread the boards again. He'd reached the depths of his despair, and would have killed himself if he'd had the courage. At least he still had the chance to perform at Temple Street. It was then that Meng Hung heard what he was doing, and flew all the way from Canada to Hong Kong, just to visit him on Temple Street. That night, they watched Leslie Cheung and Tony Leung in *Happy Together*, then he walked Meng Hung back to his hotel in Jordan.

"I want to go back to Singapore. I can't take any more of this place," he said.

"I'd like to go back too. Why don't we start over again?" said Meng Hung abruptly.

"*You want to revive the opera troupe?*" He smiled bitterly. "*I didn't think you had so much money to spare.*"

He was just telling the truth. Although he didn't know exactly how Meng Hung was doing in Canada, it was plain from his sallow, lined face that things weren't going as well as he'd hoped. (And if he was still as wealthy as before, he'd hardly be living at the Prudential Hotel.) Maybe Meng Hung was already ill then. Did he know? Had he realised this would be the last time they'd see each other? Kim Chau feels guilty for giving him such a frosty reception. He was still very angry with Meng Hung. There was no way they could start over again. Why would he even say something that ridiculous?

He responded coldly to Meng Hung, "*Our time is over. I'm old now.*"

Meng Hung stared back at him, his voice firm. "*You knew what I meant. I'm serious.*"

Meng Hung's face pops into Kim Chau's mind: the emaciated, craggy face, the startlingly large eyes. His heart aches. Yes, Meng Hung must already have been ill, and Kim Chau was cruel to him. He can still hear the meanness in his voice, "*I'm serious too. Our time is over.*" They arrived at Prudential Hotel just as he said these words. He didn't stay over at the hotel that night, but went back to Yau Ma Tei.

He can still remember his final words to Meng Hung: "*Give Lily my regards.*"

"*What did he tell you?*" he blurts out to Lily, returning suddenly to the present. His eyes remain on the costume, cradled in his arm like a cat.

"*You mean Meng Hung?*"

While Kim Chau was sunk in thought, Lily's eyes drifted to a photo hanging by the foot of the bed. Hearing him address her out of the blue, she is a little unprepared, like a schoolgirl caught daydreaming.

Yu Sau has noticed the picture too. Eldest Brother is in full warrior gear, with what looks like a battle flag behind him; Meng Hung is in a suit and tie. Both men are in high spirits. So Kim Chau had kept some of these old photographs. Grandpa was right, Eldest Brother did take these pictures with him. Where are the ones from the album? Maybe they actually did get lost when the rosewood furniture was sold off.

Kim Chau doesn't answer Lily. They are both silent for a while, until finally Lily bites her lip and says, *"I understand."* She pauses a moment. *"I've known for a very long time."*

He is quiet again, staring at the robe that he can't stop touching. When he speaks, his voice is so soft it feels as if he's forcing it from his throat. *"How did you trick him into—"* Like a movie freeze frame, he is stock still for a full minute. Then he lets out a breath, and continues stroking the costume.

The air in the room seems to solidify. From outside comes the electronic pew pew of the computer game, the kids calling out excitedly, the landlord and his wife speaking in Teochew. All these sounds are crystal clear.

After a long while, Yu Sau hears Lily say, quiet and unhurried, *"In the end, a woman needs somewhere she can call home. By the time it happened, I was no longer young."*

TRANSLATOR'S NOTE

THE OFFICIAL LANGUAGES OF SINGAPORE, ACCORDING TO ITS constitution, are Malay, Mandarin, Tamil and English. As well as English, schoolchildren are taught their "Mother Tongue", which is determined by ethnicity. Yet this elides the fact that most Chinese Singaporeans trace their ancestry back to immigrants from China who spoke, depending which part of the Mainland they were from, Hainanese, Hokkien, Teochew, Hakka and, like Ping Hung and Tak Chai, Cantonese. These are largely mutually unintelligible, and so a decision was made to adopt Mandarin as the universal Chinese language, just as on the Mainland, where it is known as *putonghua*: "the common tongue". (A data point: my parents speak Cantonese, I do not; I speak Mandarin, they do not; we communicate in English; my father also speaks Tamil, but that is a whole other story.)

The change was sudden. In her memoir *Growing Up in the Era of Lee Kuan Yew*, Lee Hui Min describes the surreal experience of coming home one day in the 1980s, and turning on the TV only to find Hong Kong stars Carol Cheng and Chow Yun-Fat inexplicably speaking Mandarin, their lips out of sync with their words. As if a switch had been flipped, all Chinese dialects vanished from television, to be replaced by badly-dubbed Mandarin.

Yeng Pway Ngon, one of Singapore's foremost Chinese-language writers, regards Cantonese as his mother tongue. His childhood was saturated with it: both parents and all his neighbours were Cantonese, and he grew up surrounded by Hong Kong TV serials, Cantonese opera, and the dialect programming of Radio Rediffusion. In *Costume*, he looks at what we have lost along with the language itself: art forms such as Cantonese opera, communication between generations, an entire way of life.

If you were wondering how language hegemony works, here's an example: the written and spoken forms of Cantonese are generally quite different; the written form (书面语) happens to correspond more or less exactly to Mandarin. This means that Mandarin speakers are able to read books by Cantonese writers with no problem, whereas Cantonese speakers are obliged to perform a tricky act of transposition each time, substituting and rearranging words to bridge the gap.

That said, there are written symbols for the characters that occur in Cantonese but not Mandarin; these are typically not used in the standard written form. In a small act of rebellion against the totalising effect of Mandarin, Yeng has left all Cantonese dialogue in the book in the original, rather than transposing it into Mandarin. The result is bracing: to a non-Cantonese speaker, these utterances become almost illegible, mirroring the effect of the government's language policy on Cantonese-speaking Singaporeans, who suddenly found themselves surrounded by an unfamiliar language. (There is a Cantonese-Mandarin glossary at the back of the original text, so readers are not totally marooned.)

There was no way to replicate this effect in translation, or at least none that I could think of. (I did find myself wondering whether, if I were translating into Spanish, it would be appropriate to use Catalan for the Cantonese dialogue—but of course, minoritised languages are not simply analogues for each other.) In the end, I went with the simplest, least distracting option: italics. This loses the effect of incomprehensibility, but the typography will at least serve as a constant reminder to the reader that some of these conversations are taking place in an entirely different language.

There are many sticking points in the shift between languages. In this case, I found the names particularly tricky. My general rule is to call characters what they call themselves; but what about places? And what if different groups of people have different names for the same places? For instance, the South Seas, the region including Singapore and Malaysia, is Nam Yong (南洋) in Cantonese, but I grew up in Singapore with the term "Nanyang" in common use: one of the most prominent Chinese schools is Nanyang Girls' High. Yet calling the territory "Nanyang" felt wrong, not just because this is the Mandarin pronunciation, but because hanyu pinyin wasn't in use in early twentieth century China. (In this case, the Wade-Giles rendering wouldn't have been far off, but "Nan Yang" still felt wrong.)

On the other hand, the city where the boys seek work is "Guangzhou" in pinyin. Applying the same rules, I should have called it Kwangchow, but then I'd have lost the resonance of its anglicised name, Canton, being the source of the word "Cantonese". Is it odd nonetheless to have Ping Hung talking about going to "Canton", which is not the name he would have known the city by? Well, yes, but then they also talk about going to "Singapore". Later on, Kim Ming talks about travelling to "Guangzhou" (and as he speaks Mandarin to his sister, that's the name he would have used). This means the same city is referred to by two different names in the book, but as these mentions take place almost a hundred years apart, I decided this was an appropriate way to mark how much has changed in that time.

Most of the novel is set in Singapore, and here the problem compounded. On one hand, many of this book's readers will know the places mentioned by their English names; on the other hand, the Chinese in Singapore had their own system of place names, ones that often had nothing to do with the other languages. In old Singapore, the downtown area south of the Singapore River was known in Chinese as 大坡 (Dai Bo), and north was 小坡 (Siu Bo). I translated those into their literal meanings, Big Town and Small Town, which I hope convey a broad sense of the neighbourhoods. The bridge that joined Big Town and Small Town was known as 吊桥头 (Diu Kiu Tao, "suspension bridge"), and has a particularly gruesome cameo in the novel; I decided to make its appearance vivid to present-day Singaporean readers by using the name they probably know it by, the English one: Coleman Bridge.

Given the subject of the novel, another challenge how to describe Cantonese opera, a maximalist art form with a great deal of stylised movement and heightened expression. (Full disclosure: I grew up with a vague awareness of Cantonese opera, having seen it performed around me, but I can't say it's something I paid a lot of attention to; luckily, there are many, many videos on YouTube that I was able to watch in preparation.) I didn't want to derail the book with constant explanation and contextualisation, so I erred on the side of giving the reader just enough information to orient themselves. I don't think any writer could convey such an intricate mode of performance merely in words, and hope anyone who isn't already familiar with it will seek out performance footage for themselves.

Once again, the problem was names. Many of the operas, arias and technical terms have simply no equivalent in English. In the end, I proceeded on the basis that if this were a novel about ballet written in English, the author would have no qualms about referring to *fouettés* and *arabesques*, never mind that not every reader would be familiar with those terms. I similarly trusted the readers of *Costume* to work out from context when a particular gesture or vocal technique is being referred to, and translated these names literally. Luckily, many of them are evocative, and you can probably come up with your own visualisation of what "pulling the cart" might look like, or how a "level voice" passage might sound. There were moments when I fudged it, using distinctly non-Cantonese terms such as *ingénue*—usually when a word from a different theatrical tradition fit particularly well, and I allowed myself to shoplift it, smuggling a moment of familiarity to give the reader a reference point.

I could go on at great length about the thought that went into how to present this world in English, and while I'm sure my decisions won't please everyone, I hope they are at least comprehensible and have not got in the way of the story, the least any translator could ask for. While I've aimed for consistency, I've also broken my own rules where it seemed best, always reaching for the tool that seemed most suited to do the job at hand.

I wanted to talk about the particular challenges presented by this translation and the reasoning behind my choices, in order to demystify the process a little for those who may not have thought much about it, and give a glimpse of the convoluted workings of moving an entire novel from one language to another. I've been doing this for a living for several years now, yet each time the mere fact of this transposition still feels to me like a particularly arcane form of magic.